2 UNFORGETTABLE ROMANCE NOVELS IN 1 BIG VOLUME!

LORI COPELAND

Author Of More ~~...~~ **t!**

WHEN L~~...~~

"I think you're ins~~...~~

"Well, that remains ~~...~~ took the plate of peanut but~~...~~ ackers and walked over to dump them in the trash.

"What did you do that for?" Fritzi asked in amazement.

"Because I would throw up if I had to eat those with my chili," he replied defiantly.

"But you said you loved peanut butter and crackers with your chili!"

"I was lying."

She propped her hands on her hips. "So what brought on this spurt of honesty?"

"It suddenly occurred to me that I'm going to have to work my buns off to get anywhere with you, Fritzi Taylor," Ryan said, grinning from ear to ear. "And the best way to start is for me to begin by being honest right now, whether you like it or not."

TALE OF LOVE

With tantalizing slowness, Garth carried Hilary to the brass bed. The soft rays of sunlight that filtered through the sheer material of the drapes reflected a glistening shimmer across her skin.

They came into each other's arms once more, and as his passion mounted, he embraced her boldly against his bare frame, a tender light shining through his eyes. His mouth moved down the length of her, sending hot shafts of desire racing unchecked through both of them.

Maybe nothing in the world could stop him from claiming her. Maybe these crazy feelings they were experiencing would turn out to be the real thing.

Maybe...she was finally in love.

LORI COPELAND

WHEN LIGHTNING
=STRIKES=
TALE OF LOVE

LOVE SPELL **NEW YORK CITY**

LOVE SPELL®

July 1995

Published by

Dorchester Publishing Co., Inc.
276 Fifth Avenue
New York, NY 10001

WHEN LIGHTNING STRIKES Copyright © 1986 by
Lori Copeland

TALE OF LOVE Copyright © 1988 by Lori Copeland

WHEN LIGHTNING STRIKES

CHAPTER ONE

There was one thing for sure: It wasn't a fit night for man nor beast outside.

A weary Fritzi Taylor sat in the small office of Concerned Volunteers of the Community, CVOTC, and listened to the sleet hitting the double-paned windows. The weather bureau was predicting that a mass of Arctic air headed their way would bring with it twelve to sixteen inches of snow, and the temperatures would drop to record low levels before morning.

She rose and casually strolled over to peer out the window, absently rubbing the small of her back, which had been nagging her mildly all day. Her eyes grew concerned as she saw the worsening conditions. At least it had held off until most of the party-goers had made it safely home, she mused thankfully.

It was New Year's Eve, and as a volunteer of CVOTC, she, along with her fellow workers, had manned the phones continuously for the last few hours. The organization offered free rides home for those who had celebrated with the gusto normally associated with the holiday, and since midnight had long passed, business had now slacked off. In a few more minutes she felt it would be safe to close the office and go home while she could still travel the streets. The other workers had left a few moments earlier, and all that was left to do was to lock up and get herself home. A swift feeling of pride overcame her as she reached for her coat. Another successful holiday had been concluded, and as far as she knew, there had not been one single car accident on the streets of town tonight.

Smothering a tired yawn, she turned from the window and began gathering up her purse and gloves. The temperature was already beginning to plummet, and she silently promised herself that the moment she arrived back at the ranch she would build a roaring fire and let the warmth thaw out her chilled body before she went to bed.

Reaching for the set of keys on the desk, she was momentarily startled when the phone shrilled loudly, breaking the peaceful silence of the room.

Egad! She hoped it was a wrong number.

"Good evening. CVOTC, may I help you?"

"Well, that's entirely possible," an inebriated male voice said, slurring suggestively. "What'd you have in mind, cupcake?"

"Do you need a ride, sir?" Fritzi was used to varied, sometimes risqué, responses to her question, so

8

she calmly ignored the innuendo in his voice and the "cupcake." Considering his obvious condition, she knew he couldn't be held accountable for his actions at the moment. "If you'll give me the address where you are, I'll send a car right over," she offered pleasantly. Normally she would turn this over to one of the drivers, but since she was the only one left in the office, she would have to be the one to provide the service at this late hour. She was concerned that it might be a bit risky for her to go alone, but since Fritzi Taylor had never been an overly cautious person to begin with, the unexpected request didn't bother her. She figured she could be the good Samaritan and pick up the caller, then deposit him safely on his doorstep before she headed for home.

Besides, he was probably so drunk, he wouldn't be able to find his rear end with both hands, let alone try anything funny with her.

There was a moment's pause on the other end of the line while she waited patiently for his answer.

"Sir? Can you tell me your address?" she prompted.

"I don't know where the devil I am," he confessed irritably. "Some party, I think . . . no, wait— I left the party and was looking for my car. But I can't find it . . . someone must have stolen it. . . ." His mind was becoming increasingly muddled, and Fritzi realized he must be out in the cold sleet; his teeth began to chatter like an adding ma-

9

chine. "To be perfectly honest, I don't know where the hell I am," he concluded lamely.

Obviously he was going to need more than a little help. "Are you calling from the party?"

"No . . . I'm pretty sure I left there a few minutes ago," he supplied helpfully.

She frowned. "Then you're calling from a public telephone?"

"I don't know . . . maybe. Let me look." There was the sound of rustling on the other end as he tried to figure out where he was. "It must be . . . Someone handed me your phone number as I went out the door . . . Yeah, it's a pay phone, all right. Here's the slit where I put my money—" His voice broke off again irritably. "This no-good . . ." She frowned as his tone suddenly turned agitated and he began to give a colorful and extremely descriptive opinion of what he thought about the instrument he was using. Seconds later he began to bang on the side of the phone with the receiver.

"Sir, what are you doing? Sir!"

The pounding increased in intensity until she was forced to hold the receiver away from her ear. After several more authoritative whacks she could hear him grumbling under his breath.

"Sir?" she inquired again calmly.

"What?"

"What are you doing?"

"I put a quarter in this darn phone and it didn't give me back my change," he complained.

"Is that any reason to destroy it?"

"I wasn't destroying it. I was only trying to get my change back," he said, defending himself in a surly tone. "Listen, I think I'll just try to find my car and get on home. Talk to you later."

"No, wait!" she demanded. "Now listen to me. You're in no condition to be driving. If you'll only tell me how to get there, I'll send a car for you right away."

"If *I* don't know where I am, how the devil am I going to tell *you* how to get here?" he protested, then giggled. "Don't say anything to anyone, cupcake, but I think I've had one too many," he confessed in a secretive whisper.

"I agree. That's why I want you to promise me you won't try to drive yourself home. You're going to have to concentrate and help me figure out where you are," she argued, hoping he wasn't so far gone that he would refuse to listen to reason. "Now, we established you're using a public telephone. Are you inside or outside?"

He looked around him blearily. "Outside, standing under a gigantic thousand-pound monkey," he relayed in a voice that had suddenly turned paralyzed with fear. "Meanest damn monkey I've ever saw in my life . . . Lady, you're not going to believe this, but that sucker's spittin' rocks at me!" By now there was outright panic dominating his voice.

"Those aren't rocks. It's sleeting," she said, trying to comfort him, and relieved that she knew exactly where he was. The gigantic monkey that was terrorizing him was a trademark of a car dealership in town. Fritzi heaved a sigh of relief that the mysterious caller was only a mere ten minutes away from the office. "Stay right where you are and don't move a muscle," she instructed. "I'll be there in a few minutes."

Not waiting to hear if he would comply or not, she slammed down the receiver and scooped up her purse and car keys. Sprinting toward the doorway, she flipped off the lights and turned the safety lock on the door as she closed it.

The sleet was falling heavier as she rushed out to her car and got in. The wipers labored across the heavy crust of ice that had already formed on the windshield as she sat huddled behind the wheel waiting for the defrosters to clear the glass enough for her to see. She could only hope the caller wouldn't take it upon himself to try to drive home as he had earlier suggested.

A few moments later Fritzi pulled out on the icy street, thankful there was very little traffic at this late hour. The small, picturesque town was nestled in the foothills of Colorado, and while it was a thriving tourist town in the summer months, the winter months brought a huge sigh of relief to the town residents that all had settled back to normal until another season was upon them.

Fritzi tensed and eased her foot off the accelerator as she felt the car try to go into a skid as she made her way around the hazardous mountain roads, praying that her mission would not be a futile one. As bombed as the caller had been, she seriously doubted that the man remembered a word of her caution two minutes after he had hung up the phone.

She silently scolded herself for not bringing the jeep tonight, as her brother, Neil, had encouraged, when she had to tap the brake several times with her foot to avoid another hazardous skid. Miraculously the small car straightened once more and proceeded on down the deserted road. In just a little under fifteen minutes she pulled into the drive of the car dealership and came to a skidding halt beneath the feet of the gargantuan monkey. The tiny ice pellets stung her cheeks as she got out of the car, her eyes searching hopefully for the male caller. Then she saw him crouched down beside the phone booth, still clutching the receiver in his hands.

He stirred and grinned lopsidedly as she hurried in his direction. "Hi, there, cupcake!"

"Hello yourself," she said as she tried to help him to his feet, which was no easy task for a person her size.

Barely able to lay claim to being five feet and a hundred pounds, she tugged on his arm as he lay limply at her feet, still grinning up at her stupidly.

"I was hiding from that monkey," he confessed in a hushed whisper. "Shhh . . . don't let him see you."

"The monkey isn't going to hurt you," Fritzi said, trying to get him up once more. He was big, and she didn't know if she could get him to move or not. "Can you stand up?"

"Sure I can stand up, but I don't want to. The monkey will get me."

"No, he won't. I promise. Now take my hand and I'll pull. You're going to get pneumonia if you stay out in this much longer."

Eyeing the gigantic monkey fearfully, he obviously didn't know whether to trust her or not. That thing looked dangerous to him no matter what she said.

She extended her hand to him pleadingly. "Please, I'm getting drenched."

"Well . . ." He cast one last apprehensive glance in the monkey's direction and decided, since it seemed to be looking the other way at the moment, that he would attempt to make his escape. "All right. But someone ought to call the zookeeper. That thing shouldn't be running loose," he warned. Grasping her hand, he started to pull himself up, but his strength was so much greater than hers that she found herself toppling down on him a few seconds later.

A scream of terror rang out as he clutched frantically at her struggling body. "It's got me! That devil's got me!"

Realizing that in his drunken stupor he thought the monkey had actually attacked him, Fritzi stumbled to her feet and made an effort to calm his shattered nerves.

"No, no, the monkey hasn't got you," she assured him gently, trying once more to heft him to his feet.

"Yes, it has! It jumped on me, I know it did!"

"No, it didn't. I fell on you when you tried to get up. Here, let's try it again." Her hand went out to him once more, and she pulled with all her might as he finally opened his eyes and peered at her hopefully.

"Are you sure?"

"I'm positive. Will you hurry a little? We're both going to die of exposure if you don't cooperate."

She could have sworn that his face turned an even deeper shade of red than it already was from the stinging sleet and rain as he glanced hurriedly down at the front of his soaked trousers. "I'm not exposing anything, am I?" he asked guiltily.

It was her face that turned crimson now. "Oh, no —I didn't mean expose in that way. What I meant to say was that we'd both get pneumonia if we didn't get in out of this weather."

Relieved that he had been saved the embarrassment of such an unsavory incident, he let out a sigh of relief. "Oh, good!" In a matter of seconds he was on his feet, leering down at her drunkenly. "Say, you're nice. What's your name?"

She peered up at him expectantly, surprised to see that he wasn't nearly as tall as she had first thought. He wasn't anywhere near six feet, she was sure of that. He was stockily built with a broad chest and thick, well-muscled thighs. He wasn't wearing his suit coat, only a long sleeved dress shirt, tie, and charcoal trousers that by now were soaked. And although the sleet was falling so hard that she couldn't get a good look at his features, she could tell he was close to her age.

"Come on and get in the car," she urged, hurrying him along. "My goodness. You haven't even got a coat on. Where is it?"

"I don't know." He giggled again and she tried to brace herself as he slumped against her slight weight, but they both went down on the ground again.

"Oh, Lord! It's got us both this time." He panicked, clutching at her neck protectively once again.

"No, it hasn't!" she snapped, and struggled out of his tight embrace and back to her feet once more. That darn monkey had him so psyched out, she would never get him in the car! By now she was as soaked as he was, and her lips were beginning to turn blue as she tried to pull him to his feet. "Come on . . . we only have a few more steps to go," she pleaded.

After what seemed a hopeless mission, she finally got him back on his feet, and a few minutes later she was cramming him into the passenger side of the car. Heaving a relieved sigh as he tumbled into the front seat, she slammed the door and bounded around the front of the car and got in on her side, quickly starting the motor. Her teeth were knocking together as she pushed her wet hair out of her eyes and let the warmth of the heater try to penetrate her near frozen state.

"The heater will only take a few minutes to warm up," she said, chattering between clenched teeth. "The car hasn't had time to cool off yet."

He was resting his head on the back of the seat, and when she spoke, his head rolled limply over in her direction. He grinned happily. "You're really nice," he said again. "Really, really nice to come out here and get me safely home." She could tell that the liquor was making him feel sentimental and emotional. "Most people wouldn't come out on a night like this and take me home. Why are you being so nice to me? Do I know you?" he asked expectantly as he leaned forward in his seat and peered at her closer.

"Say, didn't I take you to the party?"

"No." She saw no reason to try to explain why he happened to be in her car at the moment. In his condition he would never understand.

"Huh." He leaned back puzzledly. "Then someone's sure going to be mad at me, because I could have sworn I had someone with me."

"Maybe it was your wife?" That would be terrible, Fritzi thought. The poor woman would be wandering around worrying about what had happened to her husband!

"No, I'm drunk, but I *know* I don't have a wife," he mused.

"Well, it wasn't me. Perhaps you brought a date. I'm sure someone will see that she gets home safely." She put the car in gear and started forward. "I'm just here to see that you get home safely."

"Oh, that's nice. You're really very, very nice. Coming all the way out here and taking me home safely . . . that's really nice." Suddenly he started singing under his breath, some catchy little song warning not to "mess with his toot-toot" as she pulled out on the street.

"I don't suppose you have any idea where you live?" she asked hopefully. It was plain to see that the events of the evening were not putting a damper on his festive mood.

"Nope. Not an inkling."

"Then hand me your billfold." He would undoubtedly have a driver's license from which she could get his address.

Obediently he dug in his back pocket and within moments had produced the requested item. Pulling over to the side of the road, she flipped on the dome lights as he leaned up and peered interestedly over her shoulder.

"Where do I live?"

"On Spruce Drive."

"No kidding? That's one of my favorite streets," he told her happily, then he gave her that devastatingly cute grin once more. "You're really nice . . .

really, really nice . . . to take me home like this. Have I said thank you?"

"Yes, you have, and believe me, it's perfectly all right." She had to smile at his winning way. He was a doll even though he was drunk, and it suddenly struck her that she had seen him somewhere before.

"You know, I can't help but think I've met you before," she prompted. "Have you always lived around here?"

He shrugged hopelessly, his grin widening. "At the moment I don't even know where I am, let alone how long I've been here."

Still chuckling at his obvious confusion, she started to pull back on the highway when suddenly there was the sound of a horn being frantically beeped. Slamming on the brakes, Fritzi shut her eyes and braced herself for the jolt she knew would be coming. Seconds later the sound of twisting metal filled the air as the car spun around in the middle of the road and came to a sudden halt.

"Ho boy!" The jarring effect sent her passenger flying over into her seat, where he landed in her lap dazedly. Shaking the fuzz from his head, he sat up and looked around him before he dissolved in a fit of giggles again. "What happened? Did the monkey get us again?"

"Oh, my gosh! We've just had an accident!" Not one single accident on the town's streets tonight and *she* had to be the one to break the record! Bounding out of the car quickly, Fritzi began to apologize profusely to the shaken motorist whom she had just pulled out in front of. He had gotten out of his car and, with both hands on his hips, was grimly surveying the damage to his dented fender.

"I'm so sorry," she blurted out. "It was all my fault. I pulled right out in front of you!"

The other motorist grunted as he straightened up to face her. "Are you hurt, lady?"

"No, not at all. How about you?"

"No, just gave me a sudden jolt."

"Hey!" A loud whistle rent the air. "You want me to come out there and punch him in the nose for you?" Her male passenger had rolled down the window and stuck his head out to yell at her. "She's a nice lady, mister, she's getting me home safe. You want me to come out there and take care of him for you, lady?"

"No, you just stay where you are," she said in warning.

"Listen." The man's eyes narrowed suspiciously. "Have you two been drinking?"

"No!" she shot back defensively. "I mean . . . at least I haven't been. I'm a volunteer worker and I was just driving that man home . . . safely." She felt very foolish in view of the circumstances, but it was the truth.

The motorist grunted again. "Safely? Well, that's rich." He glanced around irritably. "Wonder if there's a pay phone around here so we can call the police?"

20

"Yes, over there under the monkey," she volunteered quickly.

His demeanor instantly turned defensive again. "What monkey?"

"The one over there on the car lot, see? The great big one." She could hardly see how he could miss the stupid thing. It had certainly terrorized her passenger!

The man took another impatient drag off the cigar he had been smoking.

Fritzi hurried to point out the object in question, knowing that the man thought she was as stewed as her passenger. "Really . . . right there. Can't you see it?"

The man shaded his eyes and peered through the falling sleet, barely able to make out the outline of the tall figure looming in the darkness. "Oh . . . yeah. I can see it now. Well, I guess one of us had better go make the call."

"Uh, listen, would you mind?" She knew without a doubt that she would never be able to get her passenger even remotely close to the monkey again without him falling to pieces. She nodded her head discreetly toward the man sitting in her car and explained in a hushed voice, "He's terrified of the monkey."

"He is? Why? It's just a statue, isn't it?" he grumbled as he cast a wary glance back over in the direction of the car lot.

"Oh, yes. It's not real, but he thinks it is and gets terribly upset every time we get close to it."

"Good God! A bunch of fruitcakes . . . both of them!" Fritzi could barely make out the man's garbled words as he turned and stalked off in the direction of the telephone. "Okay, okay, I'll go make the call. You stay here and watch the cars."

While he went across the street Fritzi returned to her car to see how her charge was doing.

He was still in a state of oblivion, having gone back to singing his little song concerning his "toot-toot." It wasn't a risqué song but rather a popular little ditty with a Cajun beat made popular a few months earlier by Rockin' Sydney.

"Qué pasa? Oh, hi there," he said, greeting her, his face breaking into a wide grin again.

"Hi. I'm sorry about the delay. Are you cold?"

"Nope. I feel pretty good right now."

Obviously, she thought resentfully. As pickled as he was, the whole world was a barrel of laughs.

"And how are you?" he inquired solicitously.

"Cold and miserable, but this shouldn't take too long," she assured him.

It was forty-five minutes later when the details of the accident had been taken care of and she was on her way once more. She had been embarrassed to death when she had been forced to take a sobriety test, indignantly insisting that she hadn't had a drop of liquor all evening. The police had been unimpressed with her pleadings and administered the test, anyway. When she had passed with flying colors, it was all she could do to refrain from pointing out that she had told them so to begin with.

It was with a great sense of relief that she pulled up in front of the apartment house on Spruce Drive a few minutes before two and prepared to help her inebriated charge to his doorway.

The man had roused up from his catnap on the way home and began to sing his little song again as she put her arm around him for support and led him into the building. Then he broke out in a rash of giggles once more. It was strange. She had never met a man who giggled!

"Shhh," she warned as they made their way down the deserted hallway. "You're going to wake up all your neighbors."

Instantly the singing ceased, and he buried his face in her shoulder and tried to smother his glee. "I'm sorry," he said repentantly, his body shaking with a new round of mirth. "I've got the giggles and I can't stop. Every time I drink I get this way, and then, when I get to thinking about you taking me home so I wouldn't have an accident, then *you* having one, I crack up."

It was very hard to keep a straight face when the person with her had gone totally bananas, but Fritzi tried . . . really tried. But by the time they reached his apartment, they were both beside themselves with peals of laughter.

"You have to get yourself under control," she

said with a gasp, trying to cover his mouth with her hand. "I know it seems funny, but I *was* trying to get you home safely."

Her words only served to make him laugh that much harder, and before she knew it, they had both slumped down on the floor in front of his door, holding their sides as they fought to regain control of their shattered composure.

"Listen, we have to stop this." Wiping at the tears streaming down her cheeks, she tried to make her voice sound stern, but she couldn't quit laughing long enough to pull it off.

Finally, when she was sure they would both be thrown out in the street, she managed to get her hand over his mouth again. "Shhh . . . now stop," she pleaded.

"Okay, okay. I'm all right now," he vowed, but they both immediately broke out into another round of laughter.

When he finally gained control of himself once more, he pulled her head onto his broad chest and held her contentedly for a moment. "You're nice, you know that? Really nice . . . and your hair smells so good." He breathed deeply. "Like wildflowers after a summer rain."

"Thank you." She felt her breath catch as her gaze became mesmerized by his. Suddenly his face became tender as he reached over and caught her face between his two large hands. For a moment she found herself lost in the nicest pair of brown eyes she had ever seen, and her pulse suddenly took a faster cadence. He wasn't exactly handsome, but there was something about him that uncharacteristically made her heart thump a little faster. Slowly his mouth moved cautiously down to touch hers. It was a soft touch, but it was as if an electrical wire had seared her flesh. They both quickly decided that one touch was not enough, and their mouths met hurriedly and lingered for a long and more satisfying kiss.

"I think you'd better be getting inside so I can go home," she whispered in a shaky voice a few moments later.

"Yeah . . . I really should, but you be careful," he said, warning her protectively. "It's awfully bad out there. Maybe I should drive you home."

"No, I don't think so," she said, refusing nicely. "I think I can make it home all right."

"Well, whatever you say," he said, obliging. "Let me give you my card before you leave," he insisted. "Maybe I can do something nice for you someday." He began to search his pockets absently. "I know I have one here somewhere . . . Can you help me find it?"

"I guess so. Where would it be?"

"I think it's in my billfold." He leaned forward as she reached over and extracted his wallet from his back pocket.

"Is this it?" She held up a beige business card for his bleary inspection.

"Yeah, that's it," he said, acknowledging it with a relieved sigh.

Holding it out before her in the dim light of the hallway, she read aloud, "Waterbed Bonanza, Ryan E. Majors, Proprietor."

"I can make your nights memorable," the small print promised.

"You can make my nights memorable?" She looked at him and grinned. "That sounds interesting." She glanced at the card once more. "Ryan E. Majors. I guess that's you?"

He giggled that infectious giggle again. "That's entirely possible . . . although I couldn't swear to it."

"Well, Ryan E. Majors, I think you should be getting to bed now." She rose to her feet and helped him to do the same. A few seconds later she had the door unlocked and was gently easing him into the darkened apartment. "Go straight to bed."

"I will. And thanks again . . . what was your name?"

"Fritzi Taylor."

"Fritzi? That's a strange name for a woman."

"I know." She had been teased about her name all her life. "My grandfather's name was Fritz, and my parents named me after him."

"Well"—he reached out and touched her cheek in a gesture of tenderness—"I like it. Happy New Year, Fritzi."

"Happy New Year, Ryan."

"Fritzi." He smiled sweetly as he repeated her name once more and yanked his tie loose from its restricting knot, then almost fell into his darkened apartment before she could grab him. "You're okay, Fritzi Taylor," she heard him announce as he finally got the door shut.

She was still smiling as she hurried down the quiet hallway a few minutes later on the way back to her car.

Ryan E. Majors wasn't bad himself!

CHAPTER TWO

It was ironic, but Fritzi *had* been thinking about buying a water bed lately. In fact, there was one in her treasure-mapping book, a lovely solid oak one with beveled mirrors.

Fritzi sat at the kitchen table the next morning savoring her coffee and thumbing through the scrapbook she had started many years ago.

At that time she had inadvertently attended a lecture on treasure mapping instead of the accounting class she thought she was scheduled for and had found it so interesting that she had remained glued to her chair all evening.

The woman giving the lecture explained the positive thinking, visualization technique with such zest and enthusiasm that Fritzi had rushed home and immediately started her own scrapbook, pasting in a book images of what she wanted to do or achieve in life, then proceeding to believe that those things would actually happen.

The speaker suggested that the book should be

placed where it could easily be seen by the owner, therefore keeping one's goals in mind daily. After all, the motivational speaker had pointed out, treasure mapping was a simple way of making an itinerary of life. "A person wouldn't start out on a long trip without having the proper road map. Our minds can't hope to achieve our goals until it has a clear image of what it's supposed to do," she had reasoned.

And Fritzi had found herself nodding her head enthusiastically. It made sense to her.

So, over the years she had meticulously cut out airplanes, hula girls, and palm trees and put them on the page marked HAWAII. She had always dreamed of going to Hawaii, and seeing the picture before her gave her calm assurance that she actually would someday.

The book was filled with such other dreams as a tanned, healthy woman portraying the picture of good health; to Fritzi's way of thinking, if a person had their health, they had much to be thankful for.

There were also pictures of a red Corvette, a personal computer, and a handsome man lounging in the sun advertising suntan lotion, whom she supposedly would someday meet and marry. She had carefully made a special note in ink under this particular picture emphasizing the fact that he wouldn't necessarily have to be selling suntan lotion to please her, but it certainly wouldn't break her heart if he looked as devastatingly male in his swimsuit as this guy did. Then there was a picture of a glass kitchen table with four brass chairs; a lovely house from the pages of a home-decorating magazine; an oak water bed with beveled glass sitting on a high pedestal; a picture of a hand that had long, gorgeous finger-nails; a video recorder; and so on. All those pictures represented what she hoped to achieve someday, and by using the power of positive thinking, she would happily thumb through her scrapbook and wait for the day that they all became hers.

There were those who chided her and predicted that it would never work, but Fritzi knew better. It worked for those who believed it would. She not only believed it would work, but she had actually seen it happen to other treasure mappers, so she was able to ignore the scoffers and go on, purposely mapping out her goals.

With a deep sigh of contentment she settled back in her chair to enjoy the rest of her coffee and watch the heavy snow that was falling outside the window that morning. Her thoughts turned to the new suede coat she had given herself for Christmas. The lovely coat was just another prime example of how trea-sure mapping really worked. A suede coat had been one of the first items she had pasted in the book, and now what was once only a dream was hanging neatly in her closet, ready to show off at the first possible occasion.

Yes, everything was falling into place just as she had carefully planned it. Next she would acquire the water bed, then the table and chairs, and in five years she would have managed to reach all her goals. Then, at thirty-two, she would start thinking about marriage and a family.

The old ranch house was snug and quiet, with only the occasional sounds of Neda vacuuming in the other rooms to break the silence as Fritzi sat daydreaming. Neda, a full-blooded Sioux Indian, had been the Taylor housekeeper for more years than Fritzi could remember, and she smiled fondly as she thought how comforting it was for Neil and herself to have Neda around while her parents were gone.

Earl and Maxine Taylor had owned and operated the Circle J Ranch for over thirty years. At one time it had been one of the biggest cattle ranches in southwest Colorado, but ten years earlier, they had turned part of the ranch into a tourist attraction. From the middle of May until late September tourists could come for a tour of the grounds, then stay for a typical cowpoke's dinner of beef cooked over an open pit, beans, homemade biscuits, and apple pie. Of course, the apple pie wasn't authentic, but the guests never seemed to complain since a good time was had by all. At the end of the evening a group of cowhands would entertain with songs around the camp fire before the guests would leave with full stomachs and satisfied smiles on their faces.

The day after Christmas, Earl and Maxine always

took off for Florida to spend the winter, leaving Fritzi and her older brother, Neil, to oversee the duties at the ranch while they were gone.

Her gaze wandered back to the business card lying on the table. A water bed. Everyone had told her that she would love one. She rubbed her aching back thoughtfully. They were supposed to be marvelous for any type of back problem, and no one could argue the fact that they were excellent for the circulatory system.

Fritzi pondered the card thoughtfully. She still had a little money left in her savings account. Turning the card over in her hand, her mind conjured up the owner of Waterbed Bonanza, Ryan E. Majors.

She would bet that he had a doozy of a hangover this morning, and selling a water bed would probably be the last thing on his mind. An amused smile tugged at the corners of her mouth as she thought about Ryan. She wondered what *would* be on his mind. Tiny goose bumps broke out and raced across her skin as she remembered the touch of his mouth on hers the night before. He really seemed like he could be a very pleasant person to be with under ordinary circumstances.

"What are you so happy about this morning?" Neil walked into the kitchen and strolled over to the coffeepot to pour himself a fresh cup as she sighed and laid the card back down on the table.

"Nothing earth-shattering," she confessed. "I was just thinking about buying a water bed."

32

"A water bed?" Neil chuckled as he dumped a couple of teaspoons of sugar in his coffee and took a cautious sip. "Why would you want one of those things?"

"Why not?"

"Well, as far as I'm concerned, you're wasting your money. I wouldn't have one if it was given to me."

Fritzi glanced up in surprise. "Really? Have you ever slept on one?"

"Yeah, Susan and I slept on one a couple of times. It was like sleeping in a vat of hot jelly."

That didn't sound too enticing, and at the mention of Neil's estranged wife, Fritzi turned away and busied herself with putting more cream in her own coffee. The subject of Susan Taylor had been strictly taboo lately, and she was surprised to hear Neil bring her up, but since he had . . .

"How is Susan these days?"

For a moment a fleeting shaft of pain flashed across Neil's face before he managed to regain control of his composure and take another drink of coffee. "She's okay."

Although her brother and his wife had been separated for well over a year, there was still a lot of bitterness left in Neil. Susan Monroe had married Neil on the rebound from a previous love affair, and when her old flame, Tyce Williams, had come back pleading for reconciliation, Susan had become so confused about whom she loved that she had finally begged Neil for some time alone to think about their hasty marriage. Neil was hurt, but he had allowed her that time. It hadn't taken Susan long to realize that it was Neil she truly loved, but by then Neil had decided to be stubborn and have doubts of his own. The separation had dragged on.

In Fritzi's opinion, if Neil would have planned his life more carefully, he wouldn't be having all this trouble. Still, she was surprised to hear him mention Susan's name.

"That's good," Fritzi replied, picking up the morning paper to leaf through the home section. "If you want some good advice, you two should stop being so pigheaded and sit down and talk this thing over. You'd both be a lot happier."

As far as Fritzi knew, neither Neil nor Susan had dated anyone else since they separated, and she knew for a fact that they were both miserable, but neither one seemed willing to do anything to change their situation.

"Why is it that it's always easy for outsiders to give such 'good' advice," Neil said, grumbling.

"Because outsiders can usually see what the problem is," she informed him loftily.

"Well, it so happens that we are talking," Neil replied calmly. "In fact, Susan and I are having dinner together tonight."

Fritzi's face brightened, for she loved both Neil and Susan and always hoped for their reconciliation. "You are? That's great!"

"I don't know how great it is, but we've been going to a marriage encounter group for the last three weeks."

"Oh, Neil!" She threw her napkin down on the table and jumped up to give him a big bear hug. "That's wonderful!"

"I don't know, Fritzi. Some of those people are real strange." Neil grimaced.

"Strange? How?"

"I don't know how to explain it . . . just strange." He shuddered as he thought about the therapy sessions where they were supposed to let their hostilities out in the open. Sometimes it turned into a knock-down drag-out between other couples while he and Susan looked on in stunned silence. "I think Susan and I could work this thing out by ourselves if she would try, but she insists on going to these sessions."

"And I think she's right," Fritzi said encouragingly. "I'm just so happy to hear that you're both working to save the marriage now. I've been very concerned that you'd never do that."

"I don't know," he said, musing again as he stared thoughtfully down at his coffee cup. "I just don't know how it's going to work out."

"Well, I do. Susan loves you and you love her. It will all work out if you'll just give it enough time."

"I'm not at all sure Susan loves me—or, for that matter, if she ever did," Neil confessed in a low voice.

"That's only your pride talking," Fritzi chided gently. "Yes, she was mixed up for a while, but she loved you, Neil. She still does."

There had been more than one occasion in the past few months when Susan had phoned Fritzi and poured her heart out, but Fritzi had been unable to take sides. Neil and Susan were both very nice people whom she loved very much.

"Look, how did we get off on this subject?" Neil rebuked with just a trace of emotion still lingering in his voice. "What happened to the subject of the water bed?"

"Oh . . . yes, the water bed." Fritzi didn't exactly want to change the subject, but she could tell by the tone in Neil's voice that he wanted to. "Well, as I was saying, I've been thinking about buying a water bed lately, and I gave a man a ride home last night who just happens to own a water-bed store. I thought I might drop by there today and see what sort of prices he has."

"Gave a man a ride?" Neil scowled at her protectively. "I thought you were only going to answer the phone for that volunteer program. I would have had a fit if I'd known you were going to be running around by yourself."

"I did answer the phone most of the night. But this guy called as I was getting ready to leave, he was really soused, and since I was the only one left in the office, I had to go get him."

"Fritzi, that was a stupid chance to take! Do you

realize what could have happened to you?" Neil protested. "There are a lot of crazies running around out there."

"I know, but Ryan wasn't a crazy," she said, defending him. "In fact, he was rather sweet." For a brief moment her mind took her back to the hasty kiss they had both exchanged. The kiss had been . . . nice.

"Ryan?"

"Yeah, Ryan E. Majors. That's what his card said. He owns a water-bed store. Isn't that a coincidence?"

Neil shook his head tolerantly and dumped the remainder of his coffee into the sink. "Do what you want, but just remember: A fool and his money are soon parted," he predicted, his customary good-naturedness creeping back into his voice now. "Hear anything from Mom and Dad?"

"Mmm." Fritzi turned her attention back to the paper. "Mom called yesterday and said they were fine. Sarasota is having beautiful weather."

Neil grimaced and reached for his coat, which was hanging on a hook behind the kitchen door. "And we're up to our patooties in snow. What about loverboy? Heard from him lately?"

"Loverboy" was Neil's playful term for one of the ranch hands and childhood friends, Coy McAllister, who sang with the music show in the tourist season. During the winter months the group traveled doing road engagements, returning in time for the opening of tourist season at the ranch.

Coy and Fritzi had dated off and on, and although everyone had always thought they would marry someday, any serious relationship between the couple was slow in developing.

"Haven't heard from him since Christmas Day," she mumbled between bites of buttered toast. "But I'm sure he's fine."

"You should call him tonight. You've been moping around here all week," Neil chided. "Maybe talking to him would perk you up a little."

"No, I don't think so. Besides, it's his turn to call me."

Neil shrugged into the heavy wool parka and zipped it up tightly around his neck. "I'm going out to check on the stock. You'd better take the jeep if you go into town. The weatherman says the snow's going to be coming down heavy all day."

"I will . . . oh, and Neil?"

"Yes?" He paused to look at his sister fondly.

"If you get an extra minute sometime today, would you care to take my car to the garage?"

"The garage? Why?"

She shrugged sheepishly. "I had this small fender bender on the way home last night and—"

"You had a wreck last night?"

"Now, don't get that I-told-you-so tone in your voice," she said coaxingly. "It was nothing, really. I just wasn't watching where I was going, and I pulled out in front of a car. No one was hurt, and the damages to both cars are relatively minor."

Neil shook his head in disbelief. "I can't believe it. You're out running around trying to get everyone else home safely, and you have a wreck!"

"Yeah, that struck Ryan as being funny too," she admitted with a wry grin.

"Well, be careful in the jeep," he warned as his hand reached for the knob on the door. "You might not be so lucky the next time."

"I will. And, Neil, for a change, you and Susan be nice to each other tonight. Okay?"

Again that shaft of pain cut deeply into the hazel depths of his eyes before he gave a brief nod of his head, then opened the kitchen door and slipped out into the white, snowy stillness.

Turning her attention back to the paper, Fritzi scrutinized the sale pages, discovering that one of the other local water-bed stores was running a huge New Year's Day sale. Maybe she would look there too. Finishing the last of her coffee, she rinsed the cup and put it in the dishwasher, then went to get dressed for her impromptu shopping trip.

There was something about Christmas carols and gaily decorated trees that were downright depressing after the holidays were over. As Fritzi drove down the familiar streets of town, she had to fight the urge to turn around and go back home. The sights that had sent her spirits soaring with expectation only a few days ago now seemed only to increase the blah feeling that had hovered over her all week.

For some reason she had felt Coy's absence more this time than in years past. To be honest, it wasn't exactly him she missed so much, but it was the companionship he so readily offered that she longed for.

She had her share of dates, but after a while the men began to want to get serious. Since marriage wasn't in her plans for at least another five years, Fritzi hastily backed away from those relationships.

That was what she liked so much about Coy. Like her, he had no thoughts of becoming serious, and they just had a lot of fun together when they went out. He was always ready to listen to all her problems, big or small, and he felt comfortable to her, like the old pair of raggy scuffs she wore around the house. She would hate ever to have to give him up, but contrary to what a lot of people believed, they were not in love with one another.

Perhaps the thought of a long winter with only an occasional phone call from Coy to keep her going accounted for the slight feeling of depression she was experiencing this morning, she thought dismally as her eyes searched for a parking place close to the front of the store.

Because of the inclement weather, the usual diehard holiday bargain-hunters were little in evidence as she noticed a spot and maneuvered the jeep into an empty place in front of Waterbed Bonanza. Hopping out into a deep snowdrift, she jerked off one furry mitten with her front teeth and reached into her purse for a coin to feed the parking meter.

With any luck at all, by the time she left town today, one more dream in her treasure-mapping book would have been realized, she thought, her spirits beginning to rise a little.

An oak water bed with beveled mirrors.

And they said treasure mapping would never work!

CHAPTER THREE

"I'd like to speak to Ryan E. Majors, please." The pleasant warmth of the store made the tip of Fritzi's nose tingle sharply as she unwrapped the heavy woolen scarf from around her neck and glanced around the interior of the store.

"Ryan? He isn't in at the moment. Can I help you?" The pleasant-looking salesman put the morning paper he had been reading on the counter and stood up.

"Are you expecting him soon?" she inquired, trying to keep the disappointment out of her voice. For some reason she had been looking forward to seeing Ryan again.

"He should be in anytime now. Could I be of some help to you while you're waiting?"

"Well, I was sort of looking for a water bed." Her eyes traveled around the room appreciatively.

As the flashing sign outside had proclaimed, it truly was a water-bed bonanza, hosting every kind of water bed imaginable.

Her eyes were immediately drawn to an impressive display in the center of the room, spotlighting a gorgeous bedroom set constructed of dark oak and lovely beveled mirrors, sitting on a twelve-drawer pedestal. There were tiny roses etched around the center mirrors and a lovely canopy spread enticingly overhead. The matching dresser and two nightstands completed the ensemble and reeked of excellent taste and understated elegance. With a sense of exhilaration Fritzi had to remind herself that she wasn't looking in her treasure book now, that what she saw before her was the real thing!

"Oh," she crooned, hurrying over to reverently touch the glistening wood. Her fingers ran lightly over the varnished surface of the bed, her eyes closing momentarily in sheer ecstasy. But then reality sank in. Though there were numerous banners throughout the store boldly proclaiming an end-of-the-year sale, she still had the sinking feeling that she would never be able to afford this particular set. But it was exactly like the one she had pasted in her scrapbook.

"You like this little beauty?" the salesman inquired pleasantly, his eyes lighting up with what surely would be an impending sale.

When they came in with that kind of look, they nearly always went home with a water bed. Only three more sales today and he would have enough to pay off his credit card, which was groaning from the holidays.

"Oh, yes," she murmured. "It is beautiful."

"Not only beautiful but durable. Yep, this little beauty is built to last," the man assured her. To prove his point he thrummed on the gleaming wood with his fingers, his face solemnly assuring her that he knew what he was talking about. Since it didn't necessarily sound cheap, Fritzi was duly impressed.

"Oh, that is nice," she murmured appreciatively.

"You ever slept on a water bed?" he asked.

"No."

"You'll love it . . . you'll love it!" he promised in a voice that sounded remarkably like Gomer Pyle talking to Sergeant Carter. "After one night on this bed you'll never think of sleeping on anything else. Here, lie down and get the feel of it." He stood back and motioned for her to climb up on the bed.

Fritzi glanced around uneasily, not at all sure she should climb up in the middle of the bed and lie down. In fact, she wasn't at all sure she could get in the bed at all; it was extremely high off the floor! "Oh, I don't think I should—"

"Nonsense! Don't be shy," the salesman insisted. "Believe me, you're going to love it!"

Even though the bed looked absolutely lovely on the pedestal, Fritzi did have to admit that it would be devilish to get in and out of. Eyeing the bed apprehensively, she glanced back at the salesman hopefully. "How do you get in?"

"Just climb right up there," he encouraged brightly.

Still not sure if she was doing the right thing, Fritzi removed her heavy coat, then gathered her skirt up around her knees and proceeded to climb up the side of the bed, having the awful feeling that she looked exactly like a monkey in snow boots shimmying up a tree.

Egad, it was a tall bed! She cast an apprehensive glance down toward the floor, and her fingers dug tighter into the patchwork bedspread. "It's really . . . high, isn't it?" She grinned nervously.

"Yes, but that's what makes it so unique. Isn't it great? Did you notice the excellent craftsmanship of this bed? This little beauty hasn't just been assembly-lined. Handcrafted, that's what we're dealing with here. Now lie down and stretch out. Isn't that glorious?"

She had finally reached the top, and she lay staring at the ceiling for a moment, trying to catch her breath. One thing was for certain: Should she be able to afford this marvelous luxury, she would definitely have to change her bathroom habits at night; once she got in, it would be wise to stay there until morning!

The salesman fairly beamed with confidence as she obediently spread out and let the motion of the mattress sway her gently back and forth. It was a pleasant, soothing motion, and she had to admit that it was indeed comfortable as she let her eyes drift closed peacefully.

"The nice thing about this bed is that there are

two twin mattresses. That eliminates a lot of the motion you'd have in other models." He hefted himself up the side and plopped down heavily on the other side of the bed as Fritzi's eyes flew open, and she clutched the edge for support when she felt herself catapulting straight up in the air. "You won't even know when another person's in the bed, or, if they happened to get up in the middle of the night, you'll never know it, either. Count to three and the motion of the mattress immediately ceases."

She hated to contradict his sales pitch, but she definitely *had* been aware when he entered the bed. She was counting, but they were still moving like a ship in a storm-tossed sea.

"Yes . . . that *is* nice," she parroted again, fearing that if the thing took a notion to throw her, it would break every bone in her body.

"Actually, this is our best buy in the store. I'll even throw in a set of sheets and a comforter and you won't be out the extra expense of new linens when you make your purchase. A person has to consider those things when purchasing a water bed."

"I hadn't thought of that."

"Most people don't. That's why I always like to mention it. This bed also has dual heaters. You can have your side as warm or as cool as you like and never disturb your bed partner."

"I'm not married."

"Oh . . . well, a pretty lady like you certainly

will be one of these days, and I'm sure this bed will be with you a long time. Once you have it, you'll never let it go."

They were both lying on the bed now. The salesman suddenly turned his head and looked her straight in the eye. "Honestly, have you *ever* experienced such a sensation?"

"No." She really hadn't.

"It's on sale today. Half price," he said temptingly.

"Well . . . I don't know. How much is it?" she ventured timidly. It felt very strange to be lying on the bed with a complete stranger discussing the prices of beds.

"Ah! The price. I'm not going to be able to make you believe me when I tell you."

"Try," she coaxed with breathless anticipation.

"You really like this set, don't you?" he urged.

She nodded her head enthusiastically.

"It's what you've always wanted, I can tell by the look on your face!"

"Yes, it is," she admitted, thinking of her treasure-mapping book.

"And I want to see you have it. We at Waterbed Bonanza want our customers happy. A happy customer is a satisfied customer!"

She nodded her head excitedly. "The bed, how much is it?" She wasn't going to be able to stand the suspense much longer.

"The entire set? A mere thirty-five hundred," he exclaimed, as if he couldn't believe it himself.

"Thirty-five hundred!" She gasped. His face crumbled with disenchantment as she sat upright and looked around her dismally. She couldn't afford thirty-five hundred dollars!

"Can you believe it?" the salesman prompted gleefully. "We're practically giving it away!"

"Well, I appreciate your generosity, but I can't afford it," she confessed.

"You don't think it's worth it? We're talking solid oak, a fifteen-year guarantee, and baffled flotation mattress with dual control!" His face was crestfallen as he stared at her in disbelief.

"I'm sure it is, but I don't have that much money."

"How much do you have?"

"Five hundred . . . more or less."

The phone began to ring as the salesman sat up and swung his feet over the side of the bed. "Let me do some figuring," he offered, some of the enthusiasm draining out of his voice. "I'll be right back."

Thirty-five hundred dollars! Good grief! She lay back on the pillow and savored the last few remaining minutes of the delicious feeling of floating free as he rushed off to answer the phone and do some new calculations. No matter how much figuring he did, she was sure he couldn't knock enough off to satisfy her budget.

Since the store was empty of everyone other than

her and the salesman, who was busy talking on the phone, she rolled over on her stomach, spreading her arms out wide and luxuriating in the warmth of the bed a few seconds more before she climbed down and contented herself with looking at a less expensive model.

The bed did feel heavenly. She sighed contentedly and let her eyes drift closed once more.

With just the slightest motion she could set the bed to rocking gently back and forth. Without realizing it her knees began to dig in the mattress, and she impishly set the bed to swaying faster. The faster it swayed, the deeper she dug in, and in a few minutes her bottom was sticking up in the air and the bed was moving back and forth like a whirlpool.

"Are you being waited on, ma'am?" A deep baritone voice shattered her playful antics, and she froze in her ridiculous position as the bed slowly settled down.

Egads! She knew that voice.

Deciding to bluff her way out of this embarrassing situation, she flipped over on her back and grinned up at him pertly. "Oh, hi there, Ryan!"

Since he was wearing a pair of dark sunglasses, she couldn't fully see his expression, but she could tell that he was confused when she had addressed him by his first name.

Struggling to prop herself up on one elbow, she decided to be generous and help him out. "Don't you remember me?"

A tiny, apologetic grin tugged at the corners of his mouth as he stared down at her, sensing that they had met before but not having the slightest idea where or when. "You do ring a bell somewhere . . . but I'm sorry, I don't seem to recall the honor of having met you."

She smiled. Honor. That was nice. "I'm Fritzi Taylor. You know, the one who saved you from the big, mean monkey?"

"Big monkey?" His grin widened even though his face grew more puzzled.

"You don't remember the big monkey." She gasped in a playfully offended voice. "And I saved your life! I would have sworn you would be eternally indebted to me until your dying day." She put out her hand, gesturing for him to help her out of the bed.

"I'm going to take a wild guess and say you're the angel of mercy who's responsible for getting me home last night?" He reached out and carefully began to help her down from the bed.

"That's me. I'm really surprised to see that you made it in to work. I figured you'd have a lulu of a headache this morning."

"A lulu and then some," he confided with a meaningful wince. "Listen, I want to thank you again for coming to my rescue, and I want to apologize for my . . . uh . . . behavior. I hope I didn't say or do anything to offend you. I don't make a habit of drinking like I did last night, and I want to assure you tnat I'm usually in more control of my faculties."

"Oh, that's all right," she assured him. "There were a lot of people who got a little carried away last night."

"I seem to remember some sort of an accident. I hope your car wasn't damaged too badly?"

"No, it's not bad." She suddenly felt very impish. "Have you found out yet who you took to the party and then ran off?" she said teasingly.

He cleared his throat uncomfortably. "Yes, I do believe she just happened to call first thing this morning to express her . . . displeasure at the way the evening ended so abruptly." Once more his face broke out into a contagious smile as he easily lifted her the last part of her journey. "What sort of flowers do you think a guy should send a lady if he wanted to make amends?"

"A man can never go wrong with roses," she promised.

"Then roses it is."

When her feet were solidly on the floor once more, she heaved a sigh of relief and straightened her disheveled clothing. "Thanks a lot. That bed's higher than it looks."

He giggled, that same infectious giggle she remembered from the night before, and she felt herself joining in. "Well, it is! Have you ever been up there?"

"No, can't say that I have," he acknowledged, the

giggle still clearly in evidence. "Can't really say that I've ever had any desire to, either."

"Do you mean to tell me that you don't have a water bed yourself, and you sell them?" she exclaimed. She was experiencing that same warm, happy feeling she had felt the previous night when they had been together. There was a certain instant attraction she seemed to feel for him, but she couldn't pinpoint the reason why.

He shrugged sheepishly. "I know this doesn't sound very good, but I've honestly never slept in one . . . although I've been thinking about taking one home lately." Once more that pleasant, contagious grin spread across his features. "What about you? Are you really interested in purchasing a new bed?" He removed his sunglasses as he spoke and, in an absent manner, ran his hands over his bloodshot eyes. Although he was immaculately dressed and smelled as good as anything Fritzi could ever remember, his face showed distinct signs of his rambunctious partying the night before.

"I've been toying with the idea. I've had a little back trouble since I was thrown off a horse several years ago, and all my friends tell me that a water bed is exactly what I need." Her hand ran lovingly over the glistening wood she was standing next to. "This one's really lovely, isn't it?"

"Yes, that's one of our nicest pieces," he agreed. "Handcrafted, solid oak." He placed the glasses in a leather case and stuck them in the pocket of his dress shirt.

"I know." She sighed wistfully, giving one final affectionate pat to the gleaming headboard with its lovely twining roses. "But I'm afraid it's much too expensive for me."

"Oh? Well, we have other models," he offered quickly. Taking a step back, he pointed to another bed that was on sale but wasn't half as pretty as the oak one. "I could let you have this one for a little under three hundred dollars, or that one over there in the corner for even less than that. Is that more in the price range you were thinking about?"

Although her heart wasn't in it, Fritzi dutifully walked over and carefully examined the beds, her heart sinking. They were in her price range, all right, and they were okay, but her eyes kept drifting back to the first set. "The other salesman who was waiting on me is up at the desk doing some refiguring. Do you think he could come up with a better price than the thirty-five hundred dollars on this oak one?" she prompted hopefully.

His smile was genuinely polite and helpful. "Well, that's possible. About what did you want to spend?"

She swallowed nervously and grinned at him lamely. "Five hundred would be tops."

His smile went from genuinely polite and helpful to sagging disbelief. "Five hundred?"

"Yeah . . . it's probably impossible to drop the price three thousand dollars, isn't it?" She knew it was, but after all, that oak bedroom set was practically the image of the picture she had pasted in her treasure-mapping book, and she *was* talking to the owner of the store. Stranger things had happened.

"I'm afraid so," he verified before her hopes soared any higher. "Don't you like this one for three hundred dollars? I'll even throw in a set of sheets and the padded rails," he tried again, but she had already gone back to the other set.

"Just look at those mirrors," she marveled, peering up at the squeaky clean mirrors above the headboard, then blushed a pretty pink when she caught him looking at her strangely.

Glancing up at him shyly, her gray eyes widened pleadingly. "I really love this particular set. How much would the bed alone be? Maybe I could get the rest of the pieces later on."

Ryan's smile was gentle as he gazed down at her. He could tell how much she loved the bed, and he was really sorry he couldn't cut the price to fit her budget. "Look, Fritzi, are you sure you really want a water bed?" he prompted. "You know, some people don't like them after they get them home," he revealed honestly.

"Oh, I'd *love* one," she vowed adamantly. "Everyone I talk to says they're the greatest!"

"Not everyone likes them," he warned again.

"But, Ryan—"

"Okay, okay," he relented, realizing that she had

her heart set on the bed. "Let me see what I can do."

"I have the new figures," the first salesman announced as he walked away from the desk. "Hi, Ryan."

"Hi, Ed."

Handing his business card to Fritzi, Ed smiled persuasively. "I know you won't believe it, but I was able to knock even more off the sales price!"

A quick glance at the new price, which was considerably lower than the first one, assured Fritzi that it was still well out of her price range. "Oh." Her face fell with disappointment. "Well, I suppose I'll have to look around a little more. Even at that price, I can't afford the whole set."

Ryan reached over and took the card out of her hand, quietly surveying the figures written on it. "Ed, she was wondering what the bed alone would sell for," he suggested helpfully.

"The bed alone? Well, I'd have to break it all down," Ed complied willingly. "Wait a sec."

Ryan calmly edged over to the desk with him as he started to figure the numbers once more.

"Knock off another couple of hundred," he instructed quietly as Ed finally came up with a new total.

"Another couple of hundred?" Ed turned to him in puzzlement. "Are you sure? You'd be losing money at that price."

"I know, but she did me a big favor last night.

And, Ed, tell her that includes the setup and delivery price." His eyes wandered over to her as she was still looking at the bedroom set. There was a certain something about this woman that seemed intriguing. He had never been one to be overly impressed by a pretty woman, but for some reason this pretty woman had caught his eye. "If you can, arrange for me to deliver it this afternoon."

"You're going to deliver it?" Ed had no idea what was going on, but something was up. Although Ryan never shied away from work, he never voluntarily offered to do a job that he paid someone else to perform. "You don't want Charlie and Doyle to handle it?"

"No." His eyes remained glued to the shapely feminine derriere still bending over the side of the bed as he spoke. "I'll take care of it."

"Whatever you say," Ed relented, placing his pen back in his shirt pocket. "You're the boss."

When the salesman handed her the card this time, a smile of pure delight broke across her face and she eagerly nodded her acceptance of the new price. Her gaze immediately searched for Ryan, and as their eyes met, she gave him a grateful smile.

Smiling back, he winked at her and walked toward the back of the store as Ed began to write up the sale.

Fritzi was overjoyed with her new purchase, but an overwhelming sense of disappointment stole over her as she watched Ryan disappear through a doorway leading into the back room. He had a marvelous . . . tush. In fact, she had noticed it last night, and it looked even better this morning.

Strange, but she had never been impressed with a man's tush before. She shrugged the unnerving thought away quickly.

"I can have the bed delivered to you this afternoon if that would be okay," Ed was saying.

"Oh, that soon? Well, yes, I suppose so." Fritzi tried to shake away the feeling of loneliness that was now threatening to override her earlier enthusiasm as she wrote out the check. Maybe getting the new bed would help.

Casting one last longing glance at the door Ryan had disappeared behind, she gave Ed her address.

Since she couldn't think of a single reason to summon Ryan to the front again, she dropped her checkbook back in her purse and gave one final glance in the direction of her new bed before she slipped on her coat and left the store.

Ryan had said that he had never slept in a water bed, either, she thought absently, then licked her lips wickedly.

Immediately guilt filled her as she kicked herself mentally for the lustful thought that had come rushing into her mind.

Gad! Maybe she *should* call Coy tonight.

CHAPTER FOUR

"It's simply gorgeous," Fritzi bragged as she stirred a pot of chili late that afternoon. "It looks exactly like the one in my treasure-mapping book. You're going to drool when you see it."

Neil gave an absentminded grunt as he turned to the sports page of the evening paper. "I'll try to control myself."

"See that you do," she bantered. "Even though I got it at a fantastic bargain, I spent more than I intended. I'll be broke the rest of the winter."

He shook his head tolerantly. "That won't be anything new for you. You're broke the majority of the time, anyway."

Reaching in the cabinet for the box of crackers, she had to laugh at his accurate observations of her financial status. "You're just jealous because you don't have a lovely water bed with beveled mirrors and twining roses."

"You bet. Just what I always wanted. Twining roses on my bed." He groaned aloud. "Son of a gun! The Lakers blew it again!"

"You want some chili?" Fritzi flipped off the burner and proceeded to fill her bowl generously with the fragrant mixture of beans, meat, and seasonings.

Taking a quick glance at his watch, he laid the paper down and got up from the table. "No. I have to pick up Susan in a little while. I have to leave soon."

"You'd better allow extra time," she warned as she brought her bowl over to the table and sat down. "The weather is really beastly. I was beginning to wonder if I was going to get home."

"I'll make it," Neil assured her, grinning to deliberately provoke her. "I'm a man and I can do anything." He knew how much she hated his man-woman comparisons.

"You could always call Susan and cancel," Fritzi suggested, completely ignoring his chauvinistic remark. Although he would never admit it, Neil would probably crawl on his hands and knees to keep his date that night.

"No," he returned casually—too casually in her opinion. "I agreed to these sessions, and I'll see them through no matter how stupid they are."

"It seems to me that since you hate the meetings so much, it would just be easier for you and Susan to break down and admit you love each other and try to work out your problems together," Fritzi suggested. "And even if you didn't plan your life carefully enough, I think this will all work out eventually. You do love each other, and I predict you'll end up back together. I've always said that."

"Now wait a minute. I didn't say I was going back to her," he said, challenging her. "I only said I was willing to try to talk our problems through. It may not work." Tyce Williams was still a thorn sticking in his side, and he wasn't sure he could forget what he considered Susan's disloyalty. "And furthermore, I'm not at all sure I love Susan any longer."

Fritzi ducked her head and snickered as she bit into a cracker. He could stand there and deny he didn't love Susan until the cows came home, but Fritzi knew better. He was just being stubborn. Boy, was she glad her life wasn't such a mess!

"What's the snicker for?" He lifted a challenging brow.

She glanced up innocently. "Did I snicker?"

"You certainly did. What's so funny?"

"Nothing."

"Look, just because I don't run my life on a sheet of paper like you do, doesn't mean that I'm not capable of handling my problems. And just because we're going to these meetings doesn't automatically mean we're getting back together."

"I know, I know." Fritzi decided that since he had failed to listen to common sense in the past, she should try a different approach and see if she couldn't make him see the light in a different way. From now on she was going to agree with everything he said in an effort to make him see how very foolish he was behaving when it came to Susan.

"I wasn't the one who had doubts," Neil reminded her. "You seem to forget that it was she who couldn't make up her mind which one she wanted. Me or Tyce Williams." He began to pace the floor in agitation. "Lord knows I tried. I was patient far longer than the average man would be, but I'm sorry, I just couldn't play second fiddle to another man and be happy about it."

"Don't get all wound up. I completely agree. The marriage was probably a big mistake, and if the counseling doesn't work, then I say scratch it and get this fiasco over with."

"Fiasco?" He paused in his pacing and frowned. "I wouldn't necessarily call the marriage a fiasco, just poor timing on my part. . . ." His voice trailed off defensively.

"Well, I don't know what else you could call it other than a fiasco," she argued. "You've repeatedly refused to see Susan or even discuss the possibility of a reconciliation until recently. In the thirteen months you've been married, how long have you actually lived with each other?"

"Only three months—but that was long enough for her to have doubts," he pointed out. "I was perfectly happy with the marriage. *She* was the one who wanted time to 'think.' "

"I realize that. You were a real saint, and she's a temperamental worm who doesn't deserve a man like you." She took a cautious bite of her chili. "You'd better hurry. You're going to be late."

His stance stiffened almost imperceptibly, but she didn't fail to notice. "Susan isn't a worm," he said curtly.

"Perhaps 'worm' is a little strong, but nevertheless, you're absolutely right about her. A divorce might be the only solution. When it's over, Susan can go back to Tyce and you can pick up your life and start over again."

"She is not going back to Tyce," he snapped irritably. "That's all over now. It has been for a long time."

"Really?" Fritzi knew that Tyce was out of Susan's life permanently, but she was relieved to hear Neil finally admit it. "If that's true, then what's all the fuss about?" she reasoned.

"The fact that Tyce Williams is gone doesn't change my relationship with Susan in the least," he hastened to add as he noted the look of triumph on his sister's face. "Maybe that was our problem in the beginning, but there are other complications now. Complications we may or may not work out." He glared at Fritzi and absently tucked his shirttail in the back of his jeans. "But she isn't a worm," he reiterated.

"Tell Susan I said hi," Fritzi conceded with a friendly grin, knowing full well how much she was annoying him. But if it would make him stop and consider what he was about to throw away, then it was worth his anger. "Give her my love—it probably wouldn't hurt if you gave her a little of yours."

"You may think that this is all very funny, but one of these days you're going to meet a man who'll tie your stomach up in knots. Then I'll be the one standing back with the smirk on my face," he promised. To his knowledge Fritzi had never actually been head over heels in love with any man, so it was easy for her to find humor where there was none.

"Not a chance," Fritzi declared smugly. "My life is too well planned out. If you would have listened to me and done the same to yours, you wouldn't be in this pickle in the first place."

Neil shook his head disgustedly. "Boy, I can't wait for the day when you have to eat those words."

"Never." She drained the last of her coffee and set the mug back on the table carefully.

"What makes you think so?"

She grinned. "Because I'm a woman and I can do anything."

"I wouldn't be so smug if I were you. You never know what Cupid will throw your way," he warned.

Deciding that he had had more than enough of the troublesome subject, he turned and stalked to the back door, shrugging into his heavy coat on the way. "Well, I have to go. I hope you're planning on staying in this evening. If a person was smart, they wouldn't go out unless they had to."

"As a matter of fact, I *am* staying home. Didn't I tell you? The salesman promised delivery of my new bed late this afternoon. Although"—she glanced worriedly out the window at the heavy snow falling against the windowpanes—"I really doubt if they can now. It would take a team of Siberian huskies and a dogsled to get it here in this kind of weather."

As she spoke, the sound of the front door bell filtered through to the kitchen. "Was that the sound of dogs barking or a door bell?" Neil quipped, giving her a good-bye wave as he opened the back door to leave. She waved back as she popped out of her chair and headed for the living room.

When she pulled the door open, a strong gust of wind buffeted her as she smiled and greeted the delivery man.

"I'm so happy to see you! I didn't think you could—" She stopped, and her heart fluttered as she recognized Ryan Majors's delectable form huddled in a dark brown suede sheepskin coat.

"Hi, lady. I hope you have a warm fire going." He grinned.

"Ryan? Well, my goodness, come in!" she invited happily, holding the door open wider for him. Funny, but every time he appeared on the scene, her pulse decided to act erratically. "Surely you're not delivering my bed?"

Ryan's grin widened shyly. "Yes, I am . . . or at least I'm trying to."

She peered around his broad shoulders, half expecting to really see a dogsled parked in the drive. "What did you come in?"

"The delivery truck. I didn't have any trouble until I turned off the main highway. The snow is beginning to drift, and the secondary roads are in pretty bad shape." He stomped the snow off his boots and stepped into the warmth of the old-fashioned living room. A cheery blaze was burning brightly in the massive stone fireplace as he stepped closer to the heat to warm his hands.

Closing the door quickly behind him, she hurried over, trying to still her excitement of seeing him again.

"I can't thank you enough for coming out on a day like this," she said gratefully, "and I had no idea *you* would be the one to deliver the bed."

Ryan unbuttoned a couple of buttons on his coat and gave her another one of his cute grins, which made her legs threaten to buckle on her. "I don't usually do the delivering, but in this case I offered my services. I hope you don't mind."

"Mind? Goodness, no." She laughed weakly. "I don't mind." Far from it—she was *too* happy to see him, and that was beginning to worry her.

"Good." She felt her face turn pink with a warm, self-conscious flush as his gaze locked briefly with hers. "I was hoping you wouldn't."

"Well." She laughed again, breaking the tiny thread of intimacy that had suddenly sprang up between them. "I suppose you want me to show you where to put the bed?"

"Yeah, if you will, then I can get started."

"Sure, just follow me."

He trailed behind her out of the room and up a long, winding staircase. The upstairs hall was cold and drafty as the north wind rattled the shutters eerily.

"I hope the bed isn't very heavy," she said, chattering conversationally as they made their way down the carpeted hallway.

"No, it isn't," he assured her as he tried to keep his mind on the business at hand and his eyes off her jean-clad fanny. She had a darn cute fanny. "Actually, I'm only setting up your bed frame this afternoon. After you left, we discovered we only had one headboard, so it's been ordered. It'll be in in a couple of days."

"Oh?" She turned to face him, disappointment clearly written on her pretty features. "Well, I guess that will be all right. At least I'll have the bed."

Once more their eyes met, and she smiled at him timidly as her pulse raced feverishly. "It was very nice of you to make the delivery yourself."

It was more than nice. Somehow she sensed that he had gone out of his way for her, and for some reason, that made her feel extremely good.

"Like I said," he repeated softly, "in this particular case I wanted to handle it personally."

Her hand fumbled behind her for the doorknob, and she hurriedly pushed the door to her bedroom open before her knees gave way completely. Whatever strange power Ryan Majors was beginning to have over her almost frightened her. "You can just put it right in here. I've already taken my other bed down."

Ryan's gaze assessed the size of the room, and he quickly determined that he would have no trouble in assembling the bed. "Okay. No problem."

Thirty minutes later the bed was assembled with the exception of the headboard and canopy and was being filled with warm water from a garden hose connected to the faucet in her bathroom.

"These things are amazing," she said, marveling as she watched the blue plastic swell invitingly. "I can hardly wait to go to bed tonight!"

Ryan glanced up from his work and smiled. He was a great one to tease, and for a moment he toyed with the idea of making some witty, suggestive remark but decided to refrain until he knew her better. "I hope you're going to enjoy it as much as you think."

"Oh, I will," she vowed.

Ryan's smile deepened as he made a silent promise to himself to see that she did.

Fifteen minutes later he reached over to feel the hose to check the temperature of the water. "I'm afraid we've run out of hot water," he announced.

"Oh? What does that mean?"

"It means we'll have to let the hot-water heater recover before we run any more into the mattress. That is, if you want to sleep on the bed tonight. I can go ahead and fill it with cold water, but it will take at least twenty-four hours before the heater can warm it sufficiently."

"No, let's let it recover," she decided, wondering what they would do in the meantime. The hot-water heater was an old one and would take at least a couple of hours to do its job. "Would you like a cup of coffee or something cold to drink while we're waiting?"

Ryan suddenly propped both his arms on the doorjamb she was standing under, for a moment forcing her to stay in place. The butterflies in her stomach went crazy as he gazed at her with his lovely brown eyes. "Maybe later, but right now I'd like to take this opportunity to thank you properly for bringing me home last night."

His voice had softened to a husky, sensual tone as he leaned closer, their faces barely inches apart. Fritzi knew he was going to kiss her, and she stood strangely transfixed as his mouth drew closer. "I really did appreciate it. I don't know if I mentioned it earlier or not, but I don't usually get in that kind of condition. All I remember is that someone kept handing me a glass, and it was always full of gin."

She smiled, recalling how truly out of it he had been. "Really, your thanks are completely unnecessary. I was happy to do it."

"Maybe so, but I still appreciate it." His mouth inched closer. "Uh, by the way, you don't happen to have a husband lurking around in the shadows somewhere, do you?"

68

"No, no husband."

"Boyfriend?"

"No, not really."

"Good." He felt a surge of relief at her denial. He had worried all day that she already would be involved with someone.

"Ryan," she cautioned, her voice growing more breathless by the minute. "I think I should warn you that I'm not exactly looking for a new relationship at the moment." She paused, searching for a more tactful way to put it. After all, she didn't know what his intentions were at this point. "What I meant to say is, you're very nice, but let's keep this on a business level. Okay?"

"Business? Sure, no problem, but what's wrong with combining business with pleasure?" His eyes and arms continued to hold her captive, but he stepped back a fraction to allow her room to think his question over.

She closed her eyes and struggled to still her pounding heart. "Nothing, I suppose. I just didn't want to mislead you into thinking I was looking for any . . ." She took a deep breath and grinned at him lamely. "You know."

"Yes, I know." He gazed at her lips longingly. They looked very soft and inviting. "But one kiss wouldn't necessarily constitute a commitment for life, would it?"

Although Ryan had always considered himself a gentleman first—and he would never push a woman when she didn't want to be pushed—he was still hesitant to let this attraction they seemed to have for each other end so quickly. He shifted his stance only slightly and continued to block her path with his arms. "Wouldn't you agree?"

Yes, she would agree with that.

"Of course . . . I'm sorry." She smiled, relieved that the burdensome question had been solved. After all, what was one little kiss?

His mouth was already making headway toward her while she was still arguing the wisdom of her decision. Her life was running too smoothly right now to put a cog in the wheel, and somehow she had the uncanny feeling that this man might try to do just that.

"Then you agree that I should thank you properly," he concluded.

Leaning closer to him, she gave up trying to persuade herself that she shouldn't be doing this and gave way to the moment. "I am never one to argue once a person has his mind made up," she said teasingly.

"Good," he said huskily as his mouth finally captured hers. Closing her eyes blissfully, her arms crept around his neck, and she savored the feel of his mouth taking full possession of hers.

If a man had ever made her feel like this, she couldn't remember the occasion. Try as she might, Fritzi couldn't ever recall a man ever making her bones feel as if they were going to completely melt the way Ryan was doing. From the moment the kiss began progressing from pleasant to cordial to devastating, she forced herself to remember that her life *was* all planned out for her, and Ryan Majors was not in those plans!

"Ryan," she murmured as his mouth seemed reluctant to part from hers long moments later.

"Mmm?"

"Ryan . . . this is nice, but I think we should stop."

"Why? I'm not through thanking you yet."

Lifting her up against his sturdy frame, he pulled her tightly to him, making her achingly aware of the differences in their bodies. Hers was soft and rounded while his was like finely honed steel. "Do you honestly want me to stop?" he challenged as he buried his face in the curve of her neck and savored her floral-scented perfume.

"Yes!"

"Why?"

"Because I like it too much. . . ."

He chuckled at her honesty and drew her closer as his mouth hungrily took control of hers a second time.

Again it was several minutes before she could convince herself that this insanity would have to stop. Gently pushing him away, she took a deep breath to clear her muddled senses and hurriedly pushed herself out of his arms before she weakened again.

He grinned at her abrupt departure and backed away to give her some breathing space. "So, Fritzi Taylor is not looking for a new man in her life right now." He sighed and shook his head thoughtfully. "I have to tell you that I'm more than a little disappointed to hear that."

Taking a deep breath, she returned his smile with a very shaky one of her own. "Well, you know how it is. There's a time and a place for everything, and this just doesn't happen to be the time or the place to form any new involvements." Somehow she didn't sound as convincing as she should. "But that shouldn't disturb you. I'm sure a handsome man like you isn't running around completely unattached." She wanted to keep her question light and completely indifferent, but she found herself holding her breath while she waited for his answer.

"No, I'm not involved with anyone."

"No one special?" she prompted, trying to hide the elation filling her voice, although she couldn't understand why she should care one way or the other.

His eyes sought and captured hers once more. "No, no one special." The silence that followed his carefully chosen words was almost deafening. "But who knows when the right one will come along and sweep me right off my feet."

"Yes." She laughed nervously. "Who knows? Well, I suppose you'd like that cup of coffee now."

"If you wouldn't mind."

"I wouldn't mind. I might even throw in a bowl of chili if you're real lucky," she said, tempting him.

"Chili? That sounds great," he replied as they started out of the room.

"I was just having a bowl when you arrived," she explained as she skipped happily down the staircase. She suddenly felt as carefree as a schoolgirl on her first date, and she had no idea why. She only knew she thoroughly enjoyed Ryan Majors.

Ryan followed her down the stairs, his mood matching hers completely.

"I hope you have plenty of catsup," he warned. "I love catsup with my chili."

"Oh, I do too! And cold milk." Her feet paused in their descent, and she turned to face him expectantly. "Do you happen to like milk with your chili?"

He grinned happily. "Do I? I love it!"

She cocked her head and grinned back expectantly. "If you say you like peanut butter and crackers with it, I'll die."

He'd die, too, if he had to eat that combination! "You're kidding! Why, I've eaten peanut butter and crackers with chili since I was big enough to get my knife in the peanut butter jar, but this is the first time in my life I've ever met anyone else who shared that same thrill," he said with mock adoration.

"I've always eaten peanut butter and crackers with my chili!" she exclaimed.

That truly was the most revolting food combination he had ever heard of in his life, but he vowed he'd try it if it killed him. She might not be looking for a new relationship right now, but she hadn't asked about *his* plans.

"I can hardly wait. It seems that fate must have made us for each other," he commented as they walked into the kitchen.

Her smile suddenly died an instant death. Meant for each other? Her pulse increased its rhythm. Now wait a minute. He was just the nice guy she had taken home the night before and then bought a bed from today. So what if they happened to have the same taste in food and almost everything else that had been mentioned since they first met? That didn't mean a thing. She glanced at him nervously. Did it?

No, she hurriedly reasoned. It certainly did not. Although he was very nice, she would never be romantically or otherwise interested in Ryan Majors, though she kept having this nagging sensation that she knew him from somewhere. Maybe it had been in a different life when she had been Cleopatra and he had been Antony. . . . She shook her head at her wild imaginings and decided to be rational. Before last night she had never seen Ryan, and right now they were a far cry from being Antony and Cleopatra! She was just plain Fritzi Taylor, who had graciously offered a new acquaintance a bowl of chili.

But just to keep the record straight, she found

herself discreetly trying to explain the carefully laid out plans she had made for her life as she reached for the box of crackers and jar of peanut butter.

"I guess some people would laugh, but I've always believed a person should have goals in their life," she added after she had explained the basics of her plans.

"Oh, yes . . . I agree." He sat down at the table and watched her bustle around the kitchen.

"I've already got a lot of the things in my treasure-mapping book," she revealed proudly. "And the water bed is just one more dream come true."

Ryan stared down glumly at the huge plate of crackers and peanut butter she placed before him and waited patiently for the chili to follow. "Do these plans of yours include marriage someday?"

"Oh, certainly," she assured him as she switched the burner off under the pot and filled his bowl. "But that's at least five years away."

"Five years!" Ryan reached out and stopped her ramblings with a touch of his hand on her arm. For a moment she dreaded turning around to face him. Five years suddenly *did* sound like a long time.

"Five years?" he repeated incredulously. "Are you serious?"

"Well . . . yes. Very serious."

"How old are you, Fritzi?"

"Maybe I don't want you to know how old I—"

"Come on, how old? Twenty-three, twenty-four?" he asked, guessing.

A feeling of satisfaction washed over her. He had missed it by several years. "Thanks, but no, I'm a little older than that."

"Well, however old you are, don't you think you're going to be getting a late start in life by waiting another five years before you even think about becoming seriously involved with a man?"

Actually, she had never thought about it that way. "Yes, I suppose so. But I'll only be thirty-two then," she argued, letting her age slip out, anyway. "That isn't exactly over the hill."

"Surely you could be persuaded to change your mind," Ryan chided, letting that slow grin of his take over once more. "What would happen if you met that certain man who could turn your whole world around now, instead of five years from now?"

"Not a chance." Her answer came back so quickly, it threw him for a loop.

"You mean, if the right man walked into your life right now, you'd still want to hold to some cockamamie plans you made several years ago?" he exclaimed.

Suddenly she didn't like the change in his tone at all. "I certainly would. I've had those plans for a long time, and just because some man would come waltzing into my life and want to change them wouldn't mean a thing to me," she retorted stubbornly.

"Why, that has to be the most cockeyed thing

I've ever heard of." He pushed away from the table and began to pace the floor agitatedly.

Sensing that he was becoming upset with her, she busied herself with the chili. "This is a senseless conversation, Ryan. If you knew me, you'd know that I run my life on a schedule and I'm not about to stop now . . . even if I did happen to meet this so-called man who would change my whole life."

When cornered, Ryan could be as stubborn as she was. He paused in his pacing and turned to face her, a cunning look on his features now. "Just what would happen if I should be that man?"

His question took her completely off-guard, and the ladle dropped into the pot with a splash. "You?"

"Yes, me!"

"My gosh, Ryan. What a question. How in the world did we get on this subject? I only bought a bed from you! How did we get on the subject of marriage?" She was totally flustered by now.

"Surely you're not trying to deny that you haven't been feeling what I have from the moment we first met."

"No—I mean, yes! I'm not denying that you're a nice guy, but as far as anything serious developing between us, well . . ." She looked him over carefully before she totally cast him aside. There *was* something about him that was terribly appealing. "Maybe in five years . . ."

She didn't have the slightest idea what she was saying. He had her so shaken up, she could barely think straight. "Now look, Ryan, just *what* are you suggesting?"

"I'm suggesting that I might be the one to put a kink in those plans of yours and end up marrying you one of these days," he explained in a voice that suggested he was going to the grocery store for bread and milk instead of talking marriage to a relative stranger. "But I can tell you right now, I'm sure not going to wait five years to do it!"

For a second she thought she had misunderstood him as she stared back at him vacantly.

"But I'd have to give it a little more thought," he confessed. "We barely know each other, but I think I like what I do know . . . an awful lot." His eyes ran over her lazily. "Any objections?"

"Objections? To marrying me?"

"That's what I said."

"Well, hell's bells!" she sputtered, completely out of patience with his preposterous assumptions. "Of course I have objections! I think you're mad!"

"Well, that remains to be seen," he announced matter-of-factly as he stepped over to the table and picked up the plate of peanut butter and crackers. In a few seconds he had dumped them all in the trash.

"Ryan! What did you do that for?"

"Because I would throw up if I had to eat those with my chili," he said defiantly.

"I thought you said you loved peanut butter and crackers with your chili!"

"I was lying."

"So what brought on this spurt of honesty?" she demanded as she propped her hands on her hips irritably.

"It suddenly occurred to me that I'm going to have to work my buns off to get anywhere with you, Fritzi Taylor, and I'd better begin by being totally honest."

"Oh?"

"Yes. I'm going to do everything within my power to change your 'plans,'" he stated simply. "And I think you'd better be aware of that."

"You're not serious," she snapped.

"I have never been more serious in my life."

She was still dumbfounded. "Ryan, it's my life! Please don't try to mess it up. I'm perfectly happy with it the way it is."

"I know you *think* you are, but I don't think you know what you're going to be missing if you remain single for five more years." No one could have been more surprised than Ryan by the stance he had suddenly taken, but then, he had known that she was special from the moment he first met her.

"And you do?"

His smile was lazy. "I know what it can be."

"This is absolutely crazy," she reiterated. "You don't know anything about me. Why, I might be a real witch. Then what would you do?"

"If you are, I'll give up my pursuit real quick," he offered graciously.

"You're . . . you're impossible," she sputtered.

"Maybe so, but I've never felt as attracted to any other woman as I have to you, Fritzi." All humor suddenly left his pleasant features. "Regardless of how you feel, I think I owe it to myself to pursue that attraction. If it isn't right, it won't take long for me to find out. But if it is right, you'll thank me on our wedding day."

"Do whatever you want," she returned coolly, turning back to the stove. "But my plans are made. You can't change them, and there will be no wedding day for you and me, Ryan. That's absurd, and you might as well accept it."

"I beg to differ with you. I'll say it will be February fourteenth. Valentine's Day. That would be a nice romantic date, don't you think?"

"Five weeks away?"

"So?" He shrugged. "It's a lot better than five years."

"You're wasting your time." She carried the bowls of chili over to the table, willing her fickle heart to be still. He was talking nonsense and she knew it.

He winked at her as she marched past him. "Okay, so maybe I'll be off a day or two. February sixteenth or seventeenth wouldn't be all that bad, either."

"You're out of your mind."

He grinned and picked up a cracker and bit into it. "We'll see."

CHAPTER FIVE

February the fourteenth! Honestly. Who did he think he was?

Fritzi was still steaming over Ryan's absurd prediction two weeks later. Neat and orderly had been the pattern of her life for as long as she could remember, and she was not about to change things now.

For the past few years she had planned to the last detail what she intended to do with her life, and with very little variance she usually managed to get those things done. Whether it be professional or personal goals, she liked her life to run on schedule, and she wasn't about to let Ryan Majors change a thing.

A weak ray of January sun filtered through the bedroom window as Fritzi struggled to open her eyes. She groped blindly for the clock she had set beside the bed and groaned when she saw that it was ten o'clock already.

Willing her eyes to remain open, she struggled to

lie back on the pillow and absently reached up to rub her aching neck. If Ryan didn't drive her crazy, this bed was going to. It undoubtedly was the most uncomfortable thing she had ever slept on.

Twice in the last two weeks she had demanded that Ryan take the bed back, that she couldn't stand it another moment. Twice he had come back to the ranch and drained the bed, but at the last minute he had always talked her into trying it one more time, using the excuse that he would be out a lot of money if he had to sell the bed as a used one.

She would feel sorry for him and weaken, agreeing to try it one more time, but it was always the same old story. She hated water beds. Wiggling around on the flotation mattress irritably, she tried to pull the wad of sheets out from under her back. If it wasn't for the fact that she would have to see *him* again, she had half a mind to call Waterbed Bonanza and demand that the store take the thing back that very morning.

But if she did that, Ryan would probably come out and try to talk her out of it, and then she would be forced to see him again and, in turn, would find herself enjoying his company, as she had been with increasing regularity lately, and that had to stop. It simply had to. The situation was going to get out of hand, and she couldn't afford for that to happen.

Ryan had somehow managed to maneuver his way into her life nearly every day since she had met him, accidental meetings at the banks and local stores, meetings that in her opinion were far from accidental. He had sent bouquets of roses every other day and performed flagrant acts of downright subversion in her estimation, in order to see her.

One day she had been on her way into town when he had pulled her over on the side of the road and practically kidnapped her for the entire afternoon. He had brought along a basket filled with wine, cheese, and fruit, and they had spent the afternoon in the snow-covered mountains having a picnic, of all things.

A slow smile spread across her face as her mind drifted back to that almost perfect afternoon. Ryan had a way about him—she couldn't deny that. She could never remember wanting a man as badly as she wanted Ryan, both physically and emotionally, but her stubborn will wouldn't allow her to give in to her feelings.

Oh, she had thought about letting him make love to her . . . how could she have not at least considered that tempting thought when he touched all her senses with the grace of a bull in a china shop? And he was not exactly hiding the fact that he wanted her, but she knew that if she should take the relationship a step further, it would only strengthen his belief that their association would be a permanent one. And that would be sheer folly . . . unless he changed his stubborn mind and was willing to wait around for a few years.

She sighed and let her eyes drift closed once

more. She had to confess that in a tiny way she wished he would change his mind, even though they spent most of their time arguing over the fact that she wouldn't discard her plans. She repeatedly warned him that she was sticking to her plans, come hell or high water, but he had a way of looking at her that turned her insides to apple butter, and he not only knew it, but also used it every chance he got.

She stirred and forced herself to snap out of her daydreaming. Even with the minuscule chance that she should be falling in love with him, she would fight that attraction tooth and nail. She wasn't about to screw up her life the way Neil had.

Neil . . . he and Susan were absolutely nauseating the way they had done a sudden about-face and were now calling each other "cutie pie" and "sweetums," she thought resentfully.

The way they were acting lately, it was enough to make one throw up. Neil had stopped fighting the marriage encounter group, and now he was as strange as he had first accused the other members of being. They were positively so nice to each other, it was like drowning in a room of saccharin when they were around.

Summoning up enough courage to pull herself out of bed, she threw back the covers and started to climb out. After considerable grunting and groaning, she managed to get her feet on the floor. Trying to work the kinks out of her neck and shoulders, she eyed the bed with hostility.

True, her back didn't necessarily ache, but everything else did!

Neil was just coming up the stairs with a cup of coffee in his hand as she pulled on a robe and slipped out of her room.

"Morning, sleepyhead," he said in greeting as they passed each other.

"Morning, cutie pie."

"Hey, watch it. That's Susan's name for me," he said, rebuking her in an offended tone.

"Sorry."

"How's the water bed?"

She wrinkled her nose in distaste and proceeded down the stairway, trying to ignore his snickers and I-told-you-sos.

The smell of freshly brewed coffee met her dulled senses as she entered the kitchen and walked over to the cabinet to retrieve a cup.

"Good morning, Neda."

The housekeeper looked up from her place at the sink and smiled. "Good morning, dear. I see you slept late again this morning."

"Yes. As usual, I had trouble getting to sleep last night." Picking up the sugar bowl, Fritzi spooned two heaping teaspoons into the black mixture. Sneaking a guilty glance at Neda, who was cleaning vegetables for a stew she was preparing, Fritzi quickly added another teaspoon for good measure before she put the lid back on the bowl and placed it in the cabinet.

"Too much sugar is bad for you," Neda scolded with her back still turned. "The water bed still bothering you?"

The woman had eyes in back of her head! "Yes." Slumping down at the table, she took a cautious sip out of her cup and rubbed her aching neck. "Is it going to snow again today?"

"The weatherman is predicting another big storm."

"Oh, great. Just what we need."

"By the way, there's a telephone message for you by the phone in the living room."

"Oh, really? Who called?"

"He didn't say. He just left a number and wanted you to return the call when you got up."

Picking up her coffee cup, Fritzi strolled into the family room, almost afraid to look at the message. Somehow she knew it would be from Ryan. She wasn't going to return his call. She had distinctly told him after the movie he had insisted on taking her to a couple of nights ago that she would not see him again. And this time she was going to remain firm.

For a moment she stood staring at the set of digits neatly written in Neda's handwriting on the notepad. Actually, the number wasn't Ryan's. Her curiosity aroused, she continued to study the number, but it didn't look at all familiar. Perhaps it hadn't been Ryan and this was something important.

Her hand reached for the phone and then faltered. But if he had called and was trying to trick her like he had one other time when he left the number of a friend and Ryan had answered, she would be falling right back in his little trap and she didn't want that, either.

While she was still wrestling with her decision the phone rang, nearly making her jump out of her skin.

Relieved that the decision had been taken out of her hands if only for a moment, she lifted the receiver on the second ring.

"Hello?"

"Hi. Did you finally get up?" a familiar male voice said in greeting.

"Ryan." She gave a hopeless sigh and sank down on the chair next to the phone.

"Well, you don't have to make my name sound like a four-letter word," he said teasingly.

"It *is* a four-letter word," she pointed out.

"Yeah, come to think of it, I suppose it is." He chuckled. "How did you sleep last night?"

"Don't ask. I feel like I've wallowed around in hot soup all night. And if you say that I'll eventually get used to it, I'll scream."

"I wouldn't do that," he proclaimed. "What seems to be the problem this time?"

"Have you got a couple of hours?"

"That bad, huh?"

"That bad," she agreed.

"Maybe I should spend a night in it with you to see what you're talking about," he suggested hopefully.

"Forget that."

"Oh, all right, spoilsport. Is the water temperature comfortable?"

"I can't seem to put my finger on exactly what's making me so miserable, but something is. I barely closed my eyes all night—again."

"That's too bad. Are you doing anything today?"

"Yes, I am."

"Uh-uh. That was too quick," he chastised, not buying her excuse. "You're lying and you know it."

"I am not lying. I happen to be very busy," she lied.

"Oh, that's too bad. I thought I might come by and try to straighten out your problem. It's probably something very simple this time, but if you're too busy . . ."

"You couldn't straighten out my problem," she said. "You've tried for two weeks already."

"I think I could this time."

"How?"

"There are lots of things that I couldn't possibly explain to a layman," he reasoned. "Too much water, not enough water, too much heat, not enough heat, too much . . ."

He was probably feeding her a line of bull ten feet long again, but the thought of him actually being able to do anything about the bed got the better of her. "Oh, all right. Come on by, but if you can't figure out what's wrong with the thing this time, you're going to take it back!" she snapped. "And you're not going to talk me out of it."

"You're a hard-hearted woman, Fritzi Taylor." He sighed. "Okay. I'll take it back without a moment's hesitation if I can't straighten out the problem."

"You bet you will, and you'd better bring your truck, because I don't think you're going to be able to satisfy me."

"I beg to differ with you there," he teased in a suggestive voice.

"Ryan!" she snapped again. "If you're going to talk like that, send one of your men over. Come to think of it, that's what you should do, anyway. Send Ed, the man I bought the bed from."

"And miss out on my daily tongue-lashing from you? No way. I'm coming myself," he declared.

She stuck her leg out before her and studied the furry scuff on her foot, trying to keep from losing her temper with him. He was right; she had been giving him his daily share of tongue-lashings lately . . . but he deserved them!

"If you don't like my tongue-lashings, why do you keep coming back to get them?" She was sparring now.

"Beats the hell out of me. You're really turning out to be the old witch you said you might be."

"Then stay away from me."

"No, I can't do that. You're as mean as sin right now, but I figure that when I wear you down, you'll be worth the wait. Now don't go to all the trouble to get prettied up for me. I like you the way you are."

She slammed the receiver down and kicked both scuffs off in complete exasperation. She was purposely going to look like the wrath of God when he came!

But when he did ring the door bell an hour later, she found herself dressed in her nicest tailored slacks and an apricot-colored sweater as she went to let him in.

"Hi, beautiful. How's it going?" he asked calmly as he breezed in and planted a kiss in the middle of her forehead. "Still love me?"

"Oh, for heaven's sake!" she exclaimed impatiently. "Just get to the bed!"

"Ms. Taylor." He paused and gave her his most offended look, realizing that he was growing very tired of her persistent uncaring attitude toward him. "Would you care to tell me why you insist on being such an ass in my presence?"

"I think you know why," she said, forcing her tone to be more civil this time.

"No, I'm afraid I don't. You make it sound as if it would be a personal call instead of a business one," he pointed out, deciding to give her a taste of her own medicine.

"Well, it is." She felt her face flush warmly at her

lack of discretion in the matter, but she also felt it was time to put a stop to this nonsense once and for all.

"Why would you feel that way?" His voice had taken on a certain sharp edge to it now, one she had never heard him use before. "I thought I was coming over here to straighten out a problem with your bed."

"I know that's what you're supposed to be doing, but I think it's just another way of throwing us together," she accused, not knowing exactly how to say it tactfully without hurting his feelings. "I've told you a hundred times or more, *nothing* can come of our relationship," she said, finishing lamely. "I'm not going to get serious with any man for at least another five years."

"I'm more than aware of your plans," he returned in an unruffled tone. His tone may have been unruffled, but she could tell that he was getting angry.

"Then why don't you stop this nonsense?"

"Do you really want me to leave you alone, Fritzi?" His eyes were pleading with her to dispute that statement, but she couldn't. She just *couldn't*.

"Yes, that's what I really want, Ryan."

Pain flashed deep in his eyes, then he stiffened and his expression became bland. "Then you've got it, lady. From now on I won't be bothering you again. I'll get to the bed so I can get out of your way." He started up the stairway as she stood gaping at him. Had she heard right?

"Ryan?"

He kept on walking as she started up the stairs after him. "Ryan, wait a minute. Are you serious?"

"I am."

"Oh, Ryan." She was beginning to have second thoughts about her nasty mood. The last thing she wanted to do was hurt him. She loved him—no, wait! She liked him a lot, and she couldn't hurt him this way. "I didn't mean to be so hateful and I'm sorry. I know how you feel about me, but I know it just can't work out, so you force me to be nasty and ill-tempered. I *have* to set you straight. Don't you see? If we go on this way, you're only going to end up getting hurt, and I couldn't stand to do that to you. You want marriage and the whole works right now, but I don't. Can't you see how useless our relationship is if we have such different views of our lives?"

"Fritzi"—the ice in his voice now was a living, breathing thing—"let's not ride a dead horse, okay? You want me to leave you alone and I've agreed. Let's leave it at that."

"But I don't want to leave it that way, Ryan! You've goaded me and pushed me until I can't think straight any longer," she explained. "Can't we sit down and discuss this like two adults and try to come to some understanding about this?" She was puzzled and hurt by this new Ryan who was stalking up the stairs before her. "You've always been so nice and understanding—"

"I can assure you, Ms. Taylor, that I try to be 'nice' to everyone," he said, interrupting her curtly. "If I have been overly nice to you or offended you in any way, then please accept my apologies. I can assure you, you have set me straight. I no longer have anything personal in mind when it comes to you."

Her face flamed even brighter at his obvious putdown. "Ryan, try to understand. I was completely honest with you in the beginning and you knew how I felt—"

"I understand perfectly. Now, I have no intentions of losing more money on this sale, so if you have no objections, I'll do my job and get out of your way."

"Fine," she returned, a touch of frost creeping into her own voice at his blatant dismissal. "Suit yourself, but I fully intend to return the bed if the problem can't be resolved," she warned.

"We'll see about that."

"Yes, we certainly will!"

Two old goats butting head to head; that's what they were at the moment, and if he wanted to play rough, then, by golly, she would too!

No longer interested in her? That thought kept flitting in and out of Fritzi's mind as she showered and blew her hair dry the following evening. Ryan had been unable to do anything different to the bed, so she had made him promise to come personally and take it back after work this evening. It was plain that he was definitely put out with her, but he had agreed, and now she found herself taking extraordinary pains with the way she looked tonight.

Reaching for her lipstick, she leaned closer to the mirror and surveyed the image that stared back at her. Just what was wrong with her that he would give up on her so easily? Granted, he had pursued her intently for the last two weeks, and she had insulted him every day she saw him in an attempt to dampen his ardor, but did he have to give up so quickly? her female ego reasoned in a hurt voice.

Maybe it was her looks. She studied her image in the mirror critically. She wasn't fat and she wasn't skinny. She just had a nice, average shape with maybe a slight edge in the bust department. Tilting sideways a fraction, she looked her generous bustline over thoroughly and decided that maybe it could be classified as more than an edge.

She frowned. Perhaps Ryan Majors wasn't a bust man. Perhaps he was one of those men who liked legs or fannies or long, flowing hair and china-doll complexions, and she had to admit that she would be a real washout in those departments.

Her ash-blond hair was cut in a perky, short wedge. It wasn't flowing down around her creamy, china-doll complexion. On the contrary, if she wasn't careful and ate chocolate too often, her very average, dry-on-the-sides, and oily-in-the-tee-zone complexion would break out and make her want to hide for days. And her fanny? She turned a fraction more to assess that part of her body more carefully. It sure wasn't anything out of the ordinary. It didn't stick out or wobble when she walked or, to her knowledge, hold any particular allure for a man. It was just an ordinary fanny.

But *his* fanny . . . now that was a horse of a different color, and she wished now that she had explored it a tiny bit more when she had had the chance.

She turned back around to face the mirror head-on again. Her legs. An audible sigh filled the air as she surveyed the slender, but shapely, expanse of bare flesh meeting her now condemning eye. Egad. If he liked leggy women, she was dead for sure.

Grabbing her blusher, she wondered why she should be wasting her time wondering what Ryan Majors liked in a woman.

By the time the door bell rang thirty minutes later, Fritzi had herself worked up into a real snit wondering just exactly what Ryan Majors's taste in women was!

"I'll get it," Neil announced as he walked by her in the hallway. He was putting on his coat to go out as Fritzi fell into step behind him.

"You don't have to bother. It's for me."

"I'm on my way out, anyway."

"Where are you going?"

"Over to pick up Susan."

"There's supposed to be another storm on the way," Fritzi cautioned.

"I heard, but I don't think the brunt of it will hit until early morning." He paused on the last step and finished buttoning his coat. "I thought I might bring her back here for a quiet evening. What are your plans?"

"To disappear into thin air?" she guessed dryly.

Neil grinned. "Well, since you suggested it . . ."

Fritzi shook her head in disbelief and headed for the front door. "Don't worry. I won't be underfoot, Don Juan. I plan to have a very quiet evening, myself." Actually, dull would be more appropriate, she thought dismally. She was already beginning to miss Ryan, and he wasn't officially gone yet.

"Then who's at the door?"

"Ryan."

"Again?" Neil cocked his head to one side suspiciously. "It seems to me that he's getting to be a permanent fixture around here lately. What gives?" A sudden look of exasperation crossed his face. "Oh, no. I hope you two aren't going to drain that bed again and then refill it. The serviceman is down there now fixing the water heater, and he says it's on its last legs."

"Don't worry. He's coming over to take the water bed back, then he won't be around anymore," she admitted with a touch of wistfulness in her voice that he didn't fail to catch.

"You sound disappointed," Neil noted.

"Disappointed? Why would I be disappointed?" She laughed half-heartedly. "I don't even like the man . . . much."

"Really?" He grinned that knowing grin only a brother could bestow on a sister who was lying through her teeth. "You could have fooled me. Oh, by the way, Neda isn't going to be around for a couple of days. With the weather so bad, I told her to take some time off, so she's decided to ride into town with me and stay with one of her daughters."

"She is?"

Neil's hand paused on the doorknob as the bell sounded once more. "You didn't need her for anything, did you?"

"No, we can batch for a couple of days."

"I thought we might be capable of doing that." He smiled and reached out to ruffle her hair, a habit since childhood. "By the way, I'm sorry to hear that Ryan won't be around anymore. I kind of like the guy." Before she could ask him why, the serviceman emerged from the basement.

"All finished," the young man informed them in a friendly voice. "I think it will last a while longer, but give me a ring if you have any more trouble."

"Thanks, we will." Fritzi returned the serviceman's warm smile as Neil pulled open the door and started out.

Ryan was standing on the porch about to ring the bell again as Neil and the serviceman nodded a greeting to him, then walked on out to their vehicles.

Neda waved at Fritzi as she finished loading her suitcase in the jeep and pointed upward to the sky.

Waving back, Fritzi glanced up and was surprised to see the dark, angry-looking clouds gathering on the horizon. They would be extremely lucky if the storm held off until morning.

"The weatherman says we're in for more bad weather," she relayed worriedly to the new arrival.

"Yes, I heard," Ryan returned politely. Too politely. She was used to Ryan being friendly and warm, and it bothered her to think that he was still upset with her.

"Come on in. It's getting colder," she invited pleasantly.

Ryan stepped into the foyer, and she took his coat and hung it on a wooden clothes tree in the hallway as he walked over in front of the fireplace to warm his hands.

"It shouldn't take very long," he promised, wanting to make sure that she didn't think he planned to hang around any longer than necessary. A couple of times he had started to ask the regular servicemen to come out and get the bed, but something always stopped him. Maybe he was a glutton for punishment, but he wanted to see her at least one more time before he gave up on her.

In a few moments she joined him before the fire,

98

and remembering her manners, she offered to fix him a cup of something warm to drink.

"No thanks."

"You're sure? It wouldn't be any bother." Once more she felt her stomach do that queer little flip-flop it seemed to do whenever he was around, and it irritated her.

"No. I had a late lunch," he refused politely once again. His eyes lingered for just a brief moment on her before he determinedly turned his gaze elsewhere. "Who was the guy with Neil?" He forced a certain air of disinterest in his voice, wondering all the while why he was asking in the first place.

"Guy?" She glanced at him expectantly.

"Yeah, the guy who just left here a few minutes ago. Was that another one of your suitors?"

"One of my suitors?" She laughed. "That was the plumber. He was fixing the water heater that we've almost destroyed filling and refilling that darn water bed!"

"Oh."

"Yes, oh. Any objections?" A tiny thrill shot through her when she realized that he had been jealous!

He shrugged his shoulders. "None at all. You can have your water heater fixed anytime you want to."

He strolled over to the window and lifted a corner of the curtain to watch the first flake of snow hit the porch railing.

A log in the fireplace broke and sent a shower of

sparks up the chimney before it fell down through the grate, and silence descended over the room for a moment.

Fritzi wanted to make peace with him, but her pride held her back. He was the one being unreasonable about the whole situation, not her.

"Have you had dinner yet?"

"No."

"I could fix you a sandwich," she offered.

"No thanks, I'll get one later." Any other time he would have jumped at the chance to extend his visit, but now he was being as stubborn as she was.

"Well, that's fine with me!" she exclaimed impatiently. "Honestly, Ryan. Don't you think you're being a little impossible?" She began to pace the floor in agitation. "It would be different if I had led you into believing that anything serious could develop between us, but I was honest from the very beginning. *You* were the one who wouldn't take no for an answer, and now you're all bent out of shape because I'm going ahead with the plans that I made long before I ever met you." She paused and waved her arms in the air, groping for the right words. "Can't we just be . . . friends? Surely you can't seriously expect me to throw everything away just because we've got the . . . the hots for each other!" There! She had said it. That was the real problem. This crazy, asinine, mind-boggling attraction for him was just pure, unadulterated sexual chemistry! That's all it could be.

He surveyed her, pacing nonchalantly. "The hots for each other?" He frowned in dispute. "I have no idea what you're talking about. I'm only here to get the bed, not climb in it with you."

She whirled around angrily. "And what would you find so distasteful about that? Oh, wait a minute. Don't tell me, let me guess. You *are* a leg man!" she challenged hotly, suddenly letting all her earlier speculations about the sort of woman that attracted him rise to the surface.

He looked at her blankly. "A what?"

"A leg man—you know! You like long, shapely legs. Well, too bad!" She turned her back on him petulantly. "I have short, squatty ones."

"What are you talking about?" he demanded.

Still keeping her back to him, she clarified her statement. "Legs! You like your women to have legs, don't you?"

"Well, I never thought about it, but I suppose they would come in handy at a roller derby or a wine-making party."

It was apparent that he had missed the point. "That's not what I mean and you know it."

"I'm sorry, but I must be dense, and you have a tendency to talk like a weirdo at times," he said, apologizing. "You're going to have to spell it out for me."

"The reason you're not attracted to me any longer is because I have short, squatty legs and you like long, slender ones. Admit it!"

"Not attracted to you?" he asked in disbelief. "I thought you didn't *want* me to be attracted to you! And what am I supposed to admit?" he said in exasperation. "You're not making sense."

"Admit that you like long, slender legs!"

"All right. You've got it. I like long, slender legs!" When he saw the immediate hurt flash across her face, he backtracked quickly. "But I like short, squatty ones too," he finished meekly.

"You mean, like mine!"

"How should I know? I've never seen yours," he said challenging her. "But I hardly think they could be described as short and squatty."

"Oh, really! Then have a good look, Mr. Majors." Without thinking, she jerked up her dress until it almost touched her thighs and displayed what he thought was a darn sexy-looking set of legs. "Short and squatty, aren't they?"

His eyes ran longingly over her slender ankles and calves on up to her shapely thighs. "No, they're not short and squatty. They're very beautiful," he said, letting his gaze linger far too long.

Guiltily she let the hem of her dress drop back into place as his gaze slowly moved up to meet hers. "Then if it isn't my legs that you don't like, what is it?" she asked in a small helpless voice. "My hair?"

He had no idea what kind of game she was playing this time, but he wasn't going to play it with her. "As I said earlier, Ms. Taylor, I'm only here for the bed. Nothing personal. You've made it abundantly clear that you don't want me to be attracted to any part of you—legs or otherwise—at this point in your life. I'm only trying to comply with your wishes. Unless you've changed your mind."

The impersonal tone of his voice hurt more than if he had said the words harshly, and she felt herself instantly rebelling. "I have not changed my mind, and you are absolutely right about us remaining impersonal." It may kill her but he was right. "Now, if you're ready, you can load that rotten bed up and take it back where it came from."

Turning on her heel, she started to lead the way up the stairs, her feelings still smarting from his attitude. Still, she couldn't help but feel a tingle of anticipation when she thought about the way he had looked at her legs. Maybe, just maybe, he hadn't thought they were all that short and squatty. He certainly didn't look as if he had.

Well, if it wasn't her legs, then it had to be her hair. She made a mental note to pinpoint him on that later.

CHAPTER SIX

No matter what Fritzi tried to deny, there was no disputing the fact that she still thought he had the cutest tush she had ever seen on a man, and her eyes seemed determined to linger on that particular part of his anatomy as she followed him up the staircase.

"I hate to mention this," Ryan said, "but since we're being so honest with each other, it seems to me that you have always been unduly fascinated with my posterior. Any particular reason why?" He paused on the stairway to let Fritzi catch up with him.

"What?" Her face flamed beet-red at his observation.

"I said," he repeated patiently, *"If,* as you claim, you're not interested in me personally—for at least five more years—then why is it that you keep staring at my backside? Does it hold some sort of fascination for you?"

Trying to ignore his smirking face, she was determined not to let him goad her into another confrontation. "Your wild imagination almost exceeds your colossal ego, Mr. Majors. I was not staring at your . . . backside."

She had been and she knew it—and *he* knew it—but she certainly didn't have to admit it. Quickly deciding that she was going to have to watch herself more closely, Fritzi swept past him as regally as possible under the circumstances and made her way on down the hallway.

"Ms. Taylor," he said as he fell into step and began to follow her, "call it ego if you like, but there are a few things a man takes note of. A good-looking woman being unduly preoccupied with his tush on more than a few occasions is one of them."

"I can personally guarantee you that your tush holds no attraction for me whatsoever," she retorted defensively as her face flamed even more.

"Come now, Ms. Tay—"

"And stop calling me Ms. Taylor!" she demanded, turning to face him angrily. How he could have seemed so nice when she met him and then turn into such a rat so quickly amazed her.

He stepped back, faking mock surprise at her anger. "But I'm only trying to get our relationship strictly impersonal. That's all I'm trying to do," he said calmly.

"I don't want our relationship to be anything," she clarified in an icy tone.

"Oh, right. For a moment there I forgot." His

tone became as glacial as hers, and his brown eyes surveyed her accusingly.

Realizing how she had trampled on his feelings once again, Fritzi tried to soften her earlier approach. "Look, I'm sorry . . . I didn't mean to sound so callous." Because his face still held such a vulnerable expression, she found herself growing defensive again. Why oh why did this man have to come along right now? "All I want from you is to remove the bed and give me my money back," she finished lamely.

"If you'll kindly step out of my way, that's what I intend to do."

"Oh, Ryan," she whispered. "Do we have to keep arguing all the time?" How could one man hold so much power in his gaze? she wondered miserably. When he looked at her the way he was doing right now, it made her want to throw her plans out the front door. "I really do care for you . . . a lot."

Her plea sounded so wistful that he found the anger slowly beginning to drain out of him as his footsteps slowed and he turned to face her. "And I . . . like you. Look, I'm sorry I've been acting like a jackass. I'll get the bed down and get out of your way as soon as I can."

"You don't have to hurry," she protested.

"I know, but if you haven't noticed, I'm not in the best of moods tonight."

"Well, I guess you noticed that I'm not, either." She stuck her hand out invitingly. "Truce?"

He accepted it without hesitation. "Truce."

"Good. Now, what's wrong with my hair?"

"Your hair?" He looked at her head. "Not a thing. Why?"

It wasn't the hair, either? "Uh . . . no reason. I just wondered if it looked all right." She fussed with it nervously. "I've barely had time to comb it today."

"Looks great." He turned his attention back to his work. "Can you get me the hose?"

"I'll be glad to. Be right back." She turned and skipped down the stairs, relieved that he was willing to call a halt to their hostilities, and her hair and squatty legs looked great to him.

As she walked past the dining room window on her way to the basement to get the hose to drain the bed one final time, she noticed the snow was coming down heavier. As she had feared, it was not going to hold off until morning.

For the next hour they both worked at taking down the bed and draining it, but it was a slow task.

"It's going to take forever to drain at this rate," Fritzi complained, noting the slow trickle of water that was oozing out of the hose into her bathroom tub.

"If you recall, it does take awhile," Ryan noted dryly. This was the third time he had drained the bed, and she should know by now that it wasn't a fast process. He plopped down in the middle of the bed with a weary yawn. "I'm tired. I think I'll kill two birds with one stone and rest while I'm helping things along."

The water started running much more freely as he applied his weight, and Fritzi grinned at him. "Well, it so happens that I'm tired too. Mind if I join you? Wouldn't it run out faster with both of us in there?" Funny, but she felt as free to join him on the bed as she would have if they'd been married.

"It would." He moved over willingly. "I just hope you don't snore."

She laughed and laid down, handing him a magazine as she did so. It was a lazy time of the day, so she figured that they may as well relax while they worked. "Here, entertain yourself."

"I can think of more ways to entertain myself in a water bed than by reading a magazine," he noted sorely, but he obediently thumbed through the pages for a few minutes until he finally lost interest and cast it aside.

Fritzi glanced over at him. "What's the matter?"

"Nothing. I just have no particular interest learning new techniques with my eye shadow."

She laughed, realizing that she had handed him a woman's magazine. "Really? Well, no wonder. Your makeup is always flawless," she said teasingly.

"Thanks," he replied in a terrible imitation of a feminine voice. "I always try to look my best, sweetie."

They both laughed as Fritzi tossed her magazine

up in the air and stretched out comfortably on the bed. "Wow. This feels good."

"I thought you said you hated it," Ryan corrected.

"I do, to sleep in. But it's rather nice just to lie on," she confessed.

"Yeah, it is, isn't it?" he agreed, setting the bed into a swaying motion. "I may have to get me one of these things yet."

"Take mine, *please,*" she urged with exaggerated desperation.

"You'd better get up and check the flow of the water," he suggested a little while later as they both began to grow drowsy. The snow was floating by the windows in big cottony fluffs as darkness descended on the cozy room.

She had been lying on her side in a semiconscious state, staring into the fireplace that stretched across the west wall of her room. Its flames were sending rosy shadows dancing across the wall. She had no idea what Ryan was thinking about as he lay beside her with his back turned to the wall. He was so close yet so very far away. But she couldn't keep herself from wondering what they would be doing in bed together if circumstances had been different.

"Are you trying to get rid of me?" she murmured drowsily.

"It isn't me who wants to get rid of anyone," he murmured back. "I believe it's the other way around."

She sighed at the implication in his words. She didn't want to argue with him again. "I thought we had called a truce."

"Sorry. We did."

"You're forgiven, but as penance, *you* get up and check the water."

"No, you do it. I'm already half asleep."

Groping for the glass of water on her bedside stand, she carefully turned over and let a few drops trickle down the collar of his shirt.

"If you're doing what I think you're doing, you're in trouble," he warned as the cold liquid ran down his back in chilly rivulets.

"What am I doing?" she asked in the most innocent of voices.

"Pouring water down my back."

"No, never," she denied. "Are you going to check the water? You sound like you're more awake now," she offered as she tipped the glass over farther and heard his sharp intake of breath.

Before she knew what was happening, he had rolled over on top of her and had taken the glass out of her hand, setting it back on the table.

"Ryan, you're crushing me," she protested with a laugh.

"No, I'm not. I'm preparing to break your neck. *Then* I'm going to crush you," he threatened as he held her firmly in place.

They tumbled around on the bed playfully as she

tried to get away from him, but she soon gave that up as hopeless.

"Let me go," she ordered breathlessly.

"Not a chance. You'll have to buy your way out of this mess," he informed her.

"With what?"

"What have you got?"

"All my fashion magazines?"

He shook his head.

"My new water bed?"

"I'm not about to trade for that dog."

"My new Flamingo Red fingernail polish?" she said, bargaining.

"No." His mouth moved closer to hers. "But I would consider your new Flamingo Red lipstick . . . if you were wearing it."

Suddenly all playfulness drained out of both of them as Ryan's hold slackened. His hands slid down her arms, and he moved her closer against him.

"Ryan, please don't start that again. I *can't* fall in love with you," she blurted out helplessly.

"Who asked you to fall in love? All I want is a taste of your lipstick," he argued.

"But I have plans . . ." She could feel them slipping farther away every moment as his mouth continued to draw nearer.

"Is that a fact?" His voice had lowered to a defensive nature as he moved against her suggestively. "Well, lady, I think the time has come to give you a few good reasons why you should have second thoughts about your plans."

"Now, Ryan . . . don't you dare." She could tell by the predatory look in his eyes that he was going to compound the situation even more.

" 'Now, Ryan, don't you dare,' " he mimicked as she proceeded to back away on her side of the bed. But he was not to be deterred. He moved over with her and tried to draw her slowly back into his arms. "Come here, coward. You know as well as I do that you want me to kiss you."

"Wrong. I do not—"

"Keep lying to yourself if you want. It won't phase me any."

Her eyes continued to grow wider as she noted the determined look in his eyes now. "You kiss me and I'll—"

"Enjoy every minute of it, just like I'm going to," he finished.

"Ryan," she warned as he edged closer. "Stop this or I'm—" She didn't have time to finish her threat before his hand snaked out and pulled her roughly against him.

"Or you're going to what?" he said, interrupting her and noting with great relish the way her eyes turned soft and smoky when he drew her closer to his broad chest.

"Or I'm going to enjoy this too much, and I just can't," she finished hopelessly, moments before his mouth closed over hers hungrily. She began to tremble as his powerful arms encased her tighter, and together they sank down in the warmth of the mattress.

The last rays of twilight were lingering in the room as the water bed closed around them, wrapping them in a cocoon of sensuality. Their mouths blended sweetly as his hands soothed up and down her arms, coaxing her to relax and let go. It was strange how comforting and how . . . right, how very right it felt to be here in his arms, no matter how much trouble it could get her into.

When he heard her moan softly and whisper his name, he buried his hands in the thickness of her hair and rolled them over in the middle of the bed. Now it was he who spoke her name in a voice grown thick with desire as their kisses deepened and lingered. She could feel the mounting pressure of his desire as his lips recaptured hers more demandingly each time, and he was leaving her no time to try to regain her senses.

Instinctively she snuggled closer to his body, firing both their needs for each other to painful and frightening proportions. Once more his mouth captured hers in a ravishing kiss, sending all her objections scattering like wheat chaff in the wind.

She should stop him . . . she should stop him . . . she should stop him . . . Her mind kept warning her, but somehow she couldn't listen as she wrapped her hands around his midriff and held on to the tempestuous storm that was threatening to blank out all reason. He was arousing her in a way she never knew was possible, and just for the moment she was willing to let him . . . just for the moment.

As the light from the window faded into darkness his lips brushed tenderly across her swollen lips and he groaned as he pressed tightly against her and whispered hotly against her ear, "You'd better remind me again of how long five years is, because in another few minutes I'm going to make love to you," he vowed.

"No, Ryan," she pleaded, as much in need of him as he was of her, but sanity was beginning to return oh so slowly.

"Don't keep saying no, Fritzi. It's right . . . you know it is. How can you continue to deny what we both obviously feel for each other?" he implored softly as he soothed the strand of hair that lay against her cheek. "Is it a question of morals, because if it is, I can sympathize. You have to know I'm falling in love with you."

Her hand quickly reached out to smother his unbridled confession with the tips of her fingers. "Oh, Ryan, don't."

"Why?" Once again his eyes begged her for a reason as she saw the confusion in their warm depths. "It doesn't make sense to be so stubborn."

"Ryan." She sighed and turned over on her back to stare dismally up at the ceiling. "How am I going to make you understand?"

"I don't think you ever can, but I'm willing to listen. You have to have a reason other than some damn plans you've made. Tell me what you're afraid of, Fritzi. Let me help you."

"I don't want to mess my life up like Neil has," she confessed tearfully, surprised to hear herself finally voice that fear. Maybe it wasn't so much her plans as it was seeing the mistake her brother had made by being impetuous.

"Your brother? What has he got to do with us?"

"Everything, don't you see?"

"No, I'm afraid I don't."

"Neil jumped into a hasty marriage to Susan, and it's turned out to be a nightmare for both of them."

"So? I still can't see what that has to do with us."

"Their marriage has been a complete disaster. Susan married Neil on the rebound from Tyce Williams, and they didn't live together but a few months before she was confused about which man she really loved."

"She didn't love Neil?"

"I don't know if she did or not. And she didn't, either. She went through a period when they were first married that she had some doubts. When she told Neil about those doubts, he got all puffed up with pride the way all men do, and he got stubborn and then they separated. Now they're involved in this unbelievable marriage encounter group that's purely nauseating, trying to save a marriage that I'm not at all sure can be saved."

"What's wrong with a marriage encounter group? It sounds perfectly sensible to me if they're having trouble."

"Oh, I agree, if it's a good one, but this particular marriage group seems a little off the wall. They have some really strange people in it from what Neil has said."

"Well, I can't say that I blame Neil feeling the way he does," Ryan said, sympathizing. "I doubt that any man would want to think his wife was in love with an old flame. Where Neil made his mistake was ever letting her have those doubts in the first place."

"How could he have stopped her?"

"Believe me, if it was my wife, I'd find a way to show her who the better man was," he predicted smugly.

"Pretty sure of yourself, aren't you?"

"I used to be . . . before I met you."

"Well"—she sighed and cuddled closer in his arms—"that's just one more reason why I feel we shouldn't jump into anything hasty concerning each other."

"So, it isn't necessarily your plans that are holding you back. You're afraid of jumping into a relationship too quickly?"

"Yes, that's what I'm afraid of," she admitted honestly.

"I don't see how you could gauge what we feel for each other by the way Neil and Susan have messed up their lives," he argued. "Maybe they didn't try hard enough to salvage their marriage, or maybe they weren't meant for each other in the first place."

"In all honesty, they haven't tried to save their marriage until lately, but that doesn't change anything. If Neil and Susan would have used their brains and not jumped into marriage, they might be happily married to the right person now instead of running around driving everyone crazy with their little cutesy terms for each other like 'cutie pie' and 'sweetums.' I'm telling you, Ryan, it's enough to make a grown person cry."

He laughed at her indignation of the affectionate terms. "Well, Susan and Neil will have to work out their own problems." His arms tightened around her possessively as his mouth nibbled hers once again. "At least I know what I'm fighting now, and you're willing to admit that there is something between us."

"I'm not going to admit that. It will only complicate things," she said, denying it, but she knew he was right. She was already in love with him and just wouldn't allow herself to accept that fact.

"You may as well. It's as plain as the nose on your face," he persisted as his hands caressed her boldly.

"My nose is not plain—wait a minute! Is that it? You don't like my nose?" she asked expectantly. Funny, she hadn't thought there was anything wrong with her nose!

"There's nothing wrong with your nose," he protested. "And stop trying to change the subject."

"Ryan, yesterday you distinctly told me you were no longer personally interested in me. Can't you stick by that?" she urged.

"I said that because I was ticked off at your attitude, and you know it. I do care about you. In fact, it could go much deeper than that if you'd let it."

"This has to stop." She plucked his foraging hands away from her and sat up. "Even if it weren't for Neil and Susan *or* my plans, I couldn't fall in love with you right now. You're not in my treasure-mapping book," she quipped playfully.

"What are you talking about now?" Undeterred by her protest, he calmly pulled her back down on the bed and snuggled her close to him.

"You're impossible," she scolded, but her heart wasn't in it. "You're going to make me mad if you keep this up."

"Okay." He released his hold on her promptly. "I won't touch you again until you ask me."

She looked at him warily.

"Don't look at me that way. I mean it. If you're serious about wanting me to leave you alone, I will." He reached out and touched her cheek with the tip of his finger. "You have my word on that. Now, what's a treasure-mapping book?"

She could hardly believe that he was serious in his new avowal, but she had no other choice but to accept his word at the moment. "Oh, it's a book I've kept for the last few years." In an effort to lighten up both their moods, she let her finger trail down to the first button on his shirt and pause. "I might let you see it someday . . . if you'll be nice."

The light of passion returned to his eyes as his hand reached down and trapped hers against the front of his shirt. "I'm always nice . . . what are you doing?" he asked suspiciously.

"Me?" His hands loosened their hold as her fingers began toying lightly with the button.

"I'd better warn you, I don't like women who tease."

"Oh?" Their mouths moved an inch closer as the first button came undone. Fritzi had no idea why she was provoking him this way. It was unforgivable and she knew it, but . . .

"I'm not teasing."

"Then take it off, Fritzi," he ordered in a voice that had grown husky with desire.

"Your shirt?" she asked innocently. "Or the button?"

"Whatever turns you on." He nibbled her lower lip. She sighed, happy to hear that he was taking all this teasing lightly. But he soon shattered that fallacy. "I'm willing to let you do anything you want to me as long as you don't insist on completely locking me out of your life."

The lightheartedness suddenly drained out of the moment, and she realized that her playfulness had

119

taken her too far again. Ryan was fully aroused and was making no effort to conceal that fact.

"And if I were willing to let you make love to me, Ryan Majors, would you then in turn expect a permanent commitment from me?" she asked softly. Never in her life had Fritzi used sex indiscriminately, but that was before Ryan. . . .

"That would depend," he countered. "I might be persuaded to let you love me and leave me—if you think you could honestly do that."

Her fingers moved automatically to unfasten the second button. "Ryan, I'll be honest. I want you as badly as you want me," she confessed, letting her fingers slip inside his shirt and touch the dark hair that lay like soft silk on his chest. "But it would only be for this moment . . . and I wouldn't want you to read anything more into it."

"In other words, don't get my hopes up, huh?" She could almost feel his anger rising within him, although his words were still almost gentle.

Her hand paused in its exploration at her daring proposal. "In a way I guess that's what I'm saying . . . not that I don't care for you very deeply, but you know my position on the subject."

"Oh, I see. You just want to fool around with no strings attached."

"Only with you. I mean, that's rather crass, but I guess you could say that pretty well sums it up." It hurt more than she had expected to hear him state it that way. She didn't want what they had to be dirty or soiled in any way. And not for the first time, it suddenly occurred to her just how much she cared for him.

"Oh, I see. I'm different."

She nodded, relieved that he seemed to understand the situation more clearly now. "Very different. I hope you understand that."

"Oh, I do. Perfectly. You want your cake and eat it too."

She sighed in exasperation. "Yes, if you insist on looking at it in a crude way instead of in the way it really is—that I simply don't want a commitment in my life right now—then that's what I'm saying."

"Okay, let me get this absolutely clear so we don't misunderstand one another." He reached out and unbuttoned the remaining buttons of his shirt, allowing her full access to his bare chest. Her heart thumped painfully against her ribs as once more his hands guided hers over his curly, dark hair. "I am free to make love to you as long as I don't make anything serious out of it."

"Ryan, why are you being so clinical about this? Do you or do you not want to make love to me?" She couldn't imagine what his problem was this time.

"I do not," he stated emphatically, sitting up and rebuttoning his shirt angrily. "In fact, I'm insulted that you put such a cheap price tag on what we have with each other."

She looked up at him in confusion as he stood

and stuffed his shirttails into his trousers. "An arrangement like that would be tacky and meaningless, and I wouldn't have to be clairvoyant to see which one of us would end up getting hurt. Let's just call it quits right now, before we get in any deeper."

"But, Ryan—"

"No buts. I'm serious, Fritzi." She could tell by the angry look on his face that he was. "The bed is almost drained. I'll have my bookkeeper send you a check in the mail first thing Monday morning, and we'll let our relationship end right here and now."

"A check? Ryan!" She suddenly snapped out of her lethargy and raised on one elbow to face him angrily as he impassively continued to straighten his clothes. "What do you mean, you'll send me a check? What about . . . us?"

"What about us?" he asked coolly.

"What about us! You can stand there and ask that when not a few minutes ago you were acting as if you couldn't live without me? And now you're willing to send me a cold, impersonal check in the mail and that's that?"

"That's that," he stated firmly.

"But why? I mean, granted, I won't marry you, but I thought we had agreed we could perhaps—"

"Hop in the sack together?" he returned bluntly. "No thanks, sweetheart. It suddenly occurs to me that you've been right all along. I have been moving us along too quickly, and I really don't know you at all." The way he was looking at her now was the way he would look at a complete stranger, and it tore painfully at her heartstrings.

"Ryan . . ." Her voice sounded as if someone had just shot her dog, although he was saying the exact thing she had been saying since they met.

"What?"

"You can't mean it."

"Yes, I do." His demeanor softened for just a flick of an eye. "As long as you feel the way you do about me, it's for the best, Fritzi."

"You're really serious about this, aren't you?" she asked in disbelief. She couldn't understand how they had been so close a few minutes ago and now he was acting this way.

"Yes, I'm serious," he confirmed. "Now, if you'll get off the bed, I'll take it down."

"Not on your life," she snapped.

"What do you mean, 'not on your life'?"

"I mean, I've changed my mind."

"You've what?"

"I said I've changed my mind. I want to keep the bed." She was grasping for time until she could think this mess through. If she let him take the bed back, she would probably never see him again, and she wasn't at all sure at this point that she could live with that. No, she had to have time, and the only way to gain it was to keep the bed.

"You've changed your mind again? Are you a mental case or something?" he exclaimed. "For the

123

last two weeks all you've done is complain about this bed, and now that I'm willing to take it back, you've changed your mind? Well, no way, lady. I'm taking it back this time!" He leaned over and jerked the hose out of the mattress and threw it in the tub.

"Changing her mind is a woman's prerogative. Don't you dare touch that bed!" She picked up a pillow and whacked him across his shoulders angrily.

He shrugged away her assault in complete exasperation. "And you're the one who told me that once you have your mind made up, you never change it. Okay," he said, giving up. "But don't come whining to me in a couple of days and demand that I take the bed back. I've offered and you've refused!"

He turned and started out the door, and she fell in step behind him. They descended the stairway in a strained silence. It was on the tip of her tongue to beg him to stay, but she realized that it would be useless. She wasn't going to change her mind, and apparently he was dead set on his obstinate view.

"You're being pigheaded about this," she accused as they marched down the stairs.

"Look who's talking."

The door swung open as they approached the living room and a near frozen Neil and Susan stomped in.

"Hi." Fritzi greeted half-heartedly as she walked over to retrieve Ryan's coat. "Is it still snowing?"

"Is it ever," Neil acknowledged. "The snow is beginning to drift so badly that we couldn't get up the drive. Susan and I had to walk about a mile to get here."

Fritzi's hand froze on Ryan's jacket as she heard Ryan ask worriedly, "The road's closed?"

"That's right."

"But I was just getting ready to leave."

"Ha!" Neil shrugged out of his coat and turned to help Susan with hers. "Afraid not, old man. Here, sweetums, let me help you."

"You mean, we're snowed in?" Ryan asked sickly.

"That's right." Neil glanced at Susan and smiled intimately.

"Neil! We can't be!" Fritzi protested. If she was snowed in here with Ryan Majors . . .

"Well, we are." Neil turned around and draped his arm around Susan affectionately. "Susan and I are going to have a cup of hot chocolate. Anyone care to join us?"

CHAPTER SEVEN

Twenty-four hours was not that long—unless, of course, one had the unfortunate luck to be snow-bound in a house with three other people who were bent on testing one's sanity. Then it seemed as if it were twenty-four hundred hours.

Ryan had gone out of his way to avoid her during this forced period of incarceration, which both pleased and annoyed her at the same time. Actually Fritzi couldn't blame him for avoiding her. She knew she had hurt his feelings, and she was sorry for that. If only he could understand her position in this matter and be a little more understanding, it would make things easier.

The house was big enough for the two couples to have plenty of breathing space, so Ryan and Fritzi had actually seen very little of each other except at mealtimes.

It wasn't that she necessarily wanted Ryan's attention, she kept reminding herself; it was just that she couldn't stand this new air of aloofness he had seemed to develop toward her. It hurt and she couldn't deny it.

After she nearly got down on her hands and knees the night before and begged him to refill the water bed, he had finally complied but not without a lot of complaining. She knew that he was getting as sick of the bed as she was.

When he had finished, he had parked himself on the sofa in the den and watched television the rest of the evening, flatly refusing to join Susan and Neil when they fixed a late-night snack in the kitchen. It was as if he blamed Fritzi for the snowstorm and his inconvenience. Around ten she had determinedly marched into the den and told him where the guest room was, then marched out again when he didn't say a word.

It was now late afternoon of the following day, and the atmosphere had not changed all that much. The four had had breakfast together and casually talked about the way the snow was still falling with no letup in sight and grumbling about running out of hot water for their morning showers. Neil's I-told-you-so about the old water heater not lasting through another fill up of the water bed didn't exactly make for friendly chitchat, either. But outside the windows, the ranch looked like a scene on a Christmas card, a breathtakingly beautiful winter wonderland. The boughs of the blue spruce trees lining the drive drooped heavily with layers of freshly fallen snow as birds happily scrimmaged at the ranch feeders.

Ryan was still going out of his way to avoid her, and Neil and Susan had been positively revolting with their sickly sweet nuances to each other as evening descended.

Fritzi had the strange feeling that her brother and sister-in-law were beginning to get on each other's nerves, although they were very careful to smile and agree with whatever the other one said. She could be wrong, but she thought she had caught Neil with a look on his face she had seen only once before—when he forcefully had been made to do something he didn't want to.

When they had been small children, both he and Fritzi had been made to sit at the table until they both had finished their Brussels sprouts. Neil hated force, and he hated Brussels sprouts even more, so it had taken the better part of a whole day for Martha Taylor to fulfill her oath that her son would not leave the table until the sprouts were gone. Fritzi had hurriedly stuffed hers down and then ran upstairs to quietly deposit them in the bathroom commode, but Neil decided to hold out.

Though his mother eventually won out and not one Brussels sprout was left on his plate before he was excused from his chair, Neil had made everyone in the house miserable before the despised vegetable was finally consumed. The look he gave his sister as he had passed her on the way to his room was one of sheer defiance; it was the same look Fritzi had seen at the breakfast table this morning when Susan made a comment that clearly irritated him, but once more he let it pass without incident.

In a way it seemed to Fritzi that Susan and Neil were trying to stuff Brussels sprouts down each other's throat, and in her opinion it was only a matter of time before they blew their tops.

Deciding that the silence of her own room was beginning to get to her, she went into the bathroom to freshen her makeup and run a brush through her hair. She hated to admit it, but she wanted to be with Ryan, even though he obviously didn't return the feeling. Laying the brush down carefully, she decided to swallow her pride and try to make peace with him.

She found him stretched out on the sofa in the den watching a basketball game, giving no thought to her whatsoever.

"Hi."

Barely glancing up at her, his eyes remained glued to the action on the set. "Hi."

"Are you busy?"

"Yes."

"No, you're not," she disputed.

"Okay. No, I'm not." The last thing he wanted was another argument with her.

Gliding over to the window, she gazed out on the frozen hillsides for a moment, hoping that he would show a little interest in her being there. "It's still snowing."

"I know."

"I suppose you've let someone know where you are," she rationalized. To her knowledge he hadn't made any phone calls, and that puzzled her.

"I tried to call the store first thing this morning, but no one answered. Ed must not have been able to get into town." Ryan stretched and yawned lazily. "I'll try him at home later on."

"I heard the weatherman on the radio a few minutes ago. He says the snow will be with us for a few more hours."

"Yeah, I know. There was a special weather bulletin on TV earlier."

"I hope all this hasn't interfered with your personal plans too much," she said, apologizing. "I'm sure that as soon as the storm breaks, Neil can have the roads plowed in no time at all." It would be interesting to see how he answered. Just how did Ryan Majors spend his free time?

He went back to watching the game without comment.

Running the tip of her finger along the frost on the inside of the windowpane, she thought about her next question for a moment, then went ahead and asked it, anyway. "No one other than Ed will be wondering where you are?"

There was a long moment before he decided to ease her curiosity. "I guess I should call Mona."

"Mona?" Her finger paused. "Who's Mona?" she asked, trying to keep her voice indifferent.

"Mona lives in the apartment next to me."

"A next-door neighbor?" She turned to face him, a pleasant smile on her lips. "Why would you have to let a neighbor know where you are?"

"She likes to mother me."

"Oh, really?" Her pleasant smile was still intact. "Is she an elderly lady?"

Ryan's chuckle was downright wicked. "Mona, elderly? Hardly."

"Middle-aged?"

"No."

The pleasant smile began to wilt. "How old is she?"

"I don't know . . . around my age, I guess."

"Was she the woman you took to the New Year's Eve party?" she demanded, all pleasantness deserting her now.

"She was." He glared up at her pointedly. "Why?"

"No reason . . . I just wondered." She walked over and, to his dismay, flipped off the television, then perched on the side of the sofa where he was lying. "I thought you said you weren't serious about anyone."

"I didn't say I was serious about Mona, I just said I took her to a New Year's Eve party." He sat up and ran his fingers through his hair and yawned again.

"Are you in love with her?"

"In love with her?" He laughed in disbelief and got to his feet. "We date each other on occasion, okay? Nothing more."

Too restless to sit in one place, Fritzi was back on her feet pacing the room. She had no idea why it upset her to find out that Ryan had a neighbor named Mona who liked to mother him. Why should she care?

"I suppose she's pretty?"

"No. She's as ugly as sin," he disputed dryly. "That's what first attracted me to her." She knew he was being facetious, but she wasn't going to let it bother her. After all, she was asking for it by questioning him like she was, but she had to know about this Mona.

Turning from her place at the window, she moseyed back over to where he stood.

"Seriously, Ryan, is she nice-looking?"

"I really don't know. I've never . . . well, she sure has a nice set of . . . uh, yeah." He grinned. "She's gorgeous."

"So!" She whirled and pointed an accusing finger at him. "You *are* a chest man!"

"A what?"

"A chest man—you know. You're one of those men who go for the bosomy type," she accused.

He shook his head in disbelief. "Are we on that subject again? Why are you so hung up on what parts of a woman's body I like?"

"I'm not. I'm just trying to figure out what you . . . do like in a woman," she said defensively, her voice filling with guilt now.

"Pardon me for pointing this out, but don't you think your time would be better spent on worrying about something else? Obviously, it wouldn't change your mind about anything no matter what part of you I liked."

"I'm only trying to make conversation," she returned coolly. "I don't mean anything personal by it."

"Well then, in answer to your question, I haven't made up my mind what parts of a woman I like best. But I'm still thinking on it. . . ." He found his voice trailing off suggestively as his eyes made a slow perusal of the jeans and T-shirt she was wearing.

"Why don't you help me clean out my fish tank?" she coaxed, in an effort to change the subject. He was beginning to make her nervous with the way his eyes were slowly undressing her.

"No way. I hate smelly fish." He strolled back over to the television and turned it back on.

"Smelly? My fish are not smelly. The tank just needs to be cleaned."

"Thanks, but I'll pass."

"Suit yourself." She waltzed past him, well aware that he was still fascinated by her tight T-shirt. "But you could take a page out of Neil's book and be nice to me like he's trying to be to Susan," she pointed out. "After all, I didn't ask to be snowed in with you, so we might as well make the best of it."

"Be like cutie pie? Uh-uh. Mark my word, that's not going to last much longer. Sweetums is going to lose her cool," he predicted. "And it can't be soon enough for me."

His tone of revulsion made Fritzi laugh. "Didn't I tell you they were sickening?"

"Do they really think all that mush is really helping their situation?" he asked. "Couldn't they go to a sensible marriage counselor and try to work this thing out with a little more maturity? I don't know them that well, but from what I've seen they do seem to genuinely care for each other."

"They do. They just seem to be having a hard time putting their love into words," she said absently. "Their marriage started off on a shaky footing and just stayed there."

Once more Ryan's eyes found hers meaningfully. "But that doesn't mean that they aren't meant for each other. I hope they work it out."

"I do too." And for a tiny moment she let herself wish that she wasn't so stubborn.

"You know, I believe you're right," he confessed with just a hint of teasing in his voice now. "After giving it a little thought, I believe it's entirely possible that I may be a bosom man." His eyes lingered wistfully on the rounded softness straining against her shirtfront. He wiggled his eyebrows appreciatively. "Your shirt is indecently tight, Ms. Taylor, and I do hope you're wearing it solely for my benefit."

"Don't be silly." She blushed. "I never gave you a thought when I put this on." Even as she said the words she knew that she was lying. "But if you're enjoying it, then I'm glad." She grinned at him impishly. "I really don't want you mad at me, Ryan, especially while we're snowed in together. I'm willing to call another truce if you are." She lifted her brows hopefully. "Let's try to find something to do together—something decent," she clarified quickly as new hope sprang alive in his eyes.

He sighed and shrugged his shoulders, resigned to the fact that she was a very obstinate woman. "Okay. I'm bored too. What did you have in mind?"

"Well, if you're dead set against helping me clean the fish tank, let's go out to the kitchen and make a pizza."

"Sounds okay to me."

She paused and looked him over carefully, surprised that he was clean-shaven and smelled delicious. "You look awfully nice. Did Neil lend you some clothes?"

"Yes, I took a shower a short while ago, rather quickly I might add, since the water heater had barely recovered to less than lukewarm, and used his razor. You know, I kind of like your brother," he admitted as they started for the kitchen.

"He likes you too. He said so yesterday when he was leaving."

135

"Maybe we should try to take his and Susan's minds off their problems for a little while after we eat," Ryan suggested. "Do you play Monopoly?"

"I haven't since I was a child, but Neda still has all our games stored on a shelf in the basement. Monopoly might be fun."

"Yeah, if we can just get them to agree."

"Why wouldn't they?" Fritzi grimaced. "They've been agreeing to *everything* lately. But let's go ask them. I think they're in the living room having another one of their therapy sessions."

"Oh, brother. I'm not sure we want to get in on that."

They quickened their steps down the hallway. "If they don't want to play Monopoly, then let's talk them into taking a walk. It probably wouldn't hurt any of us if we went out for some fresh air," Fritzi noted conversationally. "I don't know about you, but I'm getting cabin fever."

"I am, too, but let's eat first. I'm getting hungry." Ryan's footsteps paused as the sound of angry voices reached their ears. "Uh-oh. What's that?"

"Oh, dear. It sounds like an argument," Fritzi said in a hushed voice.

"Cutie pie and sweetums?" he said, scoffing in mock disbelief. "Never."

"Shhh. Listen." Two sets of eyes peered around the corner into the living room where the distinct sounds of the floor being systematically whacked

136

with a blunt object filled the air. Their eyes grew larger.

"What the devil are they doing?" Ryan murmured.

"It looks like they're hitting the floor with rubber bats," Fritzi whispered.

"Rubber bats!"

"Shhh. They'll hear you," she warned.

"Rubber bats!" he exclaimed, but he lowered his voice. "Have they gone off their rockers completely?"

"No. It probably has something to do with letting their pent-up aggressions out. I've heard them discussing it before." She let out a low whistle under her breath. "Will you look at that?"

The angry voices grew louder as they huddled closer to the doorway to hear better.

"We shouldn't be listening to this," Ryan cautioned.

"I know . . . we'll leave in a second."

Whack! Whack! Whack! "And, furthermore, I am sick to *death* of the way you drink your coffee!" Susan's voice informed hotly.

"What's wrong with the way I drink my coffee?" Whack! Neil's response was just as heated.

"Slurp. Slurp. Slurp." Susan enunciated hatefully. "The way you slurp your coffee is disgusting!"

"If I slurp my coffee, it's only because I'm trying to take my mind off your sloppy housekeeping," he returned defensively.

Whack! "What do you mean by that dirty crack?"

"Well, if you really want to know"—Neil straightened his stance defensively—"when we were living together, our apartment always looked like a pigsty. How was I supposed to be Rhett Butler when I had to live in a pigsty!"

"A pigsty?" she shrieked as the bat went into action once again on the floor. "Of all the nerve! I did the best I could with what *you* provided me with. You must remember, Mr. High and Mighty, I'm not Joan Collins, and it wasn't exactly *Dynasty* surroundings we were living in."

"That's true," Fritzi mumbled out of the corner of her mouth. "Their apartment was the pits. He should have rented a nicer one."

"Maybe so, but she shouldn't be throwing that up to him," Ryan defended. "Maybe it was the best the poor guy could do."

"It so happens that that was the best that I could do at the time," Neil said, arguing in a loud voice.

"See?" Ryan smiled smugly. "What did I tell you?"

"That's not true. He could have afforded better. He's just so tight, he squeaks," Fritzi argued.

"The only reason we had to live in that—that dump—was because you were so tight, you squeaked. You held on to a dollar so tight, you could hear George Washington gasping for air!" Susan exclaimed.

"Darn!" Fritzi snapped her fingers. "Wish I had thought of that one."

"Tight? Tight? Well, it's news to me that you didn't like living there." He glared at her angrily. "And it's a good thing one of us had a little common sense when it came to finances or we wouldn't even have had the 'dump' to live in," Neil pointed out. "Because you were sure lousy at handling a buck."

"What handling? I never had a buck to handle," she said accusingly. "*You* always had control of the purse strings, and believe me, you sure pinched them until they squealed!"

"Oh, so now I'm the one who was the ogre. Just because you don't have the brains to add two and two and come up with four isn't *my* fault."

Susan gasped indignantly. "You dare to say that to me when you know how horrible I am with figures!"

"I know . . . that's what I meant to say." Neil began to back down a little. "I didn't mean to say that you were dumb, honey, but let's face it, when it comes to handling money, you're . . . stupid," he said, finishing with a lame grin and realizing immediately that he had chosen the wrong adjective.

Whack! Whack! Whack! "You rat! You wretched rat!"

"Oh, boy. It *was* dirty for him to bring that up," Ryan sympathized in an undertone. "If the poor woman's bad in math, she can't help it."

139

Fritzi punched him in the ribs painfully. "Maybe so, but he's telling the truth. Susan has always been downright stupid when it comes to handling money."

"Ow!" Ryan glared at her soundly. "Okay. So she might be dumb when it comes to handling money, but if he wants to make points with her, I don't think this is the time to point that out."

Fritzi glared back. "Really? Well! Why are you so defensive of Susan all of a sudden?" She felt a surge of jealousy surface full-force.

"Defensive? I'm not defensive," he proclaimed. "I just agreed that the woman has a point when she said he shouldn't have brought up how bad she was in math."

"Well, perhaps if she and Neil can't work their problems out, you can be there to comfort sweetums," Fritzi returned frostily.

Ryan looked at her in disbelief. "Are you implying that I'm interested in Susan? Why, I barely know the woman—"

"I'm not implying anything," she said, interrupting curtly. "But if you are, let me warn you: No matter what Neil says, he loves Susan, and I seriously doubt that he'll ever permit a divorce," she said in a lofty tone.

"Oh, good Lord." Ryan slumped against the door frame. "If I had a rubber bat right now, I'd use it on you . . . nutsy." His grin was devilish. "Besides, how could I be in love with Susan when not fifteen minutes ago you accused me of being in love with Mona?"

"If I had the bat, *you* would be the one begging for mercy," she snapped.

Neil and Susan's voices had risen to a fevered pitch again as Fritzi and Ryan turned their attention back to the battling duo.

"Listen, I think this has gone far enough. They're going to kill each other," Ryan said fretfully a few minutes later as both bats went into heated action once again. "I think we'd better go in there and put a stop to this nonsense."

Fritzi bit her lip worriedly. She hated to interfere in a marital dispute, but Ryan was right. Therapy or no therapy, they were getting carried away. Something needed to be done—quickly.

CHAPTER EIGHT

"Hi! Anyone for pizza?"

Neil and Susan lowered their bats and glanced up guiltily as Ryan and Fritzi entered the room to try to put a stop to the loud fracas.

"Oh . . . hi," Susan said in greeting, her voice showing very little enthusiasm for the unexpected interruption.

"Hope we didn't interrupt anything," Fritzi said brightly. "But Ryan and I were about to make a pizza and we thought you might want to join us."

"Oh . . . sure." Neil shot a warning look at his wife as he took the bat out of her hand and laid it on the couch. "Pizza sounds good, doesn't it . . . darling."

Neil's "darling" sounded a bit strained, but not half as much as Susan's, "Yes, dear, it does sound good."

Neil laughed nervously as he turned to face Ryan and Fritzi once more. "I guess you and Ryan heard us. We weren't really quarreling, were we, sweetums?"

"Oh, goodness no. Cutie pie and I were just . . . expressing ourselves," Susan explained lamely, but Fritzi could tell that she was making a supreme effort to appear pleasant.

"Oh, we understand," Fritzi and Ryan assured her in one voice.

Neil and Susan were both still glaring at each other as Fritzi smiled weakly at Ryan, then clapped her hands together decidedly. "Well, I guess we'd better get started!"

Without a word Neil and Susan pivoted and left Ryan and Fritzi standing alone.

Ryan gave a low whistle under his breath. "Oh, boy. I can tell that this is going to be a barrel of fun."

Eyeing the deserted bats lying on the couch, Fritzi sauntered over and quietly picked one up. "It won't be bad. They'll cool down in a few minutes."

"I wouldn't bet on it."

With the speed of lightning she reached out and whacked him on his backside.

Jumping back from the unexpected assault, he rubbed his tush painfully. "What did you do that for?"

"That's for Mona," she announced smugly. "I don't like her." She dropped the bat back on the couch, dusted her hands off in satisfaction, then calmly stepped around him to follow Neil and Susan into the kitchen.

Seconds later she felt a bat being vigorously ap-

143

plied to her own backside. Startled out of her wits, she whirled around to face a grinning Ryan.

"That's for your stubbornness. I don't like that, either." He whacked her once more, a little harder than she thought necessary. "And that's for general purposes, cupcake!"

Jerking the bat back out of his hands, she whacked him on his shoulder. "And that's for selling me that rotten water bed!"

Running over to the couch where the other bat was lying, he snatched it up and took after Fritzi, who had decided she had better run.

But she was no match for his speed, especially when she was laughing so hard that she could barely walk, so he easily trapped her between the stairway and the entrance to the kitchen. Bump! went the bat again. "That's for accusing me of having a personal interest in your sister-in-law. Shame on you," he said, scolding her.

"Ryan! Stop it!"

He had her backed up under the stairway now, and both their bats were being used in a fencing manner in a flurry of frenzied activity.

Whack! Whack! Whack! The bats dueled.

"Ouch! That hurt!" he yelled when she missed and hit him by mistake.

"You started it," she shouted.

"All right. You've had it. *En garde, mademoiselle!* Prepare to defend yourself to the death." He drew himself up in a dramatic fencing pose as her bat came crashing down and hit the top of his head, nearly knocking him to his knees.

"Good grief! That *hurt!*" He lunged toward her and, with an ease that astounded her, had her pinned snugly against the wall in the blink of an eye.

"Now." His face was so close to hers, she could reach out and kiss him without moving . . . if she had wanted to. She found herself wanting to very badly.

"Now what?" she prompted in a voice made breathless by all their playful exertion.

"Now, *mademoiselle,* you have had it," he warned. "I am going to kees you until you die . . . I em or quite possibly I shall die first from the sheer bliz of ze moment."

She giggled at his playful antics. "When? When? When?" She laid her hand against her brow in a mock swoon.

His eyes grew tender as he reached out to gently smooth away a lock of stray hair. "Whenever you say," he coaxed in a suggestive whisper that sent her pulse racing.

"Now, now, now," she whispered back eagerly.

Their mouths touched as lightly as the brush of butterfly wings. "Come here, my lusty wench. Help me decide if I'm a chest or leg man," he encouraged huskily.

Her arms went eagerly around his neck, and his mouth took hers as he molded their bodies tightly against the wall.

Desire, as she had never experienced it, raced through her veins as he continued to deepen the kiss. Fritzi sighed and leaned against the wall for total support as his hands moved slowly along her rib cage, on the verge of taking liberties he knew she would object to.

His hand touched, then briefly cradled, one of her breasts in his hand before it moved on down to caress the length of her right hip and thigh, then moved exploringly on down her leg.

"No good," he said, groaning against her mouth. "I can't tell which one I am. I like them both. We'll have to research this more." Again his mouth took hers hungrily, and they forgot all about the pizza they were supposed to be making until Neil stuck his head out the kitchen door a few minutes later and called to them.

"Hey! I thought we were going to have pizza," he snapped.

Springing apart guiltily, Fritzi was immensely relieved that their ardent embrace had been hidden by the stairwell. "Coming!" she called back.

"Maybe we should forget the pizza and let me carry you off to the tower of my castle," Ryan murmured as he stole another lingering kiss from her.

"I'd like that," she confessed, letting her tongue brush lightly against his. "But we did invite them to join us."

Ryan sighed and reached out to touch her cheek wistfully. "I suppose you're right. I'm not doing a very good job of keeping my hands off you, am I?" He grinned guiltily.

"I don't mind," she assured him softly as they kissed again.

"Hey, you guys! Wanna move it? We're hungry," Neil shouted from the kitchen again.

"Gad. He sounds testy." Fritzi hurriedly moved away from the lingering kiss. She reached over and smacked him across his backside. "Better move it, Majors."

Quickly replacing the rubber bats where they had found them, Fritzi and Ryan grinned at each other and headed for the other room.

The tension in the kitchen was so thick, it could be cut with a knife. Susan was standing at the bar, rolling out pizza crust, and Neil was sitting at the table, slicing pepperoni.

It was plain to see that neither one was talking to the other.

"Oh, you've already started," Fritzi said. "Here, let me slice that, Neil."

"No thanks," he returned curtly. "I can do it."

"Then let me help you with the crust, Susan, and Ryan can set the table."

"Sure," Ryan agreed. "What plates do you want to use?"

"That won't be necessary," Susan said to Fritzi. "I'm perfectly capable of rolling out pizza crust. You can set the table."

"Well . . . it's no trouble," she offered lamely.

"Apparently I'm an atrocious housekeeper, but I don't think anyone in this room can find fault with my cooking," she went on, shooting a scathing look in the direction of the table. Slamming the rolling pin down on the crust, she began to maneuver the wooden tool vigorously back and forth.

The object of her wrath never looked up, but the distinct sound of his knife increasing in tempo filled the air as pepperoni slices began to fall more quickly on the cutting board.

"Not to mention how lousy I am at handling money," she muttered under her breath. "I can't add two and two, you know."

"Let's both set the table," Fritzi nervously suggested to Ryan.

He quickly pulled her aside in the pantry. "Don't you think we should leave them alone? I don't like the looks of things."

"No, I think that would probably upset them even more. Let's just play it by ear," she offered. "If it looks like they need time alone, then we'll leave."

"Want to hear me?" Susan was persistent as she slammed the crust on the pizza pan loudly. "Two plus two equals five!"

"That's enough, dear . . . therapy's over," Neil reminded her through clenched teeth as he laid the knife down and began to arrange the pepperoni in neat little stacks.

"Oh, sorry, darling!" Sarcasm dripped from her voice. "I must still have a tad of aggression left in me." She opened a can of tomato sauce and angrily poured in on the crust. Half of the sauce spilled out on the counter, but she didn't seem to notice.

"I can certainly understand why," Neil noted tightly. "I seem to be suffering from an overload myself."

"Think I should go get the bats?" Fritzi asked Ryan out of the corner of her mouth as they put glasses and silverware on the table.

"I think we should get out of here," he reiterated uneasily. It seemed to him that Neil and Susan were a powder keg of dynamite ready to blow up at any moment.

"Then I think it's high time you got that aggression out of you." Susan announced in a deadly calm voice. She had paused in her work, and Fritzi noted the slight tremble in her hand as she threw down the gauntlet to her husband.

Neil stood up slowly and turned to face his wife. "I think you're right. Only this time, no rubber bats. This time we're going to be honest with each other and say what's really bothering us."

"What you mean is, you want me to crawl on my knees and confess that I was all wrong to have doubts about our marriage, isn't it?"

Neil's stance grew defensive, forgetting that they were not alone. "That would do for starters."

"And you want me to say that you had every right to act the way you've been acting because you

149

feel you've been unduly wronged by those perfectly honest doubts?"

"It would help," he returned stubbornly.

Susan's eyes snapped with blue fire. "And Tyce? You want me to apologize for Tyce ever being in my life?"

"Maybe all I ever wanted was a little honesty out of you where Tyce was concerned!"

"Oh, boy. Here it comes," Ryan grimaced as he and Fritzi sank down into the kitchen chairs, hoping to make themselves as inconspicuous as possible.

"Honest? You want honesty?" Susan's hand slid under the pan of pizza and gripped it tightly. "Well, here's honest! I'm sick to death of hearing about Tyce! If you can't recognize the fact that no matter what I felt then, it's you I love now, then you can go fly a kite, you—you *man!*"

"Listen, you guys." Fritzi popped up out of her chair and scurried over to the stove in an effort to avert the inevitable. "Ryan and I have decided that we're not very hungry, so I'm just going to make us some popcorn and take it to the den so you two can finish your discussion." She hurriedly rummaged around in the cabinet and, seconds later, threw a large pan on the stove, turned on the burner, and dumped oil and popcorn kernels into it.

"Darn it, where's the lid?" she mumbled as the tension in the room began to fairly throb. She crawled back under the cabinet and began frantically searching for the cover to the pan.

"There's no need to pop corn," Susan objected, never taking her eyes off Neil. "There's plenty of pizza . . . isn't there, darling?" She hefted up the pan, and Fritzi gasped as it went sailing across the room and landed with a loud thud in the middle of the table where Ryan was sitting.

Ryan's eyes grew wide as tomato sauce splashed onto the front of his shirt.

"Of course, *dear!* But you've forgotten the pepperoni. Petulantly Neil began lobbing handfuls of pepperoni on top of the pizza, making a disgusting mess as he tried to stare her down.

"Popcorn's fine with me," Ryan insisted, reaching out to try to retrieve some of the pieces of meat that had missed the crust. He nervously began to rearrange the meat in a neater manner. "I think I've lost my appeti—"

His words were cut off when a barrage of mushrooms came sailing in his direction. He quickly ducked as he heard them hitting the table.

"Hey, you guys! This is getting out of hand," he said reproachfully as he began gathering up the mushrooms. "There's no use in ruining a perfectly good pizza," he grumbled.

"Well, I *am* sorry about the mess, but Neil likes mushrooms on his pizza, don't you, dear?"

Fritzi gave up on finding the lid and crawled out of the cabinet. She stood up to survey the messy table with growing dismay.

Neda was going to kill all of them when she came

back to see what they had done to the kitchen in her absence.

She realized now that she should have listened to Ryan and left ten minutes ago.

"I love mushrooms, but I wouldn't want to disappoint you, dearest." He scooped up a handful of green peppers he had been cleaning and heatedly threw them at the table, daring her with his eyes to say anything. "After all, what's a pepperoni-and-mushroom pizza without green peppers?"

Ryan calmly reached up and intercepted one of the airborne pieces of vegetable and munched away nervously as green peppers flew all over the floor. He was now resigned to the fact that war had broken out.

Fritzi hurried over to his side and pulled him toward the doorway. "I think you were right. Let's get out of here."

"Now?" His face took on a look of boyish disappointment. "I think the cheese was just coming up next and I love cheese," he said, protesting.

"Come on, Ryan, let's go!"

"What about the popcorn?"

"Oh damn!" The sound of corn popping began to saturate the air, and the two couples diverted their attention to the pan on the stove where a white flume of kernels was shooting up in the air like Old Faithful.

"You didn't put the lid on the pan!" Ryan shouted above the melee.

"I couldn't find it!"

"Hold on and we'll make a run for it!" Ryan yelled as he grabbed for her hand.

Minutes later they had stumbled into the sanctuary of the den where they huddled until they felt that the storm had blown over.

"I think it's all clear." Fritzi cautiously peeked out from behind the door of the den and listened for any sounds of disagreement coming from the kitchen. When complete silence met her ear, she eased the door open farther and peered out into the hallway expectantly. "It's okay to come out now."

It had been over an hour since they had left Neil and Susan, and Ryan was beginning to complain of hunger.

"You'd better be sure, cupcake," he said, mock teasingly. "I don't want to get in the middle of a pizza-slinging contest again."

"Come on, scaredy cat. It's clear." She tugged on his hand and pulled him out into the hallway.

"Good. Let's go see if we can salvage that pizza," he suggested.

"I think we'd better clean up the kitchen first," Fritzi told him in a hushed whisper as they tiptoed down the hall. "Neda would have a fit if she came home and found it in the condition it's in."

"Why are we tiptoeing and whispering?"

"Because we don't want them to hear us."

"Why not? We're not the ones arguing, they are."

As they passed Neil's bedroom Fritzi paused and pointed to the closed door, a hopeful grin forming on her mouth. "They must be talking," she mouthed silently.

Ryan reached down and picked up Susan's blouse and held it out on one finger. "Talking?"

Fritzi blushed as she surveyed the blouse. "Well, they *are* married," she said in defense.

"Hey." He held up both hands innocently. "I've been telling you all along, if I were Neil, that's how I would have handled her to begin with."

Continuing on to the kitchen, Fritzi thought about ignoring his comment, but her curiosity got the better of her. "You mean, if we were Neil and Susan, you'd just haul me off to bed and that would settle everything?"

"If we honestly loved each other, that would settle everything important . . . at least until we could sit down and iron out the small problems."

When they entered the kitchen, they both stepped back and tried to overcome their shock at the condition of the room. The floor was covered with popcorn and various articles of men and women's clothing that apparently had been discarded in haste. Remnants of the pizza littered the table and countertops, and it looked as if a bomb had been dropped in the middle of the room.

Fritzi put her hands on her hips in disgust. "Holy cow. It will take us hours to clean this up."

"Yeah . . ." Ryan shook his head dismally.

"Well, let's look on the good side. I don't think Susan and Neil were arguing when they left."

For the next hour and a half they both worked hard at putting the room back in order. Most of the pizza had been salvaged, and it was bubbling away in the oven when Fritzi finished mopping the floor.

"There." She stood back and surveyed the now spotless kitchen, her hand rubbing her aching back. "It looks as good as new."

"Your back hurting?" Ryan asked as he sponged off the counter.

"Yeah, it always does when I mop."

Flipping the sponge in the sink, he grinned and motioned for her to come over to him. "Come here, let me give you one of the famous Majors backrubs. Guaranteed to cure all ills."

She went to him gratefully, and for the next few minutes he massaged the small of her back. It felt heavenly.

"You really should be lying down for this," he coaxed, letting his fingers rub and knead until she felt the pain begin to ease.

He was holding her almost flush against him now, and she relaxed and wrapped her arms around his neck. "Not a chance, Majors. I have a feeling that you would have more than a backrub in mind."

He chuckled and brushed his mouth against her ear affectionately. "Feel better?"

"Yes, much."

He kissed her mouth softly, then set her aside with reluctance. "I think I smell the pizza burning."

An overwhelming sense of disappointment came over her when he left her arms and went to check on the pizza. She would have gladly forfeited the pizza for something more stimulating.

After dinner they went back to the den and watched television for a while. The storm had finally broken, and it looked as if their incarceration would be over by the next morning.

"You're awfully quiet over there. What are you reading?" Around ten-thirty Ryan glanced up at her from his reclining position on the sofa and smiled at her.

"My treasure-mapping book." The book had been on her mind all evening, and around nine she had gone to her bedroom to retrieve it.

"Oh, that? Why don't you bring it over here and let me see it?"

"You wouldn't be interested," she said, declining.

"Yes, I would. Bring it over here." He sat up and motioned for her to join him. A few minutes later they were thumbing through the pages, and she was once more explaining her goals in life. "And this glass table with the brass chairs, aren't they nice?"

He leaned down and peered at them more closely. "Yeah, they are. In fact, I have a set nearly identical to them."

"You do?"

"Bought it last year."

"Don't you just love it?" Her eyes sparkled with enthusiasm.

"Not really. The table has dust on it all the time, and it's impossible to keep fingerprints off it."

"Really?" She glanced back down at the page disappointedly. "Hmm. I hadn't thought about that. Well, what about this video recorder? Pretty nice, huh?"

"I have one of those too."

"Do you like it?"

"It's okay, but those movies are a lot of trouble to go out and rent, then take back the next day. Especially when the same movie usually shows up on television the next week."

They continued to browse through the pages, and Fritzi was amazed to find that Ryan already had the majority of things she had only dreamed of.

"You have a personal computer too? What about Hawaii? Ever been there?" she asked, challenging him in an almost defensive voice.

"I'm going there on my honeymoon," he promised, "but I hear it's a tourist trap."

"Oh, you!" She picked up a sofa pillow and smacked him across his chest. "You're a real pessimist."

"I am not! I'm only telling you what I've heard," he said, protesting.

"Well, I bet I know one thing you don't have."

He cocked his brow in a challenge. "What?"

"Long red fingernails." She flipped to the page

where the hands were portrayed and smiled smugly. "There. I've always wanted my fingernails to look like that."

"Oh, good grief." He groaned and rolled his eyes prettily. "I had fingernails just like those until last week," he said, scoffing. "I had to cut them off because I kept scratching myself something terrible every time I shaved."

"You big buffoon." She pinched his arm and made him confess that he was lying.

"What's so hard about having fingernails like that?" he chided. "All you have to do is go to one of those nail places and have them glue some on."

"Yeah, and you have to keep going back every two weeks to keep them on. I couldn't afford it." She looked at him sternly. "How do you know about such things?"

He shrugged. "I've dated women who've had them. Personally I can't stand the things. They look like claws."

"Does Mona have them?"

"No, Mona doesn't have them," he said, mimicking her, then leaned over to kiss her before she could protest.

The book was now lying open to the page where the man of Fritzi's dreams was portrayed. Ryan's eyes immediately seized upon the picture. "Hey, what's this? A picture of me in your book?" he exclaimed, leaning closer to get a better look.

"Of you? Don't be silly."

"Silly?" He peered closer at the photograph. "It may not be me, but it sure looks like me."

"It does not!" She snatched the book away from him and opened the book wider to get a closer view.

For a moment she was so stunned, she could barely speak. The picture did bear an uncanny resemblance to Ryan. The man had the same coloring and stocky build as Ryan. Even his hair had the same lush, brown waves that Ryan's had. Her fingers hesitantly touched the picture, running lightly over the man's delectable posterior. *That* was even the same.

No wonder she had kept having the feeling that she'd known him from somewhere before!

"See? He does look exactly like me," Ryan challenged. Leaning back on the sofa, he placed both hands behind his head and smiled. "Well, well. How interesting. I'm in Fritzi's wish book." He grinned. "Can you beat that?"

Slamming the book shut, she jumped up from the sofa and hugged the book protectively to her chest. "Well, I guess I'll go to bed now."

Ryan was still at his place on the sofa, and a slow, devilish grin was spreading across his face. "Yeah, I guess you'd better."

She turned around and faced him angrily. "What's so funny?"

"Nothing." The smile dropped off his face instantly. "Did I say something was funny?"

"Listen, just because I happen to have a silly pic-

159

ture in my treasure-mapping book that just happens to resemble you in some tiny way, you'd best not try to make anything out of it," she warned.

"No, I wouldn't do that," he denied in the most innocent voice, but his eyes told her that he definitely would if he could.

"Just see that you don't," she snapped as she turned on her heel and scurried out of the room before he could say another word.

"Hey, Fritzi!"

She paused at the door as she heard him call her name, but she refused to turn around and face him. "What do you want?"

"Don't you find it strange that the picture does resemble me? I mean, think about it. You must have pasted that picture in there years before we ever met."

"The man in the swimsuit represents the man I'm going to marry in the future," she said curtly. "It has nothing to do with you."

"But the man in the swimsuit does look like me," he pointed out again.

"Pure coincidence."

"Ha."

"What's that supposed to mean?" She whirled around to face him.

"It means, ha! Face it, sweetheart. I'm the treasure you've been waiting for. Even your little book agrees."

He was still smiling as she slammed the door in his face and hurried on down the hall.

Good grief! What was this world coming to? Even her treasure-mapping book had turned against her!

CHAPTER NINE

"See you around, cupcake." That's what Ryan Majors had had the gall to say to her the next morning as he prepared to leave. He had planted a friendly kiss on her forehead as he had breezed by her and told her to keep in touch.

Neil had been out early and plowed the road leading to the ranch, so there was nothing to detain him further.

She had stood at the window and watched Ryan trudge through the heavy snow to his truck with mixed feelings. In a way it was a relief to know that she had finally made him understand how important it was for her to stick with her plans, but she had to admit that did nothing to ease the feeling of loneliness that overcame her as she watched him drive away.

She dropped the curtain back in place and glanced around the empty room that had been so filled with his presence for the past few hours.

A tiny smile broke out as she thought about the

incident with the rubber bats. Her hand absently came up to touch her mouth, and she closed her eyes for a moment to savor the memory of his kiss during their playful antics. He always tasted so good.

Her eyes closed tighter as she began to be more aware of exactly what she had just let go.

Just like that. "See you around, cupcake." Not one word about where they would go from this point, so she could only assume that they would go nowhere. And all because of her.

"Ryan get off okay?" Neil's voice interrupted her misery as he walked into the room to throw another log on the fire.

"Yes. He just left."

Neil had noticed the look of sadness on her face when he first entered the room, but he was hesitant to ask what was troubling her. He could guess.

"Want to drive into town with Susan and me to pick up Neda?" he asked.

"No thanks. I have some bookkeeping to catch up on."

"Can't that wait? There isn't that much going on at the ranch right now. Why don't you go with us? We'll stop at Grady's for hamburgers and malts on the way back," he said, trying to tempt her.

She moved slowly away from her vigil at the window and stood before the fire. "Thanks for the invitation, Neil, but maybe another time."

"Got it bad, huh?" He stood up and held out his

163

arms to her, and after a moment's hesitation she flew into them, breaking out in tears as she buried her face in the comfort of his broad shoulder.

"Oh, Neil. I'm so miserable!"

Neil's chuckle was not exactly a balm to her aching heart. "I never thought I'd see the day when a man had Fritzi Taylor in a stew." He patted her comfortingly. "Hurts like hell, doesn't it?"

"It's killing me," she said with a sob. "And I don't know what to do."

Gently guiding her over to the sofa, he sat her down and reached in his pocket to extract a white handkerchief and hand it to her. "You're in love with the guy, aren't you?"

"Yes," she wailed, "but I can't be!"

"Why not?"

"Because I have my life all planned out and—and —this just isn't the time to fall in love and get married."

"One thing nice about plans," Neil consoled, "they can always be changed to suit the occasion."

"But I don't want them to change," she protested, blowing her nose and wiping at the stream of tears cascading down her cheeks. "If they change, I'll run the chance of messing up my life—" She caught herself just in time.

"Like me?" he supplied for her.

"I'm sorry, but, yes . . . like you." She peered at him miserably. "Don't you see, Neil? My life was clicking along like clockwork. I had a good start on the things that I wanted to accomplish, and in another five years they would all be mine with no problem. Then I would think about getting serious with a man and settling down. But Ryan had to come along and try to blow all that to Hades. Now, because of him, I don't seem to know what I want anymore."

Neil sighed and shook his head at her logic. "You and your harebrained plans. I've always known that your penchant for being so darn organized was going to get you in trouble. You think that planning your life out to the last detail is going to make you any less susceptible to making mistakes?"

"Well, maybe not from making mistakes, but it certainly should cut down on the size of the ones I make."

"Fritzi, do you love Ryan?"

"Yes! But that doesn't make any difference at this point."

"Does he love you?" Neil persisted.

"Well . . . he said he did." She glanced at her brother sheepishly. "But I'm not at all sure he still does."

"I have a strong feeling he still does. But if you don't throw those rigid set of plans away and start living one day at a time, I think you run the chance of losing him permanently."

"If he loved me all that much, he'd be willing to wait for a few years to marry."

"Five years?" He knew her plans by heart now.

She flinched at his loud exclamation of disbelief. Funny, but that had upset Ryan too.

"Well . . . maybe not five years," she said, backing down. "But certainly not *this* Valentine's Day like he wants!" she said defensively.

"When or even *if* you should marry Ryan is not the point of discussion here. The point is that you're too stubborn when it comes to making changes in your life. Face it, Fritzi, we all have to make changes whether we like it or not, and if Ryan really means anything to you, you'd better take a closer look at those plans you hold so dear and see if there isn't some room for adjustment."

Her tears started flowing again as Neil's words began to find fertile ground.

"You can't actually expect the man to wait around five years while you're out gathering up your dreams. What about *his* dreams?" Neil continued to drive his point home. "I hate to add to your misery, but if you love the man, you'd better shape up."

Wiping ineffectually at her eyes, she tried to let the look of tenderness in his eyes soften the brunt of his words, but it was hard.

Kneeling down in front of her, he took her hands and forced her teary gaze to meet his purposeful one. "And if it's my and Susan's marriage that's scaring you out of a meaningful relationship with Ryan, then don't let it. We had a long, serious talk last night—the first, I might add, that we've had since we got married. I think we see things a whole lot clearer now than we did before." A small hopeful smile tugged at the corners of his mouth. "I think we're going to make it."

Fritzi placed her hand over his affectionately. "I'm glad, Neil. I've always thought that you and Susan loved each other."

"We've had a lot of growing up to do, and our problems aren't over yet," he confessed. "But you know something? Through it all we've held on because we loved each other. Dreams are nice, Fritzi, but sometimes reality is a whole lot better."

The wisdom of Neil's words did not fail to affect Fritzi. Dreams and plans *were* nice, but she suddenly discovered that all her dreams were about Ryan. Each night she would pull her treasure-mapping book out and gaze longingly at the picture of the man who resembled Ryan, and her heart would ache to think how foolish she had been to be so stubborn.

Neil had been right when he said she was going to have to shape up, but was it too late?

Though she was now more than willing to change her plans to include Ryan, would he still want her? Apparently, since he didn't bother to come around, he had finally accepted that she didn't want him in her life at this point, when nothing could be further from the truth. But how could she swallow her pride and ask him to take her back, especially when she had been so adamant about what she had thought she had wanted?

Bone-chilling January turned into miserable February, and the weather seemed to grow more nasty as she went passively about her daily living.

Ryan finally did call but only to ask about the progress she had made in adjusting to her bed. She still hated it, yet it seemed to be a small remnant of him to hold on to, so she bit her tongue and told him she loved it now. If he still had hopes that she would change her mind about their relationship, he never voiced them in that short, impersonal conversation, and she couldn't find the words to tell him what lay so heavily in her heart.

Day after dreary day passed until suddenly she woke up one cold February morning when the sleet was pelting against her windowpane to discover that she was tired of mourning a lost love.

Miraculously she felt her old go-out-there-and-get-'em spirit coming back to her as she jumped out of bed and raced for a hot shower, plotting feverishly in the steamy mist. There was no longer a shortage of hot water since Neil had ordered a new heater installed before their parents returned home, so she had plenty of time to organize her new plans. The belated thought had suddenly occurred to her that if she was that crazy over the big oaf, then she was going to have to do something about getting him back.

Now her life took on new purpose as she sought ways to have seemingly accidental meetings with him without letting him know that their chance meetings were carefully planned by her.

Since the town wasn't that large, it was easy for her to hang around the shops and watch for him to go to the bank or on one of the various errands he ran every day.

When another week had passed and he still showed no visible signs of wanting to renew whatever it was they once had, Fritzi gritted her teeth and put her thinking cap on a little straighter. She had already gained two pounds from eating the blue-plate special where he had lunch every day, but if it took another two to accomplish her mission, then so be it.

Through it all Ryan seemed oblivious to the fact that she was chasing him now, even though she couldn't imagine how he could miss the fact.

Although he was always polite, he never did more than ask "How are you?" or say "The weather's lousy, isn't it?" when those meetings would occur, then go on his way.

Late one afternoon, two days before Valentine's Day, she was sitting in a booth of the local pub where she knew Ryan stopped occasionally, trying to enjoy a cup of hot tea, but her taste buds weren't functioning properly. She had come down with a horrible cold two days earlier, and this was the first time this week she had been able to pursue him.

Actually she never should have come today, she thought, mentally berating herself. Especially in view of the atrocious way she looked. Not only were her eyes red and weepy, but also her nose was chapped from continuous blowing and so stuffed up that she felt as if she were hearing everything from within a deep cave. She also talked with a nasal twang that was nothing short of disgusting.

Perhaps it would be better if she remained inconspicuous and tried to gain his attention when she looked a little more presentable. Yes, that would be wisest, she decided. Reaching for her check, she started to slide out of the booth, then froze in place as she saw Ryan enter the bar with another man.

She scooted back in the booth and pulled her hat down lower over her face as Ryan and the newcomer took a seat at the counter.

After what she considered a safe interval, she peeked out from beneath the brim of her hat and groaned out loud when she saw that he had spotted her and was walking her way.

"Hello," he said as he paused before her booth. "We meet again."

"Hello," she mumbled.

"I almost didn't recognize you there for a minute, with your hat pulled down over your face that way."

"It's a little drafty in here," she said, justifying her appearance and pulling her coat up a little tighter around her neck as she felt a chill assault her.

"Funny how we keep bumping into one another."

"Yes, isn't it." She grinned weakly and motioned toward her teacup. "I had been doing some shopping, and I thought I'd have a cup of tea before I went home."

He looked at her oddly. "Are you sick?"

"Just a bad cold." She fumbled with her wadded tissue and blew her nose once more.

"Oh . . . well, it was good to see you again. You're looking great," he offered, letting his gaze linger hungrily on her flushed face.

"Thanks. You are too."

"Well, see you around . . . and take care of that cold." He ambled back over to the bar as she ducked her head and tried to concentrate on her tea.

Looking good! She blew her nose loudly and took another sip of tea. Hopeless. That's what this was. Simply hopeless!

Half an hour later her temperature had gone back up, her tea had grown stone-cold, and she was shaking until her teeth knocked together, but she still held on to the small hope that he might stop by her booth again on the way out.

Although Ryan had not paid the slightest bit of attention to her since he had walked over, she still hovered in her booth and stole secret, yearning glances at him every now and then.

The man he was sitting with appeared to be a

salesman, and from the small snatches of conversation she was able to overhear, he was trying to sell Ryan a new line of water-bed accessories.

She had just about decided to give up and go home when she saw Ryan turn around and look in her direction, then turn back to say something to the bartender in a quiet voice.

Minutes later a mug filled with amber liquid was being set in front of her. "I didn't order anything," she informed quickly.

"The gentleman at the bar wanted you to have this, ma'am. It's a hot toddy, and it will do wonders for that cold."

Her glance flew over to Ryan as he smiled at her and raised his near empty glass in a silent toast.

She smiled back gratefully and picked up the glass to return the toast. "Tell the gentleman thank you. I appreciate it very much."

The warm liquid burned going down her raw throat, but she obediently took a second sip.

"This is pretty strong stuff, isn't it?" she remarked.

"It needs to be to help that cold."

She eyed the glass thoughtfully. "Well"—she tipped it up again and took another swallow—"here's to good health."

Ten minutes later a new glass was set before her, and she glanced apprehensively over at Ryan. She was not a frequent drinker, so one drink would be

172

all she could handle and still be able to drive herself home.

He smiled once more and nodded his encouragement as he forced his attention back to the presentation the salesman was trying to make. She shrugged and tipped the new glass up for another sip. The bartender had been right. It *was* strong.

Thirty minutes and three hot toddies later, she was staring glassy-eyed at the large shiffelera plant next to her when she heard Ryan's and the bartender's voices beside her.

"I didn't make them as strong as I usually do, Mr. Majors. Apparently she isn't used to drinking."

Fritzi turned and grinned stupidly, then wrapped her arms around Ryan's neck. "Hello, there. I'm much better, thank you."

"Hold on, sweetheart. You've had too much to drink, and I'm going to have to take you home," Ryan said soothingly.

"Oh ho! I think you'd better," she agreed, contentedly snuggling her head against his broad shoulder. It was like offering a cup of cool water to a man dying of thirst in the desert for her to touch him and to smell his very pleasing and familiar scent of soap and after-shave. She had missed that so very much. "I don't feel so well," she confessed in a tiny voice.

Sliding her gently out of the booth, Ryan carefully stood her on the floor before him and proceeded to button her coat and arrange her hat more securely. Then he scooped her up in his arms and made his way across the dimly lit room. "Don't have her car towed away, Jackson. I'll send someone over for it later on."

"Sure thing, Mr. Majors."

The frigid blast of wind that buffeted them as they walked out the front door made her snuggle down more protectively into his arms.

"Are you cold?" he shouted above the wind.

She nodded affirmatively and tipped her head back so she could see his face. Reverently she touched his cheek and sighed with pleasure as he hugged her up more closely and quickened his pace. "You're nice to take me home. You know that? Very, very nice."

"I should be shot for sending those toddies over to you," he said, fretting.

"They were delicious," she said, objecting strongly. "Simply delicious. I've never had one of those before."

"One was all you needed," he rebuked, more to himself than to her.

He told her that his car was parked behind the water-bed store, but Fritzi was barely aware of his words as he rounded the corner and hurried toward a black sports car.

When they were settled in the car a few moments later, she refused to relinquish her arms from around his neck as he started the car and let it warm up for a few minutes before leaving.

"How am I going to drive with you on my lap?"

174

he teased as he let his gaze drink its fill of her pretty, flushed features.

"I don't know, but I don't want to move. I've missed you, you big oaf." She brought her cheek up against his and squeezed his face affectionately. "I think I'm in love with you."

"I'm glad you finally realized that," he said with just a touch of smugness in his voice.

They both let out a sigh of deep pleasure as they savored the moment. It had been a long time since they had been in each other's arms.

"Oh, honey, you have a fever," he said with a groan, took off her hat, and let her hair fall loosely through his fingers. He buried his face in the silken mass and closed his eyes to relish the exquisite feel of her. "I've got to get you home."

"Ryan, I know I have pneumonia, but kiss me," she demanded in a tiny voice.

Cold or no cold, he didn't need to be invited twice. His mouth hungrily searched and found hers, then took it in a kiss that was so masterful, it left her begging for more.

"Again," she pleaded as her mouth consistently refused to leave his.

Groaning at her unusual ardor, Ryan complied willingly with her pleas, and for five minutes they sat in the car, which was now becoming warm, and exchanged kiss after long kiss.

"No more," he begged in a strangled voice when

his passion had finally reached its limit. "I can't take any more, Fritzi."

She felt a desolate sense of rejection at his words. "Oh, Ryan . . . I need you," she beseeched sincerely. "Don't push me away this time."

"Fritzi . . . stop." He groaned and shifted around as her mouth found his again and again.

With a determined effort he put the car in gear and eased the car out of the lot.

"Are you taking me home?" she rebuked. "Oh, Ryan, please don't take me home. I love you . . . and I'm sorry I've been so stubborn." He wasn't sure how much was her talking or the liquor, but at the moment he didn't care. All he could think of was getting her somewhere alone and out of his car.

"And if you'll only forgive me, I'll try to do better," she was still pleading as he pulled into his garage and braked ten minutes later. "I don't see why I have to give up *all* my plans. You could stand to do a little readjusting of your own, and then we might be able to work things out. . . ." She took his mouth with a kiss that threatened to put him over the brink.

Gathering her up in his arms, he slid out of the car and kicked the door shut with his foot.

"Ryan! Say something," she demanded.

"Here, blow your nose and be quiet." He handed her his handkerchief. "You're going to disturb the neighbors," he warned.

While she was still babbling something about the

176

fact that she didn't care who she disturbed, he carried her up a flight of steps that led into the kitchen of his apartment and slammed the door.

"Where are we?" She looked around and didn't recognize a thing except the lovely glass table with four brass chairs she had in her treasure-mapping book.

"Oh! I love your table," she said as he stalked through the kitchen. "It's beautiful."

"Glad you like it."

"And you've got a big video recorder!" she exclaimed with delight as they marched through his living room.

"I told you I did."

"You did? Oh. Well, I love it." She glanced back over her shoulder expectantly as he carried her on to the bedroom. Then she sighed and peered up at him lovingly as he gently laid her on his bed. "It wouldn't matter to me, you know, if you had them or not. Those are only things. I used to think I wanted a glass table with brass chairs and a video recorder, and a hundred other things, but now—" Her voice broke off whimsically. "I found out those things aren't important to me anymore." She reached out and touched the tip of his nose adoringly. "Are you finally going to make love to me?"

"Yes, but I'm going to hate myself in the morning for doing it."

Her face clouded with resentment. "Why?"

"Because you're more than a little drunk, and we still have a lot of problems to work out between us."

Shaking her head slyly, she grinned and pulled his mouth back down to meet hers. "I can personally guarantee that I know what I'm doing, and as far as the problems go, we no longer have as many as you think we do."

It suddenly occurred to him that she now sounded as sober as a judge. Eyeing her suspiciously, he sat on the side of the bed and looked down at her sternly. "You little faker. You aren't drunk at all, are you?"

She grinned and shook her head negatively. "You're the only one around here who over imbibes and has big monkeys chasing you."

"You mean to tell me that you sat there and drank three hot toddies and it never even fazed you?"

"I didn't drink three hot toddies. I may have taken a sip out of each glass, but then I dumped the rest in that plant sitting next to my booth. It's probably blooming its little heart out right now."

"Well I'll be damned." He shook his head in disbelief.

"Well, don't look so floored. Why in the world would you send three hot toddies over to my table if you didn't expect to get me bombed?" she said accusingly.

It was his turn to grin slyly. "Because that's exactly what I was hoping to do. Get you to the point where you couldn't drive yourself home so I would have to."

Motioning for him to come back in her arms, he did so without further hesitation, and their mouths touched each other's lightly. "Then what in the world is all the fuss? I was merely trying to help your cause."

"We need to talk," he cautioned as he lay down on the bed and pulled her on top of him, but his heart wasn't in his suggestion.

"To heck with talking. We can do that anytime," she said as she nibbled his lips. Her fingers began to fumble with the snap on his trousers. "I'm going to seduce you."

"I hate to tell you how to do your job, but shouldn't you start with my shirt and then work down?" he suggested.

"No. I've already seen your chest." Her fingers eagerly released the snap and helped him slip out of the restricting garment.

"Oh? Then I must have something else that caught your attention?"

Her hand hesitated momentarily, then she threw prudence to the wind and explored his bare bottom adoringly. "You might say that."

"Aha! I knew it!" he said, gloating. "And you said you had no interest whatsoever in my—" His words were cut off by a shower of kisses, and a few minutes later they were both eagerly discovering the wonders of each other's bodies.

Their motions eventually slowed and became more lingering as all playfulness drained out of them and their hunger began to grow. Now that barriers had been removed, they were able to come together in an act of love that seemed as natural as breathing. They began to move in perfect, breathless harmony, as if they had been lovers in flesh, instead of mind, for a very long time. Each one seemed to sense the other's need and had no reservations about satisfying those desires. When the moment of perfect union arrived, Ryan lifted her up in his arms and incoherently murmured words of adoration for her as she accepted his gift of love in a rush of uncontrollable passion.

Later, as they lay together basking in the warm afterglow of their lovemaking, it occurred to Fritzi that this had been the most wonderful night of her life. No other man had come close to making her feel the way she had when Ryan had made love to her. She felt a tiny shudder assault her when she thought how close she had come to letting that treasure slip through her hands.

CHAPTER TEN

"Are you cold?" Ryan had felt her shudder, and he rolled over to face her, his eyes fairly glowing with love and concern. "Here, you need to cover up." He busied himself with making her comfortable, and she had to smile at his motherly clucking.

"I'm fine, really."

"No, you're not. You have a temperature, and I should be shot for making love to you at a time like this."

"I'm not complaining," she protested, and wrapped her arms back around his neck affectionately. He allowed himself to be distracted by her kiss once more, but a few minutes later he pulled away and announced that he was going to get her some aspirin.

She had to admit that the bed felt pretty wonderful as she snuggled down in its warmth. Warmth? She wiggled her body experimentally, and sure enough, the mattress wiggled with her. It was a water bed! She had been so busy earlier, she had failed to notice what they had been lying on.

"Ryan, this is a water bed," she accused as he came back in the room carrying a bottle of aspirin and a glass of water.

He giggled, that same cute little giggle she had missed hearing so much lately, and shook a couple of aspirins into her hand. "Yeah, I brought one home a couple of weeks ago."

"But I thought you didn't like water beds," she argued, sitting up to take the pills with a sip of water.

"I didn't until I had messed with yours so much. Then they sort of intrigued me."

"Do you like it?" She looked up at him anxiously.

"Actually . . ." He started to lie and say that he loved it and couldn't see what her problem had been all along. "I hate it."

A big smile broke across her face. "See? They're not all they're cracked up to be, are they?"

"Well, I can't say I hated the last hour or so on it," he confessed.

Pulling him back on the bed with her, she hugged his neck tightly. "That was sort of nice, wasn't it? Maybe if we would have done that sooner, I would have liked mine better."

"Don't blame me. I did everything within my power to offer satisfaction," he reminded her. "You were the one who kept insisting that I wasn't welcome in your life *or* your rotten water bed."

"Yes." She sighed and lay back on her pillow. "I was a real goofball."

"No, I was the goofball, and these last few weeks have taught me a lesson. You're absolutely right. I'm too impetuous. After giving it a lot of thought, five years sounds like a reasonable time to wait for marriage. I'm willing to hang around and wait for you if you'll let me."

"Five years!"

He jumped, startled at the tone of her voice.

"Yeah, five or six. Whatever you think—"

"Are you serious? You want to wait five years for us to get married?" She snapped the blanket in place and crossed her arms stubbornly. "That's ridiculous."

"But it was you—"

"I will not wait five years, Ryan! I want to get married now."

"Now?" A slow grin broke across his features. "Well, I don't know . . . I had sort of gotten used to the idea of being single for another five years, but . . ." He pretended to mull the new suggestion over in his mind with great concentration. "Tell you what I'll do. I'll consult my treasure-mapping book and see what I can work out."

She eyed him warily. "You don't have a treasure-mapping book."

"I don't have a book? How can you say that? I've spent the last few weeks pasting pictures in my book every night, and you have the nerve to lie there and accuse me of not planning out my life."

"You've never planned out your next day, let alone your life," she complained.

"Wait right here." He was out of bed and the room before she could ask what he was up to. Minutes later he returned, a bottle of paste in one hand, a book in the other, and a pair of blunt-tipped child's scissors in his mouth. "Accuse me of not having a treasure-mapping book," he mumbled irritably around the scissors as he got back in bed. "Just take a look at this, Ms. Taylor."

He thrust the flop-eared-looking book in her hand. The book still had traces of white paste smeared across the cover.

"If this is your treasure-mapping book, it's disgusting," she chided as she gingerly opened the first page. "What's this nasty paste doing all over the front of it?"

"Don't complain. At least I have one," he said, challenging her petulantly. "And hurry up. I haven't pasted my picture in today." He opened the jar of paste and waved it in front of her face. "Stinks, doesn't it? Would you believe I used to eat this stuff when I was a kid?"

Shaking her head tolerantly, she began to turn the pages, and a tiny grin curved the corners of her mouth. Ryan's book contained nothing but page after page of pictures of her. It was the same picture over and over again. An old snapshot taken of her several years ago. "Where did you get this picture?"

"Neil gave it to me. I took it to the photo store and had twenty-six copies made."

"But my picture is the only one you have in your book," she pointed out.

He slowly removed the scissors from his mouth. "It's the only thing I want. I have everything else that's important to me," he explained patiently. "I just wish it wouldn't have taken you so darn long to realize the same about me."

She glanced up at him shamefully. "I realized you were all I wanted several weeks ago, but when I tried to get you back, you weren't the least bit interested in me."

"I wouldn't bet on that." He placed the book on the nightstand and propped his pillow beneath his head, then pulled her close to him. "I knew what you were trying to do."

"You did?" She punched him in the ribs. "Then why didn't you help me out a little bit?"

"I was, as my dear old Grandmother Majors would put it, letting you stew in your own juices. I had every intention of coming after you when the time was right."

"What made you think that today was the right time? I've been beating my brains out trying to say I'm sorry, and it hasn't phased you one iota."

"Because by today I was getting worried sick over you. I hadn't seen you around all week, and I was afraid something had happened to you, or worse, you had finally decided to give up on me and go back to your treasure-mapping book."

"I haven't been around because I've been sick with this cold." She sat up and reached for a tissue. "Besides, I wouldn't have done that," she denied. "I have a confession I'd better make. When I get my heart set on something, like having you, well, I may seem pretty laid-back at times, but I can be awfully stubborn too. I wasn't anywhere near ready to give up yet."

"No kidding—you stubborn?" He looked absolutely floored. "I never would have guessed!"

"No, I know that's hard to believe, but it's true, so it probably would have taken me a long time to give up on you," she said insistently. "And I want to apologize for suggesting a long-term affair. You mean much more to me than that, and I intend to prove it to you."

"That's all very reassuring, but all you had to do was pick up the phone and call me and tell me you had changed your mind instead of trailing me all over town and catching pneumonia. I would have been there before you hung up," he vowed as he brushed back her hair and nuzzled her neck.

"Are you going to make love to me again?"

He chuckled. "Are you a mind reader too?"

"No, just very much in love."

Later they were exchanging languid kisses as her body still tingled from the effects of his passionate lovemaking. They were both sated and relaxed and didn't have a care in the world.

"I suppose that if you're going to insist on rushing me to the altar now, I think we could still keep that wedding date on Valentine's Day," he said temptingly.

"Mmm." She was drowsy with contentment. "I can't see how. That's only two days away. We have to have plans, Ryan! You know I don't like to do anything without planning it out to the last detail, and a woman's wedding day is special. We'd have to buy a ring and find a minister and—"

Ryan reached over and laid a finger across her lips. "Hold it right there. I can solve one of those problems right now. The others will all fall into place. Trust me." Throwing back the blanket, he got up and switched on the lamp beside the bed, then walked to his dresser, aware that her eyes were following his bare bottom across the room.

He turned around and grinned, catching her in the act of ogling him once again.

"You're staring at me again."

She grinned guiltily.

"I hope you're enjoying the view."

"It's marvelous," she said, complimenting him, and snuggled farther down on her pillow. "It's better than Pike's Peak and the Royal Gorge put together."

"Could it possibly hope to be the Eighth Wonder of the World?"

"Naw, I wouldn't go that far, but I like it, so that's all that counts."

"Good." He reached in the top drawer and withdrew a small box and walked back to the bed. " 'It' would like you to stick around for the next fifty years and pay homage to it."

"Oh, Ryan." She smiled up at him as he opened the box and produced a lovely diamond set in a gold band. "When did you buy this?"

Removing it from the box, he picked up her hand and slipped it on her finger. "Promise you won't laugh?"

"Of course I won't laugh." She turned her hand to study the stone as it sparkled and twinkled in the lamplight.

"I bought it the day after I predicted we would marry on Valentine's Day," he confessed sheepishly.

She glanced at him in disbelief, then burst out laughing. "You didn't."

"You said you wouldn't laugh," he said, grumbling, "and, yes, I really did!"

"But that's preposterous. How could you have possibly known you were going to marry me? We barely knew each other."

"I knew all I had to know," he reasoned. "I've always been the type to know what I want and go after it." His eyes grew tender as he gazed down upon her. "There haven't been that many women in my life, Fritzi. And there's sure never been one even remotely close to you. When you took me home

188

New Year's Eve, as drunk as I was, I knew there was something special about you. It was then that I made up my mind you were the one, so I thought positively and went after you. In a way I guess I treasure-mapped you," he confessed. "But I didn't know about such things then."

"Oh, Ryan. How sweet." Slipping out of bed, she walked over to her purse and withdrew the large treasure-mapping book that had been so much a part of her life for the past few years. She had put it in her purse in hopes of finding a moment just like this one to give it to him.

"Chest man, definitely," Ryan announced as his eyes followed her movements with more than a passing interest.

She laughed and winked at him sexily. "I suspected that all along. Here." She handed him the book and smiled.

"What's this?"

"My treasure-mapping book. I don't need it anymore."

"Don't need it?" He could hardly believe his ears.

"No, I've decided that even though I'll always have my goals, my real treasure lies with you."

Accepting the gift, he looked at it for a moment, overwhelmed that she would entrust it to him. More than anyone, he knew what the book meant to her.

"I don't know what to say, Fritzi. I'd never expect you to give up any of your dreams. On the contrary, I want to be there to help you fulfill them."

"That's what I'm trying to tell you, Ryan. I want you in my life . . . forever."

"Come here." He held out his arms, and she went back into them eagerly.

"I love you, Ryan E. Majors," she confessed as he hugged her in a tight embrace. "And I'm sorry I've been such a pain."

"I promise I'll do everything within my power to earn your love," Ryan promised. They kissed again, a long, satisfying kiss to seal that vow.

"I hope Susan and Neil eventually find what we have," Ryan murmured absently as they settled back on their pillows. "It seems a little unfair that we have so much and they have so little."

"I think they will. Neil told me they had come to a new understanding with each other, and they even went apartment-hunting this week."

"Well, I guess they're trying. That's all a person can do."

"I saw the rubber bats in the trash this week. I guess they figure they won't be using them anymore. That's encouraging, don't you think?"

"They threw their bats away? Well, as a safety precaution, you'd better salvage those. We may need them later on."

She grinned and lay her head on his chest contentedly. "We won't need them. The only way we're going to need the bats is if you refuse to give my money back on my water bed. I really mean it this time, Ryan. I hate that thing. I have to help pay for a new water heater because of that bed!"

He let out a long, defeated sigh. "Okay. This time I'll take it back with no argument."

She sat up and kissed him exuberantly. "Thank you, darling! But why the sudden change of heart?"

He grinned and patted the squishy, jellylike substance they were lying on cunningly. "I just thought of a brilliant way to regain some of the money I've lost on this deal."

"Oh, good! What is it?"

He smiled with devilish satisfaction. "I'm going to run up the price on yours, then advertize a big special this week. Buy one, get one free."

TALE OF LOVE

To Emily Reichert:
for her support, guidance, and enthusiasm

Chapter One

THE SNOW WAS COMING DOWN IN heavy sheets at O'Hare International Airport. Perched in the glassed-in birdcage that was known as the tower, weary flight controllers were going into the last hour of their shift.

It had been one hell of a night.

During the past few hours the controllers had efficiently handled close to four hundred incoming and outgoing flights. Now, the controllers were enjoying a welcome lull in the frenzied air traffic. Planes were sitting at the gates, others systematically coming down on landing strips; but the rush was nothing compared to what it had been earlier.

From his vantage point high atop the airport terminal, Garth Redmond looked out on the red beacon lights moving about the runway and wished his shift were over. The cold he'd come down with two days ago was making him feel

197

headachy and irritable. He still had another hour left before he'd be free to go home, kick back, and relax.

Garth glanced at the ground-surveillance radar and suddenly sat up straighter. A quick reading on the bright display indicated that a Pan American Boeing 747, still ten miles out, was coming in faster than usual. Garth quickly flipped a switch on the panel before him. "Approach, this is Ground. Clipper 242 looks to be coming in pretty fast. Does he have a problem?"

"Ground, this is Approach. Yeah, he's picking up heavy ice. He's been cleared to approach."

Garth glanced at the airport-surface radar and frowned. If Tim Matthews, the Approach controller, had accurate information, they were in trouble. Garth's ground-surveillance screen indicated an unidentified radar target taxiing toward the approach end of the active runway.

Garth hurriedly reached for the binoculars and scanned the snow-covered taxiway. He swore under his breath as he saw the lighted section of a Global Airways DC-9 disappearing toward Runway 36 in the heavy snow.

"Global, this is Ground . . ." The sharp crackling at the other end took Garth by surprise. "Global, this is Ground. Do you read me?" The question was met with an ominous silence. Flipping a second button, Garth said curtly, "Local, we've got a problem. I've got a Global Airways DC-9 taxiing on parallel taxiway, and I'm not talking to him."

"What's he doing out there?" Jack Lindley shot back.

"That's what I'm trying to find out. Better advise the Clipper."

"Roger." The Local controller flipped a button on his panel. "Clipper 242, be advised we have a no-radio Global DC-9 taxiing southbound on Runway 36 parallel taxiway. Be prepared for a go-around."

Even while the Local controller was advising the Pan American pilot, Garth realized that the huge Boeing 747 coming in from Anchorage was on the final mile to mile-and-a-half approach. He seriously doubted he could go around.

"Local, what's the Global doing there?" the pilot of the Clipper demanded.

"That's what we're trying to find out."

Garth listened to the tense exchange as he kept a close eye on the runway visual-radar indicator. Visibility was down to two thousand, four hundred feet. For the past four and a half hours, the pilots had been relying solely on instruments.

Garth concentrated on the monitors. The nerves between his shoulder blades squeezed together painfully as he hit a button again.

"Global DC-9, this is Ground. Exit runway *immediately!* A Boeing 747 shot final!"

While the media focused on midair collisions and near misses midair, the more frequent problem that faced a flight controller was the kind of situation Garth now found himself monitoring. Wiping a shaky hand across the back of his neck, he eased forward in his chair as the tower supervisor threw down the papers he had been reading and came over to stand behind Garth's chair.

"What's going on?"

"I've got an unauthorized DC-9 taxiing into reserved runway, and I'm not talking to him."

Joel Anderson's seasoned eyes quickly sized up the developing situation. He frowned.

"The fool apparently thinks he's been cleared to taxi," Garth muttered. He tried to reach the DC-9 again. "Global DC-9, exit to taxiway *immediately!* Repeat. Exit to taxiway *immediately!*"

Joel leaned over Garth's shoulder and watched the screen as the two planes continued on their landing courses, both simultaneously approaching Runway 36.

"Tell Local to advise Clipper to go around," Joel warned as Garth automatically started pressing the necessary buttons.

"Local, this is Ground. Advise Clipper 242. Unauthorized DC-9 still on runway. Go around *immediately!* Repeat. Go around *immediately!*"

"Roger!" Local quickly activated another button. "Clipper 242, this is Local. Aircraft on runway. Go around. Repeat. Go around."

Garth could hear Local talking to the Clipper. Then he heard the pilot's grim refusal. "I'd love to oblige, Local, but this ain't no crop duster I'm flying!"

"Oh, hell!" Garth's voice echoed bleakly in the darkened room as he sagged back in his chair. The DC-9 was about to cross the path reserved for the incoming Clipper; and with radio contact to the DC-9 gone, it was out of the flight controller's hands and up to a Higher Power.

All Garth could hope for was that the timing

of the two aircraft would be split second and a collision would be avoided.

Joel hurriedly reached for the crash phone to alert the fire station and emergency crew to the pending crisis. Garth tried to raise the Global DC-9 again.

"Global, exit to taxiway immediately! Repeat. Exit to taxiway immediately!"

Eyes riveted to the screen, Garth and Joel watched in tense silence as the two blips on the radar screen rushed closer and closer together. The room had grown unnaturally quiet as the other flight controllers performed their duties in hushed tones.

"Well, start praying," Joel advised.

The wide-bodied Boeing 747 touched down on the landing strip and came streaking along the runway as the DC-9 began to ease its way across. The pilot of the DC-9 was still unaware of what was happening.

"Move, damn it!" Garth spoke tautly to the DC-9, then held his breath as the plane continued to roll laboriously across the path of the incoming 747.

"Get out of the way, buddy!" The strained voice of the Clipper pilot cracked over the wire as he, too, tried to will the DC-9 out of his pathway.

The dots closed in on each other as the Clipper roared down the landing strip at a speed of more than two hundred miles an hour. The blips came closer and closer.

Suddenly, they split apart, and the DC-9 eased

off the runway as the 747 shot by him in a screech of flying mud and snow.

Garth threw down his pencil angrily as Joel let out a loud war whoop.

"Holy shi...What was that?" the expletive slipped out as the pilot of the DC-9 finally came in over the wire. He was obviously shaken.

"Global, you're on unauthorized taxiway!" Garth snapped, then curtly explained what had just happened.

The pilot made his apologies, then requested to return to the terminal. "We've had a radio malfunction."

Garth granted the necessary clearance and abruptly severed contact with the pilot.

For a moment Garth fought to overcome an unreasonable sense of frustration. He fumbled for his handkerchief as Joel laid his hands on his shoulders and gave them a supportive squeeze. "Good work!"

Emotionally and physically drained, Garth could not will himself to respond to Joel's encouragement. He mopped the moisture from his forehead. There was no longer any doubt about it: The pressure of the job was getting to him.

True, Garth had experienced closer calls, but his heartbeat had never raced as fast as it was now.

"Another close one!" Garth's voice echoed hollowly in the dimly lit room.

Joel thought Garth sounded unusually tired and emotionally drained—not at all like the self-confident, cocksure young kid Joel had hired nine years ago. There had been a time when Garth would have brushed off this sort of incident without another thought, considering it just a part of the business. Tonight, though, was different. Garth seemed brooding, uncertain, troubled ...

Joel's eyes met Garth's sympathetically. Garth was one of the most competent young men he had ever had the pleasure of working with. He was alert, intelligent, a seasoned professional. But as his supervisor, Joel couldn't sit back and ignore the situation any longer.

All the symptoms of burnout were there. Anxiety, stress, and the pressures of the demanding position were obviously taking their toll on Garth.

Joel clapped a friendly hand on the younger man's shoulder. "Step into my office when you get a minute."

Garth's pulse jumped erratically. "Sure, Joel." His eyes remained fixed on the screen as he spoke, but he knew what was coming. Joel had noticed his odd behavior, and he wanted an explanation. But Garth didn't have one.

By the time he entered Joel Anderson's cluttered cubicle a half hour later, he'd decided that he was blowing the situation out of proportion. He was fine. Joel wasn't going to yell at him. He probably just wanted to shoot the breeze for a while.

Joel was on the phone when Garth arrived. He glanced up and motioned him to help himself to the coffee.

Garth shook his head. The last thing he needed was more caffeine in his system. He settled his large frame in the chair opposite the desk.

In a few moments Joel finished his conversation and replaced the receiver. "Sorry about the delay. Those idiots in the office drive me up a wall."

Garth smiled. "No problem."

Joel got up and walked to the hot plate. "I shouldn't drink another cup of this stuff. Wanda would have a fit if she knew how many I've had today...but what the hell." He poured the strong black coffee into his cup and added a couple of packets of sugar. "I'm going to die of something, so I figure I might as well go happy."

Garth acknowledged Joel's attempt at levity with a wan smile and waited patiently until he sat down again.

Joel was always worrying about what his wife would say about his bad habits but never enough to change them, Garth thought with halfhearted amusement. He just wished Joel would get on with whatever he had on his mind.

It seemed to Garth that Joel was doing a lot of fidgeting before he got to the point. "You're doing one hell of a job, Garth," he finally said, lighting a cigarette absentmindedly.

Garth glanced up, surprised by the unexpected praise. He was still half expecting to be chewed out for his performance during the past few weeks. Joel hadn't missed his edginess—Garth would bet on that. But compliments?

"Thanks. I appreciate it."

"But you're going on excused leave." The statement was firm and straight to the point.

Garth shook his head. "No...I can't. Not right now."

"Sure you can. You're on leave beginning tomorrow morning."

"Come on, Joel..." He was about to argue the point, when he saw the look of determination in his superior's eyes.

Garth realized he could sit there and argue all day, but in the end Joel would have the last word.

"No buts, Garth." His tone might have softened, but his resolution hadn't. "I've sat by and watched what's been going on for weeks now, and I think it's time we did something about it."

Garth didn't have the heart to disagree or to press Joel for details. They both knew Garth hadn't been himself lately. But, damn, his ego sure hated to accept the fact that he was stressed out.

"I'm sorry. I know I haven't been giving you my best lately," he admitted.

Joel leaned back in his chair and studied his coffee cup thoughtfully. "I've never felt that you didn't give me your best. You're one of the most valued men I have. I'm only trying to see that you stay that way. You're tired and stressed out. I want you to get a little R and R. Relax, have some fun. Forget about the job and its pressures."

"Are you worried because of what happened a few minutes ago?" Garth asked. "Because if you are, I can explain. I have this miserable cold—"

Joel interrupted gently. "No, this is a decision I've been avoiding for weeks."

"You think I'm no longer competent?" The mute appeal in Garth's eyes was hard for Joel to ignore.

"Of course not. I just think you need a little

rest." He could see that Garth was wrestling with his pride. "It's nothing to be ashamed of. We all have our limits. A few weeks of lying in the sun, and you'll be back complaining you've used up all your vacation time," Joel promised.

"Well, I can't say I agree, but you're the boss." Garth conceded, though he hated to.

"Then you agree to the leave?"

"I don't think it's a good time. It'll leave you in a bind," Garth reminded him. "I think if I could just get over this cold—"

"You will. A couple of weeks will work wonders for you." He leaned forward in his chair and stubbed out his cigarette. "Damn things are going to kill me," he complained under his breath. "Wanda would have a fit if she knew how many I've smoked today."

Garth stood up, openly disturbed by the unexpected turn of events. He felt resentful and deprived; yet at the same time he felt a strange sense of relief. Two weeks without coping ... without worrying ... without sitting on the edge of his chair ... Maybe that *was* all he needed.

"Well, I don't suppose it would do any good to argue with you."

"Nope. None at all. Soon as Randy gets here, consider yourself out of work for the next two weeks. Or longer, if you need it. You let me worry about your replacement. That's what I get paid for."

"Joel ... I appreciate this...." He reached over to shake his superior's hand, gratified for the other man's concern.

"Don't worry about it," Joel said absently.

"Oh, Lord, look at the time! I've got to call Wanda and tell her I'm going to be a few minutes late." He flashed Garth an apologetic grin. "The woman's terrified I've dropped dead if I don't get home by six on the dot."

Garth knew exactly where he would go to find the privacy he wanted: his grandparents' beachfront cottage in West Creek, North Carolina.

Silas and Grace Redmond would be in Florida for the winter, but Garth knew how to reach them.

It didn't matter that he wouldn't be able to lie around in the sun—in West Creek, it was, after all, the end of December. All he needed was a good book, a couple of packages of Oreo cookies, and complete solitude for the next two weeks.

Keep the sun and sand—give me the seclusion of that cozy three-room cottage, he thought as he drove home to pack a couple of bags.

The time off would enable him to get his priorities back in line and his head on straight again. The weather wouldn't be all that bad in West Creek, and at least he'd be able get away from all this miserable snow for a few days.

Garth wasted no time in securing a plane reservation, packing, and calling a taxi. He figured it would be better if he left Chicago before the storm turned into a full-scale blizzard. Because of the holiday rush, Garth considered himself extremely fortunate to get a seat on the next plane. Fortunately, he had connections with a cute blonde at the ticket counter.

The nine-thirty flight would take him to Raleigh,

where he'd have a brief layover before he could get a commuter hop to West Creek.

He decided to wait to call his grandmother from the terminal to ask her permission to use the cottage. If he called at the last minute, Garth knew she wouldn't have time to make half a dozen entertainment plans on his behalf.

Grace and Silas were well-meaning, but they always felt that Garth had to be entertained. Just because they were vacationing in Florida didn't mean Grace would be deterred from getting on the phone and lining up some of their friends to entertain her grandson in their absence.

At the last minute Garth made a hurried call to Lisa Matthews, the woman he'd been dating for the past few months. Lisa was another pressure that had been nagging at him lately. She wanted to get serious; Garth, on the other hand, was perfectly content to let the relationship drift along, with no strings attached. The unexpected change in plans would give him some desperately needed breathing space.

Garth hurriedly made the call, explaining to Lisa that he was going away for a few days.

She was upset but made Garth promise to call her the minute he arrived at his grandparents' cottage.

"Why don't I fly down for the weekend?" she suggested.

"No, I think I need the time alone, Lisa." They'd been spending so much of their time arguing lately that Garth felt he needed a reprieve.

"Well...if that's how you feel." Garth could

hear the petulance creeping into Lisa's voice, but he chose to ignore it.

"I'll call you later in the week." It was Garth's one concession.

"Make sure that you do."

Fierce winds blowing off icy Lake Michigan raced a bone-rattling chill down Garth's slightly feverish body as he left his apartment thirty minutes later, lugging the suitcases. He paused, sneezed, then blew his nose before going on.

A heavy blanket of snow made a dull, crunching noise beneath his boots as he trudged through the white powder to the waiting taxi. With six inches already on the frozen ground, the National Weather Service wasn't calling for an end to the storm until late tomorrow night.

Garth cautiously shuffled along what he assumed was the unshoveled sidewalk. Getting through the wet snow proved to be no easy task— but, then, nothing had been easy lately.

The sound of the cabbie impatiently leaning on the horn made Garth quicken his steps. Struggling to retain his balance as well as the luggage, he felt his temper flare when he thought of how he had waited for that cab driver for more than an hour, and now the man had the audacity to honk for *him* to hurry!

Garth reached the cab and tried to jiggle open the door, which had frozen shut fifteen minutes earlier. Hoping to free a hand and pry the stubborn latch loose, he set one suitcase down beside him, where it promptly sank out of sight in a growing snowdrift.

Expecting the door to require a hefty-sized tug, Garth obliged with a hearty jerk that sent the door flying open. He suddenly found himself lying flat on his back.

"Oh, Lord, give me a break!" Garth pleaded as he lay staring up at the cab's muddy underside. Glancing around to see if anyone other than the cabbie had seen the humiliating incident, he slowly rolled back onto his feet.

Convinced that the driver wasn't overly interested in his welfare, Garth grabbed the suitcases and pitched them into the backseat. He had to slam the door twice before it finally latched.

The plump cabbie wrestled a nasty stub of cigar butt between his lips and asked with a distinct Jersey accent, "What's ya pleasure, Mac?"

"O'Hare," Garth requested curtly. *And, believe me, nothing's my pleasure at the moment!* he thought irritably.

The cabbie shot a sympathetic glance in the rearview mirror. "Rough day, huh?" He rolled down the window and reached out to wipe the thick frost from the windshield with a large rag.

Garth viewed the action with growing dismay. No defrosters in this kind of weather? "You can see where you're going, can't you?"

"Huh? Oh, sure. The darn defroster went on the fritz about an hour ago. No sweat, though. I can get ya to O'Hare with my eyes closed." He gunned the engine, and the cab fishtailed onto the busy street.

The transmission sputtered as the driver raked through the gears. Every time the gears caught, the back of the taxi spun out, forcing Garth to grab the back of the seat for support.

"Hold on! This baby runs like a dream once you get her hummin', " the cabby called back between speed shifts.

Garth rested his head wearily against the seat and shot another squirt of decongestant up to his clogged sinuses.

As the cab neared the airport the traffic became congested and slowed to a snail's pace. Garth was sneezing with appalling regularity now.

"Sounds like you got a lulu of a cold there."

"Yeah, I think it's getting worse." Garth blew his nose, then glanced at his watch. He was going to be cutting it close. He was tempted to tell the driver to step on it, but he wasn't suicidal yet.

A good mile and a half from O'Hare the traffic came to a complete halt. Garth kept glancing uneasily at his watch. Twenty minutes later not a single car had budged.

"Hey, listen! I have an eight-o'clock plane to catch," he reminded the driver.

"Just keep your shirt on! I'll get you there, bub."

Another ten minutes passed, and Garth realized that time was running out. The plane would leave in twenty minutes, and he was still a half-mile from the airport.

Heaving a resigned sigh, Garth reached into his pocket, withdrew a wad of bills, and hurriedly paid the driver.

"Hey! Where you goin'?"

"I'll have to make a run for it." Garth sneezed again and grabbed the two pieces of luggage.

The long, cold run to the airport was a nightmare. The drifts were piling up, and the temperature was in the low teens. The tip of Garth's nose was beet-red, and his cheeks looked like two blazing cherries by the time he reached the terminal. He ran inside, wheezing like an overworked locomotive.

It was still a long sprint to his boarding gate. Garth was convinced that it was only through an act of divine intervention that the jetway was still attached to the plane when he arrived.

Stepping inside the plane, Garth was greeted by a friendly flight attendant. "Good evening. Welcome aboard American Airlines."

Garth fumbled in his pocket for his soggy handkerchief and tried to return her smile without his frozen face cracking into a million pieces. "Good evening ... Terrible weather ..." he returned lamely.

"I hope you enjoy your flight, sir."

I hope so too, Garth thought grimly as he dragged his baggage down the aisle—there had been no time to check it. He wedged the suitcases tightly into the crowded compartment at the rear of the plane.

Moments later, he sank wearily into his assigned seat. The two-year-old sitting next to him promptly started screaming as his mother tried to fasten him into a seat belt.

Short of a plane crash, Garth knew the flight had to be more enjoyable than the past four hours had been.

Chapter Two

HILARY BROOKFIELD WIPED HER teary eyes and tossed another soaked tissue into her purse. It joined nine crumpled others.

She hated herself for being so weak—so out of control—so asinine! She wiped angrily at the icy particles forming on the window and stared out of the cab into the blinding snow. Hilary had always considered herself an "in-charge person," but today's events had proved her to be anything *but* in control.

The yellow cab slowly inched its way through the snow-covered streets of Denver. The worsening weather had rendered the rush-hour traffic more snarled and congested than usual.

"How much longer before we get to the air ... airport?" she asked, trying to subdue her sobs. Her warm breath turned frosty in the arctic air.

"I'll have you there in another twenty minutes. Sorry about the heater. It was working fine an

213

hour ago. Can't imagine what could've happened to it," the driver apologized.

Hilary sighed. She could explain the malfunction—she'd been in the backseat for the last forty-five minutes of that hour. Why *shouldn't* the heater fall apart? Everything else in her life had, she thought, succumbing to another onslaught of self-pity. She bawled into her wadded tissue for a few minutes, then blew her nose again.

The taxi driver peered expectantly into the rearview mirror. If there was one thing that made Max Stinson nervous, it was a squalling female. Not that Max was hard-hearted. He was considered a real softie, but the poor soul in the backseat hadn't turned off the tap since he'd picked her up.

"Um . . . miss? Are you all right back th—"
KAABOOMMM!
Hilary squealed, then ducked at the sound of the sudden explosion.

"Oh, boy! I think we've got ourselves a flat tire, miss." The driver fought the steering wheel and finally managed to ease the cab over to the side of the road.

After bringing the crippled taxi to a halt, the man turned to reassure his passenger. "Now, don't you worry. I'll get you to Stapleton on time."

Hilary sat up and blew into her tissue again, skeptical of his optimism. Why should she hope she'd make her plane on time? Nothing else had gone right today.

She'd lost a button off her new coat and the stud to her gold earring; there had been a fifteen-hundred-dollar discrepancy in the books at work; and she'd been dumped.

A mere flat tire shouldn't upset her. Hilary leaned over and bawled harder into the tear-sodden tissue.

Every snowplow in Denver had been working nonstop for the past twenty-four hours. Six-feet-high drifts made curbside parking impossible, but the cab driver had managed to pull as far off the road as possible. There was an endless string of irritated motorists inching past the disabled vehicle. They leaned on their horns as if that would somehow even the score for their frayed tempers.

"I'll have the tire changed in a jiffy," the driver promised as he got out and slammed the door behind him.

Hilary worked to stem the flow of her streaming eyes. With yet another Kleenex having bitten the dust, she dumped it into her coat pocket and fished out a clean one.

While the driver changed the tire, she sat in the frosty silence of the cab, watching the snow drift past the car window. The hypnotic effect of the swirling flakes dredged up thoughts of the unpleasant emotional scene she'd experienced only a few hours earlier.

Lenny Ricetrum. Lenny Ricetrum the Rat, she corrected herself. The big dirty rat, she corrected herself again, as if calling Lenny names would help.

Hilary had dated Lenny steadily for the past few months. And she had grown to care very deeply for him—or at least she thought she had until this morning.

Wasn't that just like love? Hilary agonized against the cold pane of the window, indulging in her own private pity party. You think everything is wonderful, and the next thing you know ...it all blows up in your face!

Oh, she'd seen it coming, though she hadn't wanted to believe it. Lenny had always had a roving eye. Maybe that's why she'd found him so attractive, so exciting, so much fun to be with, despite his being brash and rough around the edges.

Hilary readily admitted that Lenny was a novelty. She'd never dated anyone like him, and she'd found the experience exhilarating.

But Meredith Lowry had apparently found him equally attractive.

Meredith was always hanging around the construction site where Hilary and Lenny worked. Ralph, an electrician at O'Connor's, had noticed that the bold redhead was making an obvious play for Lenny's attention. He had called it to Hilary's attention once or twice.

"Hey, Hilary! Ya better keep an eye on that little redhead. Looks like she's mapping out your man!" Ralph had tried to sound as though he were teasing, but even then Hilary had detected the underlying tone of seriousness in his words.

Hilary had kept telling herself that Lenny's case of roaming eyes was just a passing thing. Nothing to get herself in an uproar over. Besides, she'd always prided herself on not being a jealous or possessive person.

But deep down, Hilary knew the reason she hadn't confronted Lenny and demanded he put a stop to his womanizing; she thought she loved him. Consequently, the problem hadn't gone away.

This morning she'd barely seated herself at her desk when Lenny had come into her office and dropped the bombshell.

He hadn't minced words or tried to lighten the impact of his cruel announcement. Without batting an eye, he'd announced that their relationship was over. He'd left a stunned Hilary slumped over her IBM, wondering what had gone wrong.

"Hilary...I'm sorry." Michael O'Connor, the owner of the construction company, had tried to comfort her. "I was afraid this would happen."

Hilary cried on his broad shoulder, praying he wouldn't say "I told you so."

"Mr. O'Connor, Lenny didn't even say why..." Hilary dissolved into tears as Michael put a strong arm around her shoulders.

"Sh, sh, little girl." Michael gently tried to soothe her tattered pride. "Men like Lenny don't usually explain anything they do. I say good riddance to bad rubbish, as far as that bum is concerned."

Hilary tried to still her sobbing. She was a grown woman acting like a child. But at that moment, she'd felt like a street urchin. One who had just been stepped on.

At Mr. O'Connor's suggestion, Hilary had taken the rest of the day off. Sitting alone in her apartment she had knocked a big dent in her supply of tissues. She spent two hours crying, pacing the floor, crying, drinking coffee, and crying.

Realizing the situation wasn't improving, Hilary decided that what she needed was time away from the whole ugly situation. If she went back to the office, she would be forced to see Lenny at least a couple of times a day. She just didn't feel up to that right now.

With grim determination, she phoned Michael O'Connor and asked for a week's vacation to try and collect her thoughts.

"You go right ahead. A little time away is just what you need to put this thing in perspective," Michael agreed. "And don't feel guilty. Construction work is never booming this time of year. Enjoy your week."

Hilary decided she shouldn't waste precious time trying to decide where to spend her unscheduled vacation.

A good friend, Marsha Terrill, had moved to West Creek, North Carolina, a year ago. Hilary and Marsha hadn't been able to visit each other since Marsha's move, although they'd kept in close touch. Hilary decided that now would be the perfect time to visit Marsha.

The airline booked her on a nine-thirty flight. Hilary spent the next thirty minutes trying to reach Marsha. Each time she'd gotten a busy signal.

Hilary tried again before she left for the airport, but the line was still busy. Assuring herself that the layover in Raleigh would give her a chance to phone Marsha from the terminal, Hilary wasn't concerned. Marsha loved surprises, and besides, Hilary wasn't sure if she could control her emotions long enough to explain the unexpected visit.

Hilary's thoughts were interrupted as the cab driver got back into the cab. His clothing was covered with a thick dusting of snow.

"All fixed," he announced.

"Do you think we can still make it to the airport on time?"

"You bet! Even if I have to make this taxi sprout wings to get you there. I've never caused any passenger to miss a flight yet."

Yes, but you've never had me in your cab before, Hilary thought fatalistically.

Max was true to his word. He delivered Hilary to the airport ten minutes before her plane departed. What he neglected to mention was that *she'd* have to sprout wings to make it through the gates in time to catch her flight.

She raced feverishly through the crowded terminal, dodging through the throng of holiday travelers. As she breathlessly neared the boarding gate, a slow-moving elderly gentleman ahead of her dropped his boarding pass. He came to an abrupt halt.

Hilary had no choice but to do the same. She drew in her breath painfully as she felt her right ankle twist as she struggled to regain her balance. The ankle had been broken in a skiing accident three years earlier, and the renewed pain was breathtaking. Fighting the hot sting of the wrenched muscles, Hilary started trying to pick up the luggage she had dropped.

"You okay, little lady?" The elderly man

turned around, unaware that he had been the cause of her newest crisis.

"Yes...thanks...I'll be fine." Hilary gritted her teeth in agony.

"Shouldn't be in such a big hurry. That's what's wrong with the world today. Everyone's in such an all-fired hurry," the man complained as he proceeded down the corridor.

"And happy holidays to you too," Hilary muttered.

She carefully tested part of her weight on the injured ankle. The searing throb was horrible. She realized that the only way she could make the flight was to swallow her misery and hobble on.

By grace alone, Hilary managed to make it to the jetway seconds before it was detached from the plane.

Sinking gratefully into her assigned seat, Hilary buckled her belt to prepare for takeoff. She fought back the hot swell of tears that threatened to overcome her again.

Hilary, you have to stop this, she warned herself. Other women had been dumped and had lived through it. She would too.

Hilary gently rubbed her swollen ankle and wondered if she would be able to get her shoe back on if she slipped it off during the flight. Deciding to take the chance, she kicked off the two-inch black heel and wearily leaned her head back on the headrest.

If she'd had even the slightest inkling of how this day was going to turn out, she would never have gotten out of bed that morning.

Chapter Three

AT PRECISELY TEN THIRTY-SEVEN, the Boeing 727 carrying Hilary Brookfield landed in Raleigh, North Carolina.

A light snow was falling, and because it was beginning to cover the ground, Hilary couldn't help but wonder if the two-hour scheduled layover would drag out endlessly. She quickly dismissed the disturbing thought. Surely fate had been cruel enough to her today, she reasoned.

By now her ankle had swollen to nearly twice its normal size. She sighed as she thought about how she'd detained the man sitting beside her while she'd had to slowly force her shoe back on, groaning in agony.

Her ankle hung over the shoe like sagging elephant hide. If she'd thought the pain was bad before—well, it was worse now. Recalling the catastrophic course her life had recently taken, Hilary tried to summon up a hint of optimism as she hobbled painfully down the jetway.

At least I can still hobble, she told herself. *And I can still see where I'm going*, she added encouragingly. As a rule, her contacts would be bothering her by now, but they felt pretty good. Hilary limped on with grim determination.

Her improved spirits lasted until she entered the terminal. Her eyes widened when she saw the energetic preschooler who was throwing a temper tantrum. He bolted rebelliously from his mother and dashed headlong in her direction. Trying to sidestep the oncoming human missile, Hilary felt a body hurl against her. The sudden impact knocked her breathless for a moment.

Purse and makeup kit went flying at the same time that Hilary's right eye went blurry. Her hand flew up to try and catch the contact that had been dislodged, but the automatic reflex came too late.

"Frederick Lee! You stop that this moment!" The child's mother marched over to take the little boy by the scruff of the neck. "Just you wait until your father hears about this! Say you're sorry to this nice lady for bumping into her!" The woman turned apologetically to Hilary, who by now had dropped frantically down on her knees and was crawling around the floor of the terminal, searching for the missing contact.

"It's all right...I'm sure Frederick didn't mean any harm..." Hilary was as blind as a bat without her contacts. She welcomed the assistance of several thoughtful travelers who offered to help with the search. In the end, however, the contact was lost forever.

"I'm really sorry about your contact," the harried mother assured Hilary again. She had a firm clasp on the child now. Fascinated, little Frederick was watching Hilary crawl around on the floor.

"Don't worry," Hilary assured the young mother. "I have an extra pair at home." The misfortune meant that she would be half-blind during her stay with Marsha. But only *half*, she consoled herself, still fighting to hold on to her earlier spurt of optimism.

"I saweee wadeee." Frederick had turned sullen in the face of adversity.

"It's quite all right." Hilary's smile was tolerant as one of the gentlemen helping to search for the missing contact took her arm and assisted her to her feet. A renewed surge of pain shot through her ankle, and she bit her lower lip to keep from moaning. Smiling, she thanked the gentleman.

The lady and child merged into the crowd as Hilary gathered her belongings and limped steadfastly toward Gate 78.

As Garth stepped off the plane, he noticed that the runway was crowded with emergency vehicles and personnel. There were two ambulances, two fire trucks, and various pieces of emergency equipment poised on the landing strip Garth's plane had just come in on.

Garth frowned as he noticed Hank Resin coming down the jetway with a hurried stride. Hank had been employed at O'Hare years ago. He'd since married and moved to Raleigh. Garth recalled that Hank had been one of O'Hare's top mechanics.

"Hey, Garth, ol' man! Were *you* on this plane?" Hank's friendly grin was spread all over his face as he reached out to clasp Garth's hand.

"Yes. How are you, Hank?" Garth's frown deepened. "What's going on?"

"Are you serious? You don't know?"

"Know what?"

"There was a little mechanical trouble with the landing gears. The pilot managed to get them working in time...but only seconds before he had to touch down. The ol' wheels popped out of the belly like a roasted turkey!"

Garth grinned lamely, but Hank noticed that his face had turned two shades paler. "No kidding? We were coming in under emergency conditions?"

"Yeah. Flying's a real hair-raiser sometimes, ain't it?"

Garth felt his stomach grow queasy. He'd noticed that the pilot had circled the airport several times, but the idea that the plane was in trouble had never entered his mind. He felt himself go weak with relief at the close call. With his nerves already ragged, he'd have been peeling the paint from the plane's interior had he suspected he was in the middle of a "hair-raiser."

It didn't matter that it was snowing again. All that mattered was that his feet were back on solid ground. At least for now, Garth thought. In another couple of hours he would be airborne again. The flight to West Creek would surely be without incident, he hoped fervently.

As he emerged into the brightly lit terminal, Garth was mumbling under his breath a reassuring litany of statistics proving that the skies were safer now than ever before.

He had to deftly sidestep a woman who was down on her hands and knees in the middle of the floor. Garth swore under his breath and wondered where some of the weirdos he saw in airline terminals ever got the money for a plane ticket.

A few steps later he felt his shoe crunch down on what felt like a piece of glass. He paused momentarily and lifted the sole of his shoe up for inspection. He frowned as he discovered the remnants of a piece of hard candy. On closer inspection, he decided it was a contact lens.

Flicking the lens off his sole, he hurried in the direction of Gate 78.

Hilary stopped at the first pay phone she found. She rummaged in her purse for change to make the call to Marsha. All she could come up with was six pennies, a nasty-looking nickel that had part of a breath mint stuck on it, and a Canadian coin she had picked up somewhere.

By the time she had limped to the nearest coffee shop for change, and limped back, all the phones were in use again. Hilary waited patiently while a frazzled housewife gave final instructions to her husband and children. Hilary was sure the woman's family must have been as happy to have seen her leave as Hilary herself was when the lady finally ran out of time and had to dash to catch her plane.

Hilary dropped the newly acquired coins in the

slot and tapped the numbers. She breathed a sigh of relief when she heard the phone begin to ring.

"Hello! This is Marsha!" Marsha's familiar voice came over the line on the second ring.

"Hi, Marsh! This is—"

Marsha's voice continued. "I'm sorry I can't come to the phone right now. Get this—I'm lying on the warm beaches of sunny Jamaica! At the sound of the tone, please leave your name and number, and I'll return your call when I get home in two glorious weeks!" Following the recorded message, there was a beep.

Hilary clamped her eyes shut in disgust and clenched the receiver tightly in her hands. Jamaica! How could Marsha do this to her!

Hilary hooked the receiver back in place and broke out into a new round of desperate sobs. With her right hand she fumbled blindly through the muddle of wadded tissues overflowing her purse. A clean one was not to be found.

Garth was just about to call his grandparents' number, when he heard the young woman using the phone beside him suddenly burst into tears. He eyed Hilary apprehensively and continued punching out the numbers.

Hilary laid her head on her coat sleeve and cried harder, oblivious to the crowd she was drawing.

Garth watched her from the corner of his eye, noting her unproductive search for a tissue. He reached for his handkerchief and offered it to her.

"Thank you," Hilary accepted the handkerchief gratefully. She promptly wiped her eyes, and Garth resigned himself to the fact that the white linen would be soiled with black mascara. Then he turned his attention away as he heard his grandmother's voice come over the wire.

"Gram? Hi, it's Garth."

"Garthy! How nice to hear from you!" Grace Redmond's matronly voice drifted reassuringly over the wire.

"It's good to hear your voice too, Gram. Listen, I've got some time off and I was wondering if you'd care if I used the beach house."

Garth came right to the point, certain that his grandparents wouldn't object to the loan of the cottage.

"Well, of course you may use the cottage, dear. This is just wonderful! Your cousins are down there right now. If you can get there in the next couple of days, it'll give you a chance to visit with Dorothy, Frank, and the children."

Garth felt the tiny hairs on his neck bristle. Lord! Talk about topping off a rotten day. *Not Dorothy and Frank!* he pleaded silently. "They're using the cottage?" he asked.

"Yes, dear. Isn't it marvelous? They'll be there until . . . oh, dear, let me see . . . I believe until the day after tomorrow. When did you say your vacation started?"

Garth knew he couldn't tolerate two days locked inside a three-room cabin with his cousin Dorothy, her boastful husband Frank, and five of the rowdiest kids God had ever put on earth. He wasn't about to hurt Gram's feelings, but there was no way he was going anywhere near that cottage until Frank and Dorothy were gone.

"Gee, Gram, that sounds nice, but I'm afraid

I can't make it before Sunday night. I guess by then Dorothy and the family will already have left."

Garth hated to lie, but he would if he had to.

"Oh, dear, I'm afraid they will have. Frank has to be at work on Monday. What a shame! Well, maybe you can visit with them next time," Grace said soothingly.

"Oh, sure thing. Tell them I'm sorry I'll miss them."

"Well, the key's under the mat, Garthy. Now, listen, you will come and see your grandma and grandpa before the winter's over, won't you? We'll be glad to send you a plane ticket."

Garth assured his grandmother that he'd try to make the visit. He thanked her for the use of the cottage and hung up wondering what he would do for the next two days.

The thought of having to spend time in a hotel room wasn't pleasant, but it was his only choice. It beat having to tolerate good ol' hot-winded Frank and his five curtain climbers.

Hilary made a final swipe at her teary eyes as Garth finished his phone conversation. She promptly offered the return of his soiled handkerchief.

"Thanks . . . but just keep it." Garth told her.

"I'm sorry about the mascara. I think it'll come out in cold water," Hilary said, realizing why he was reluctant to accept it back.

"No, really, I don't need it," Garth replied. "Are you all right?"

"I'm fine, thank you."

Garth thought the woman looked as if someone

had just shot her dog. Glancing around for the nearest lounge to wait out the layover, he eventually melted into the crowd as Hilary hobbled over to the waiting area and sat down.

Withdrawing a magazine from her purse, she began to read to pass the time until her plane left for West Creek. She had no idea what she would do when she got there, but she supposed she'd rent a cheap hotel room and try to rest a few days while she gathered her thoughts. Then she'd be forced to make the return trip home.

What was supposed to be a two-hour layover gradually dragged into eight. The lengthy delay didn't surprise her. In view of the past few hours, nothing surprised her.

Having purchased a fresh supply of Kleenex and a cup of hot chocolate around two o'clock, Hilary went back to her seat in the boarding area. By now, she was numb with fatigue, but her ankle didn't throb as much.

Garth spent the time in the lounge, eating bag after bag of corn chips. He had no idea why he was eating them. With his cold, he couldn't taste a thing. He supposed he was bored. The chaotic turn of events he'd encountered the last few hours had numbed him. He sneezed and reached into his pocket for another couple of antihistamines.

Around seven P.M., Flight 263 to West Creek was asked to begin boarding.

Garth boarded the plane last. He walked down the aisle, pausing before seat 3a in the nonsmoking section. He glanced down, and his heart sank. He saw the woman who'd been crying at the pay phone. She was sitting in the seat next to him.

"Hello again." Garth joined her and fastened the belt tightly around his waist. Damn! He hoped she wasn't going to bawl all the way to West Creek. He'd like to catch a few winks of sleep during the short flight.

"Oh...hello." Hilary sniffed and sat up straighter, wiping at her crimson-colored nose. She fought to stem the flow of tears.

Though the endless waterworks were beginning to wear on Garth's nerves, he was determined to be nice.

She was winsomely attractive—even if her eyes did look like two burnt holes in a blanket from all that crying. Shoulder-length dark brown hair framed her face in a soft cloud. Her eyes were a large watery blue, lined with spiky black lashes. She looked like a little pup that had just been kicked.

Under different circumstances Garth would have asked her name, but right now he was bone-weary. Socializing was the last thing on his mind.

"Are you all right?" He finally grumbled under his breath as he reached for the pamphlet the stewardess was holding up.

"Oh, yes. I'm...fine, thank you."

If this was fine, I'd hate to see her when something's really bothering her, Garth thought fleetingly.

Hilary realized she was making him nervous. He was just too polite to say anything. The poor man had been subjected to her blubbering long enough. He had to be getting a little tired of it.

And he had been so nice, lending her his handkerchief and all. Hilary shut her eyes and drew a deep breath. She promised herself she would not think of Lenny Ricetrum. She would allow herself only pleasant thoughts.

"Magazine?" Garth offered, trying to take her mind off her troubles.

"No, thank you. I lost one of my contacts at the airport, and I can't see very well."

"Oh." Garth went back to riffling through the pages of the pamphlet. Hilary noticed that he suddenly paused and stared off into space. He glanced back at her, then quickly back down at the pamphlet.

"Did you lose your contact at this airport?" Garth asked in what he hoped sounded like a casual voice.

"Yes. Why?"

Garth grinned lamely. "Oh, no reason."

Settling back comfortably in her seat, Hilary tried to concentrate on something pleasant.

Moments later she found herself focusing on the man sitting next to her. He was good-looking. Crisp, clean-cut—even though he could stand a shave. His hair was a pretty chestnut color, with red highlights, and his eyes were a nice doe-brown. The build beneath the leather jacket he was wearing was impressive.

He works out, Hilary decided. She turned her gaze back to the window as she caught him looking at her over the top of his magazine.

He wouldn't dump a girl without an explanation the way Lenny had, Hilary thought intuitively. Tears began rolling out of the corners of her eyes.

231

She fumbled in her purse for a clean tissue but discovered that, as usual, she didn't have one. A few minutes later Hilary heard a resigned sigh, and another snowy-white handkerchief magically appeared in her hand. *No*, she thought as she blew her nose for the hundredth time, *he wouldn't treat a girl that way*.

When the plane touched down in West Creek, Hilary took her makeup kit straight to the ladies' room, where she applied fresh makeup and combed her hair. She was doing better. She hadn't shed a tear for almost thirty minutes, and she was optimistic that the crisis had finally passed.

Nearing the baggage pickup, Hilary witnessed a tender good-bye kiss shared by a young couple who were obviously in love. Her newly acquired "chin-up" attitude wavered, but she quickly diverted her attention and began looking for her luggage.

The revolving rack carouseled one fuzzy-looking suitcase after another past her blurred vision. Finally, Hilary thought she caught sight of two familiar pieces of Samsonite. She reached for the bags and was stunned when a large male hand hastily snaked in from behind her.

"Excuse me, but I believe this is my luggage," Garth apologized.

He groaned when he recognized her again.

Hilary turned to correct the mistaken intruder coolly. "I'm sorry, but I think you must be mistak—Oh, hello! It's you again!" Her face broke into a pleasant smile. "As I was saying, I think you must be mistaken. This is my luggage."

Garth returned her smile tolerantly. "No, I think you're mistaken. This is my luggage."

"Wait just a minute!" Suddenly Hilary had had it with being pushed around. She wasn't about to let this stranger take advantage of her, no matter how nice he'd been earlier. "This is my luggage, and I want you to let go of it!" she demanded.

"This can be settled easily enough." Garth stood his ground. "All we have to do is read the nametags. I'm sure you'll see you're mistaken. It's my luggage."

Hilary glanced around uneasily. The dispute was being closely watched by several other weary travelers eager to retrieve their own baggage. "Oh . . . yes, of course. That's the sensible thing to do."

Garth lifted the bags off the rack and carried them to the doorway. "Let's see what we have here." He silently read the first tag, and though he was disappointed to find it wasn't his, he found himself grinning devilishly. Glancing up at Hilary, he said solemnly, "I guess I was wrong. The bag isn't mine."

"I know." Hilary forced the smugness out of her voice. "That's what I've been trying to tell you."

Garth picked up the piece of luggage and extended it to her courteously. "Here you go, Harry."

Hilary accepted the bag graciously, then frowned. "Harry?"

Garth lifted one brow questioningly. "You *are* Harry Hasseltine?"

"I certainly am not."

Garth grinned, displaying two of the most delightful dimples Hilary had ever seen. "You're not. That's too bad," he said dryly, "because this bag belongs to Harry Hasseltine."

"What? Let me see that!" Hilary felt her cheeks flush beet-red. On closer examination, Hilary discovered Garth was correct. The bags belonged to Harry Hasseltine. "What about the other one?" she challenged. Hilary thought she should know her own luggage.

Garth read the other tag. This time he was less pleased with the information it provided.

"Well?"

"Yours," he conceded humbly.

"I knew it!"

"Don't gloat."

Hilary forced herself not to. "Well, I suppose my other bag is still on the rack somewhere," she conceded.

They went back to the revolving rack and waited until every single piece of luggage had been claimed. Their three bags failed to appear.

"Damn. There must have been a mix-up somewhere," Garth complained as he picked up her bag and they made their way to the baggage-claims department.

Garth noticed that Hilary was limping as they walked. "What's the matter with your foot?"

Color flooded Hilary's cheeks again. She'd hoped he wouldn't notice her swollen ankle. It strongly resembled an oversized softball now.

"I twisted my ankle earlier," she explained.

"That's too bad."

It took half an hour to inch their way to the claims window. They filled out the proper forms concerning lost luggage. Garth finished first and left a few minutes ahead of her. Hilary experienced a pang of disappointment as she watched him walk away. He'd been nice enough to ask if she needed help getting a cab. She'd gracefully declined his offer, and he'd left her leaning on the counter. He'd smiled at her and said, "Take it easy, Harry!"

When Hilary had completed her form she hobbled outside to summon a taxi. West Creek's weather was considerably better than Raleigh's. The skies were overcast, but there was no sign of snow.

"Hi, again." Hilary set her bag down on the curb. She smiled at Garth, who was still trying to hail a cab.

"Hi. Get the forms filled out?"

"Yes. I hope it doesn't take long to locate the missing luggage."

"Me too. They have practically everything I own," Garth admitted.

Several cabs whizzed by before either Garth or Hilary could bring one to a halt. Garth finally made the first catch.

He opened the door and started to hop in, when he caught sight of Hilary standing on the curb, trying to balance on one leg. With a resigned grin, Garth slid back out of the cab and held the door open for her. "You take this one," he offered. He felt he owed her that much.

"Oh, no...please, I couldn't. You take it. I'll be fine."

"I insist."

"No, *I* insist."

Realizing they'd gone this route before with neither giving an inch, Garth gave in first to save time. "Look, if we don't decide soon, the cab will leave without either one of us."

"I suppose we could share the ride," Hilary conceded. She could feel the exhaustion of the past few hours creeping up on her.

"Fine," Garth agreed. "I'll get your bags for you."

"Thanks." Hilary gratefully handed him her suitcase and makeup kit and limped over to the curb.

As the cab pulled away, Garth instructed the driver to take him to the West Creek Sheraton.

Hilary was grateful the driver assumed they both had the same destination. The hotel sounded terribly expensive to Hilary, who was quietly reassessing her limited funds, but perhaps if she were frugal, she could manage for a few days.

When the driver brought the taxi to a halt outside the Sheraton's elaborate front doors, Hilary knew she wasn't going to be able to afford the hotel.

Garth paid his fare and ducked out the door with a quick "Nice meeting you." The puzzled driver shot Hilary a questioning glance in the rearview mirror.

Hilary grinned back lamely. "Can you recommend a modestly priced hotel? One that's clean," she added quickly.

"Well, let's see...The Merrymont isn't bad.

It's a nice family-type place about a mile on down the road."

"Thanks. The Merrymont will do nicely."

About the time Hilary's taxi had pulled up in front of the Merrymont, the management at the Sheraton was informing Garth that they had no available rooms. Had he booked even a day earlier, they could have accommodated him, they said with regret. But no rooms were vacant for tonight.

The manager offered to inquire about vacancies at other establishments, and Garth wearily thanked him. All he cared about was a bed that, hopefully, the roaches wouldn't carry off during the night.

After making several calls, the manager cheerfully informed Garth that he'd secured a room for him at the Merrymont.

"That's fine. How far is it?"

"Just down the road, sir. I'll get you a taxi."

When Hilary entered the Merrymont there were plenty of rooms. There was only one minor problem: The employees of the hotel had gone out on strike two hours earlier. The management assured her that, despite the inconvenience, they would extend every effort to make her stay as comfortable as possible.

"Would you phone the airport for me?" Hilary asked a clerk as she signed the register. "The airline has misplaced one of my bags. As soon as they're able to locate it, I'd like to have it sent directly to my room."

"Yes, ma'am. Your room is 402, and we hope you enjoy your stay." The inexperienced young desk clerk made a wholehearted attempt at professionalism as he handed her the key.

At this point, Hilary didn't care if they put her on the sofa in the lobby. She had to rest her ankle.

"Where are the elevators, please?"

"Oh . . . uh . . . sorry, ma'am. That's another little difficulty we're experiencing. The elevators are out of order right now, but we've called a repairman. He's due anytime. I'm sure he'll have them running in a jiffy. If you'd like to wait in the lobby, you're certainly welcome to do so."

Hilary looked at him in disbelief. "No, thanks. I'll take the stairs."

She silently thanked the airlines for losing her other bag as she limped up four flights of stairs, lugging the makeup kit and dragging the heavy suitcase along behind her.

When she reached the fourth floor she sagged against the wall, gasping for breath. Her heartbeat had to be at least two hundred and sixty-five. She never realized how miserably out of shape she was.

Working her way down the dimly lit hallway, she found her room—the one farthest from the stairway. Hilary unlocked the door, flicked on the lamp, and fell across the bed in exhaustion. It was several moments before she could will herself to get up off the bed and close the door.

Sinking back on the bed, she surveyed the room and found it to be clean and adequately furnished.

A half hour later Hilary finally rolled off the

side of the bed and went in search of the bathroom. The thought of soaking her ankle in a nice hot tub had become her newest priority.

With the tub brimming, its tantalizing warmth inviting, Hilary was mere inches away from submerging her throbbing ankle in the healing waters when a sharp rap at the door sounded.

She groaned and grabbed for the side of the tub. "Who is it?"

The rap sounded again, and she reluctantly reached for her robe. Seconds later she hobbled to the door.

"Yes?" Hilary called from behind the dead bolt.

Silence reigned supreme now.

She waited a few moments, then slid the bolt out of place and eased the door open cautiously.

Sitting before her were three pieces of blue Samsonite.

Realizing that only one could be hers, Hilary stepped into the hall to stop the bellhop. Whoever was responsible for their delivery, however, was long gone by now.

She knelt down to squint at the tags and found that one of the bags was indeed hers. The other two belonged to a Mr. Garth Redmond... whoever he might be.

Hilary sighed and began to drag the luggage into the room. She closed the door and went back in the bathroom. When she was through with her bath, she'd call the desk and inform the clerk of the error. As far as Hilary was concerned, Garth Redmond was going to be without luggage for another hour.

Chapter Four

HILARY LAY IN THE TUB AND soaked the injured ankle for more than an hour. She finally summoned enough energy to dry off and apply cream and powder. She was relieved to have her personal articles back in her possession. She decided that the bath had been just the thing to cheer her up.

Her gaze caught the two pieces of Samsonite still sitting beside the bed. Garth what's-his-name would probably appreciate having his possessions, Hilary conceded with a pang of guilt. She should have reported the mistake earlier.

The teenybopper who was manning the front desk answered her call in a California Valley-voice that Hilary found difficult to decipher.

"Yoah! What is it?" The exuberant greeting caught Hilary off guard. The teen's voice was undergoing rapid adolescent changes. Hilary

240

wasn't sure what he'd said, much less what he'd meant.

"Yes . . . this is Hilary Brookfield in Room 402. Two pieces of luggage have been delivered to my room by mistake."

"No joke?"

"Yes, no joke. Would you please send someone to get them?"

"Sure thing, lady. Do they have a name on 'em?"

"Yes. They belong to Garth Redmond."

"Redmond, Redmond . . ." The young man repeated the name. Hilary could hear him frantically rummaging through his registration forms.

"Yeah, here ya go . . . Garth Redmond. He's in Room 404. Uh, sorry 'bout the mix-up there, lady. Tell ya what I'm gonna do. Soon as I can put a fix on that bellhop guy, I'll send him up to get 'em."

Hilary thought of the hour she'd already wasted. Mr. Redmond would want to have his personal toiletries as soon as possible. Since he was next door, Hilary decided to deliver the bags herself. She'd bet dollars to doughnuts that Mr. Redmond was a kindly old gent who would deeply appreciate her act of kindness.

Besides, there was the staff strike to consider. The few employees the hotel had managed to recruit were inexperienced and, understandably, overworked. With the elevator still on the blink, the least Hilary could do was offer to help.

"If it isn't against hotel policy, I could set Mr. Redmond's luggage outside his door," she said.

241

"Lady I don't know nothin' about no hotel policy—know what I mean? But if you're sure it wouldn't be too much of a hassle, hop to it." The clerk accepted her offer eagerly.

"All right," Hilary said. "I'll take care of it immediately."

"Gee, thanks a wad, lady."

Hilary hurriedly dressed, then gathered the luggage. Gingerly placing her weight on the injured ankle, she smiled when she discovered that the pain was tolerable. Adding just a fraction more of her weight, she suddenly winced and cried out in pain. The injury was better but far from healed. Hilary didn't need to remind herself a second time to keep most of her weight off that ankle.

Talk about weight! Hilary complained to herself as she grunted and tugged the two bulging suitcases to the door. *Poor old Mr. Redmond must have packed his respirator in one of these things!*

Hilary toyed with the idea of knocking on the door of Room 404 and abandoning the baggage. That's how hers had been delivered. Then she decided against it.

If Mr. Redmond is in ill health, she told herself, *he won't be able to manage the bags by himself.* By now Hilary had convinced herself that Garth Redmond was a senior citizen. He could even be napping and not hear the knock on the door. The bags could be stolen before Mr. Redmond realized they'd even been returned. Hilary decided to knock on the door and assist with the heavy luggage. She tapped lightly, allowing ample time for the aging man to respond.

Mr. Redmond would appreciate her thought-fulness, Hilary told herself again. And it would be nice to hear a man say thank you, for a change. Her morale could use the boost. *Perhaps he's hard of hearing*, Hilary thought as she rapped a second time.

Garth rolled over on the bed and tried to clear his mind. Lack of sleep and the multitude of cold pills he'd been taking were making him so groggy he could hardly wake up. Was someone trying to beat the door down, or was he dreaming?

Annoyed and still half asleep, Garth rolled out of bed as the knock sounded again. He stumbled toward the door, grumbling under his breath about never being able to get any rest, when his big toe found the straight pin that had been care-lessly dropped on the carpeted floor by the last occupant of the room.

"Oh, damn!" Garth sucked in his breath and dropped to one knee as he tried to identify the object that had just harpooned him. A moment later he gingerly plucked the pin from his throb-bing toe. The trickle of blood that oozed from the tiny prick made him feel light-headed. Garth had never been able to stand the sight of blood—especially not his own.

A third knock on the door brought him to his feet again, and he hurried across the room.

"Okay! Okay! Don't knock the thing off its hinges!" Garth shouted irritably. He undid the lock and opened the door a fraction.

Hilary saw one blazing eye peering back at her. "Mr. Redmond? I'm sorry to bother you, but— oh, hi there!" Hilary was shocked yet delighted to see the man from the airport standing in the doorway.

Garth finally managed to focus his bleary gaze on the person standing in the doorway.

It was her again.

"My goodness, what a surprise!" Hilary exclaimed.

"Yeah...How you doing?" Garth tried to remain civil as every bone in his body cried for mercy.

"Well, how do you like that! I thought you were an old man!" she said brightly.

"A what?" Garth sagged against the doorframe, wondering where she got her energy. He knew she had been up all night crying, but she looked as fresh as a daisy. He envied her stamina.

"Are *you* Garth Redmond?"

"I was a few hours ago. I'm not too sure right now."

"Well, I'm Hilary Brookfield. I thought you were staying at the Sheraton., What happened?"

"They didn't have any vacancies." Garth yawned.

"Well, guess what?" Hilary exclaimed.

"I haven't the faintest."

"I have a surprise."

Garth caught himself swáying forward as he felt his energy draining. "You were banging on my door to tell me you have a surprise?" He couldn't believe the woman. "Couldn't it have waited until later?"

"Yes, but I thought you'd want to know right away. Of course, I didn't know *you* were Garth

Redmond, or I wouldn't have bothered you until you had rested a while ..."

Noting his cool indifference, Hilary felt her lower lip begin to quiver, a warning sign Garth had come to recognize and fear. He was acting as if she were bothering him instead of doing him a favor, Hilary thought resentfully.

The ungrateful clod! She'd only wanted to help. All she'd gotten for her efforts was a sarcastic "You were banging on my door to tell me that?" It wasn't fair.

Hilary's injured pride ballooned as she recalled every injustice fate had dealt her in the past twenty-four hours—most of which she considered undeserved.

No one appreciated her. No one. Not Lenny Ricetrum—he'd dumped her for a redhead. Not Marsha—she'd deserted her for Jamaica. A strong wave of self-pity flooded over Hilary, and lack of sleep was not adding to her usual good disposition.

Hilary told herself that she was one giant doormat for the whole world to wipe their dirty feet on. Not even Mr. O'Connor appreciated her, she concluded. If the truth were known, he'd probably agreed to the unscheduled vacation just to get her out of the office.

And now, this ... this *ingrate* didn't even appreciate the effort it took for her to deliver his missing luggage—in person. What did he care that she had a swollen ankle, was blind in one eye, not to mention that she was still in shock from having had her heart ripped right out of her chest!

The list could go on forever and the disinterested look on Garth Redmond's face was the last straw! She began to cry again.

Garth suddenly came to life. He flung open the door and pointed his finger sternly in her direction. "Don't start that again," he warned. He knew that once she was wound up the tears wouldn't stop for hours.

"I bothered you to return your luggage, Mr. Redmond! I was 'banging' on your door because I thought you might appreciate having clean clothes." Hilary stiffened her lower lip defensively. "I can see I was mistaken."

Garth glanced down, and he saw the two bags sitting at her feet. "Oh . . . well . . . thanks." He felt like a heel for shouting at her.

"Thanks?"

Garth bristled at the sharp accusation in her voice. "Yes, thanks! I appreciate it!" Lord, what did the woman want? Blood?

"Well, all I can say is, if I had known they were your bags, I wouldn't have put myself out to deliver them," Hilary declared.

"I said I appreciate it. Do you want me to get down on my knees and say it again?"

"That won't be necessary . . . but do you realize the elevator's out," Hilary reminded him.

"You carried the bags up four flights of stairs?" Garth didn't know why she had his bags or why she would want to carry them up four flights of stairs on a twisted ankle, just to bring them to him.

Hilary refused to answer. He could come to whatever conclusion he wanted. She hadn't carried the bags up four flights of stairs, but she was feeling just neglected and irritated enough to let him think she had.

"All right," Garth conceded. "I appreciate your delivering the bags, okay? I was half asleep, and I didn't mean to snap at you." He'd feel awful if anyone had seen her dragging his luggage up the stairs—at least anyone who could connect the bags to him. She couldn't weigh more than a hundred pounds soaking wet...And with that twisted ankle...Garth flinched.

"I accept your apology, and you can rest assured I'll not be bothering you again," Hilary promised. She was still visibly miffed at what she considered his bad manners. She turned and began to hobble back to her room.

"You staying here?"

The slamming of a door gave Garth his answer; she was right next door.

Garth glanced around, feeling that he was being watched. He noted the piercing surveillance of a middle-aged woman across the hall. Her dark eyes impaled him from behind her half-opened door, and it was evident that she'd monitored the whole conversation.

"Look, I'm sorry," Garth apologized. He turned his palms up helplessly. "I didn't ask her to bring my luggage. Okay?"

The woman, whose hair was wrapped tightly in pink curlers, gave him a nasty look before she slammed her door shut as well.

When Hilary returned to her room she flung herself across the bed. The unnerving encounter with Garth Redmond had only served to remind her of how alone she was. She buried her face in the depths of the pillow and wished she had never made this miserable trip. It was just another harrowing episode on her growing list of mistakes.

Feeling a stab of homesickness, Hilary considered returning to Denver on the next available flight. Obviously she wasn't going to be able to forget Lenny. A week's vacation would have been nice, but with Marsha gone, it seemed pointless.

Hilary felt that she might as well go home and face the problem head on. It wouldn't be pleasant, but she was sure she would survive. She decided to rest just a few minutes before she called the airport...

Giving the woman across the hall a mental raspberry, Garth picked up the two bags and carried them into his room.

He realized he'd been sharp with...what was the girl's name? Hilda...Holly...Heidi? He couldn't remember, but he regretted having made her cry again.

The woman had problems, but so did he. Garth absentmindedly touched the heavy stubble on his face. What he needed was a shower, a shave, and twenty-four hours of undisturbed sleep.

The shower worked like a shot of adrenaline. Garth shaved, then dressed, but his conscience still nagged him.

Maybe he should step next door and thank the girl again for bringing his luggage. Garth shook his head admiringly. *Four* flights of stairs! With a twisted ankle, dragging two bags that weighed as much as she did!

The woman had guts.

Garth knew he would sleep better if he checked on her first. He sighed, slapped on a musky-smelling aftershave, combed his hair, and quickly left the room.

He tapped softly on the door of Room 402, praying that the woman in the pink curlers across the hall wouldn't hear him. He waited several minutes before he tapped again. Still no response.

Well, so much for chivalry, Garth thought as he turned to go back to his room. Heidi was probably down in the bar having a drink; she must have forgotten all about the incident.

As Garth entered his room again he hung the Do Not Disturb sign on the doorknob outside. Seconds later he climbed wearily back into bed. For the next forty-eight hours he was going to do what he'd been sent here to do: Relax.

Chapter Five

STARTLED BY SHOUTS AND POUNDing on doors, Garth sat bolt upright in bed. Fighting off the cobwebs of a deep sleep, he shook his head several times. He tried to focus his vision. *Now* what was going on, he wondered irritably.

If he'd felt annoyed at the earlier interruption, Garth was inclined to be furious this time. He had been so tired that it had taken him an hour to relax and finally doze off.

Garth was sure he couldn't have slept more than a moment, even if the clock on the nightstand told him otherwise. He had slept for at least ten hours. It was morning now, almost six-thirty A.M.

Grabbing the rumpled sheet, Garth gave it a good jerk and tossed it aside. His feet hit the floor at the same time a loud knock sounded at the door. He grabbed his pants off the back of a chair.

If Heidi was back again, he'd personally strangle her, he vowed as he fumbled for his shoes. Mumbling a few choice threats under his breath, he searched frantically under the bed for the missing mate. He wasn't going to take the chance of being harpooned again.

There was another sharp rap at the door, followed by a man's voice. "Open up!" he shouted.

Garth retrieved the missing shoe as another sudden loud thump at the door sent his head banging into the frame of the bed.

"Damn!" Garth ran his tongue over his bleeding lip as he clutched the shoe and crawled to freedom.

Rubbing the goose egg-sized lump that was beginning to rise on top of his head, he hopped to the door while trying to put his shoe on at the same time. He jerked the door open, vowing to take revenge on the knucklehead responsible for the invasion of his privacy. Garth was totally unprepared to see a fireman standing in his doorway.

"Yes?"

"Sorry to disturb you, sir, but we're going to have to ask you to vacate the building."

He noted the man's fire-fighting gear. The man stood, ax in hand, in the hallway reeking now with thick foul-smelling smoke. Coughing, Garth had a sinking feeling that this wasn't a fire drill.

As if his nerves weren't already dangling by threads! The thought of being fried alive didn't help the situation any!

"Oh, hell!" Garth turned four shades paler. "What's going on?"

Recognizing the panic etched on Garth's face,

the fireman tried to calm him down. "We have a small fire here on the fourth floor, sir. We're asking all the guests to vacate the premises immediately."

"Ah...yeah...sure. I just need to get my things first." Garth whirled around when the man's sharp rebuttal stopped him.

"Leave them!"

"But—"

"Look, mister, right now we've got this thing under control. But it's possible that could change."

"Oh...yeah. I'm going."

"Take the stairs at the end of the hall, buddy. *Don't* use the elevator!" The fireman warned. Then he continued down the hall to alert the other guests.

Moving in a daze, Garth headed for the end of the hallway. As he passed Room 402 the door flew open, and Hilary came rushing out. She was clutching something to her chest.

Garth noticed she was wearing her nightie. "Are you still here?" He realized that the fireman should have knocked on the door of 402 before banging on his.

"I had to go back for my makeup," Hilary said breathlessly.

"Your *what?*"

"My makeup." She looked at Garth guiltily. "I look terrible without it..." Her lame reply was drowned out by the harsh demands of the fireman shouting.

"Hey, you two! Out of the building. *Now!*"

Garth took Hilary firmly by the arm and propelled her toward the stairway. "Come on, we have to take the stairs!" As he opened the door to the stairway he drew her back protectively into his arms when he saw the cloud of thick smoke blocking the fire exit. "We can't take the stairs," he said needlessly.

"Oh, my gosh! What'll we do?" Garth could feel Hilary trembling as he drew her closer to him.

"Come on." Garth grabbed her hand and pulled Hilary along behind him. Remembering her injured ankle, Garth finally stopped and scooped her up in his arms, then raced down the hall to the outside fire escape.

As he stepped onto the metal steps, a gust of frigid air rippled up the back of the thin shirt he was wearing.

"I wish you'd brought a coat while you were at it," Garth bantered, trying to ease the look of horror on Hilary's face. He felt her arms tighten around his neck more securely.

"What's wrong?"

Wide-eyed, Hilary shook her head. "No...I can't..." She was looking down, shaking her head, her arms wrapped around his neck so tightly he could barely breathe.

"Oh, yes, *we* can," Garth assured her, trying to loosen the stranglehold she had on his throat.

Too petrified to speak, Hilary fervently shook her head, no!

"Just hold on. I'll carry you down—"

"Down? On, no! You can't..." she pleaded. "I'm terrified of heights!"

Heights! Garth thought. *It's not as though we're*

on top of the Eiffel Tower, for crying out loud!
Seeing fresh tears surfacing in her eyes, Garth
sighed.

"And I'm not overly fond of being burned
alive," he said, "so let's compromise. You shut
your eyes and don't look down, and I'll get us out
of here before the whole building goes up in
flames."

With a horrified gasp, Hilary buried her face
in his neck. "I'm scared, Garth."

"I'm scared, too," he admitted. "Just hold on."

She nodded. "Please walk slowly."

"It depends on how hot it gets." Garth hefted
her up more comfortably in his arms, then began
to ease his way down the metal stairway.

The wind was gusty, and it was getting colder.
The streets below were teeming with activity as
sirens wailed and flashing red lights lit up the
darkened sky.

"It's all right. We're only four floors up. It's
really not that high." He encouraged her as he
took each step slowly. He was careful to keep his
voice calm as he cautiously wound his way
around the narrow staircase. Heights were not
exactly Garth's favorite thing either, and the
small patches of ice he encountered occasionally
on the steps were not exactly comforting.

"Are you all right?"

"Are we almost down?"

"Not quite. Three floors to go."

"Three!"

"You're doing fine. Don't look down."

"I'm not looking in any direction."

It wasn't until his feet had touched solid

ground that Hilary stopped shaking and she dared to open her eyes.

The impact of what was happening finally hit her like a ton of bricks.

"Oh, my gosh! What about my clothes? I'm not even dressed!"

Shivering with cold, Garth set her on her feet. "I don't know. We'll have to see how bad the fire turns out to be. The fireman talked as if they had it under control."

Volunteers from the Red Cross hurried over to drape warm blankets around their shoulders. Cups of hot coffee were placed in their hands, and they gratefully sipped as they were pushed aside by the milling crowd.

They wandered across the street and sat down on the curb, drinking the coffee and staring up at the fourth floor where all their personal belongings were.

"There's an awful lot of smoke coming out of those windows," Hilary observed.

"Not that much. You know how safety-conscious hotels are. They'll have us back in our rooms in a few hours at the most," Garth predicted.

As he spoke, angry flames began to belch out of several windows on the fourth floor.

"Oh, dear," Hilary winced. "I think we've had it."

Had it they had.

The fire developed into a major one. While Garth and Hilary sat and sipped coffee, the entire fourth and fifth floors of the hotel went up in flames.

Every stitch of clothing they had brought with them, except for the few pieces they had on their backs, burned before their eyes.

Garth took the disaster with resignation. "You know, Heidi—"

"It's Hilary," she corrected him. "Hilary Brookfield."

"Oh, I'm sorry. I've been trying to remember," Garth apologized. "Anyway, as I was saying, I've had one hell of a twenty-four hours. What about you?"

Hilary nodded. "Miserable! And I came here to get away from it all!"

Garth looked at her and began to chuckle. A deep, nice sound. One that brought an immediate smile to Hilary's face. "You too?"

They both broke out into laughter, relieving the tension that had been building for hours.

"Well . . ." Garth leaned his elbows back on the curb when their amusement finally subsided. He stared up at the burning fourth and fifth floors of the hotel. "Things could be worse. Material possessions can be replaced. At least no lives were lost."

Hilary had to agree. He was right . . . It could have been much worse.

"Wonder how it started?"

"I heard someone say a man was smoking in bed."

"That's sad."

"Well . . ." Garth yawned and stretched lazily. "I don't know about you, but I could use something to eat. Are you hungry?" He smiled, determined to make the best out of a bad situation.

Hilary realized that she hadn't eaten a thing in the last twenty-four hours. "Yes, I'm starved."

Having spotted a small diner across the street earlier, they wandered away from the scene of the fire.

"I shouldn't go in looking like this," Hilary fretted. She clutched the blanket more tightly around her chin.

"No one will care," Garth promised. He ushered her into the warmth of the small building. It was almost deserted; everyone was watching the fire.

The menu didn't offer a large selection, but after pondering the choices they settled for grilled cheese sandwiches and Cokes.

Sharing a broken-down booth, they ate the meal slowly, savoring the warmth of the diner as they watched the frenzied activity outside.

Eventually the conversation drifted to the reason they were both in West Creek, and once more Hilary felt the hot sting of tears.

Garth glanced up from his plate expectantly, surprised to see that she was crying again. "Hey, what are the tears for? I thought we agreed we were pretty lucky."

"Oh, it isn't the fire . . ." Hilary fumbled for a tissue, waving one hand dismissively as she blew her nose. "Just ignore me. It'll pass in a minute."

"Look . . ." Garth reached in his pocket and retrieved the handkerchief she had used earlier. He handed it to her. "I've watched you crying for twenty-four hours. I don't know what's wrong, but it surely can't be all that bad."

"But it is," she sobbed, burying her face in the

handkerchief for another good cry. "I've been dumped!"

"Dumped?" Garth looked at her blankly. *Dumped. What was that supposed to mean?*

When the tears finally subsided, Hilary found herself telling Garth about her recent breakup with Lenny, the harrowing ride to the airport, how she'd twisted her ankle, lost a contact, and Marsha's unexpected exit to Jamaica.

Instead of dismissing her troubles as minor and unworthy of such a concentration of despair, Garth was surprisingly understanding.

"I know how you feel," he admitted. "The reason I'm here is because my boss thinks I'm stressed out."

"Well, I thought I had stress before," Hilary confessed, trying to find a dry spot on the handkerchief to blow her nose. "But since I left Denver, it's been Trauma City."

Garth nodded. "I know." It hadn't exactly been Christmas morning for him either. "Well, look,"—Garth reached over to take her hand supportively—"It's been rough, but the worst is over. As soon as we can, we'll look for new accommodations, and then we'll both get that rest we came for."

"Yes, I suppose so."

Funny, Hilary would have thought that a man holding her hand would upset her so soon after Lenny. Instead, she found the unexpected gesture comforting. Garth had nice hands, large and protective. For the first time in hours, Hilary felt the world beginning to turn right side up again.

"Do you have any idea what you're planning

to do, now that your friend is in Jamaica?" Garth asked.

"I was planning on taking the next flight home—before the fire." Hilary surveyed her bathrobe dismally. "Now, I don't know. I'll have to have clothes before I get on a plane."

"Well, I suppose we can—" Garth's words were severed in midsentence as he felt a steel hand clamp down on his shirt collar. He glanced up, and his eyes widened as he was jerked out of the booth by the scruff of his neck.

"What the—" Garth yelled as a man twice his size—twice anyone's size—dangled him in the air by his collar. The intruder glared at Garth as if he were about to disassemble him—piece by piece.

The burly character looked Garth squarely in the eye without blinking and stated in a voice that sounded like creek gravel, "The question is, what do *you* think you're doing, chump!"

By now Garth was red-faced and gasping for breath. He was clearly in no condition to answer the man's question.

"Hey! You want to put me down!" Garth finally managed to wheeze out. He had no idea who this maniac was or what he'd done to antagonize him. The only thing he *was* sure of was that he had no intention of provoking him further.

Like a bolt of lightning, Hilary sprang to her one good foot. "You put him *down* this instant!" she demanded. "Who do you think you are?"

Oh, please, Hilary don't get him any madder!

Garth willed silently as he watched her go nose-to-nose with the giant.

"I'm warning you! *Put him down!*" Hilary threatened. She snapped her fingers, then pointed at the giant authoritatively.

Maybe she knows karate, Garth prayed. His face was beginning to turn a splotchy blue. No, even if she knew karate, kung fu and had a Sears, Roebuck chain saw in the pocket of her bathrobe, Garth realized, she still was no match for this bonzo burger.

To Garth's astonishment, Hilary got her point across. The giant dropped Garth like a sack of grain, and he fell limply into the booth as the man confronted Hilary, still eye-to-eye.

Garth began sucking in deep gulps of air as Hilary spoke to the bully curtly. "Just what do you think you're doing?"

"I came looking for you, babe." The man's deep voice had suddenly taken on a tone of boyish pleading as he stepped forward and tried to take Hilary in his arms.

"Wait a minute!" Garth moved to protect Hilary, but she gently pushed him back down in the booth.

"It's all right," she said. "I'll take care of this."

"Are you sure?" Garth was confident there wasn't a lot he could do anyway—given the hundred-pound difference in size between himself and the giant—but he was willing to try.

"How did you know where to find me?" Hilary asked calmly, ignoring Garth's struggle to get to his feet again.

Garth had a tight feeling in the pit of his stomach, coinciding with the one he still had around his neck. All he'd ever heard about "a lover scorned" came rushing back to him. This undoubtedly must be "the rat," Lenny Ricetrum.

"I called the boss, and he said you'd gone to West Creek to spend some time with a girlfriend. Some girlfriend!" Lenny sneered. He glanced at Garth disdainfully, then back to Hilary and demanded, "Where's your clothes?"

"On the fourth floor of that burning hotel!"

Lenny shot a hurried glance out of the window. Assured that she was telling him the truth, his scowl began to slowly recede.

"Mr. O'Connor told *you* where I was?" Hilary demanded.

"Well, not me exactly. I had a friend call. Jake told Michael that he was your cousin from out of town," Lenny admitted.

It infuriated Hilary to think that Lenny had stooped to such low-down tactics. Especially after having treated her so badly.

"I realized I made a mistake, babe." Lenny smiled at her persuasively. "I came all this way just so we could patch things up."

"Oh, what a shame! Did you bring the little redhead too?" Hilary asked pleasantly.

Garth found it hard to believe that this was the man Hilary had wept through three boxes of Kleenex for. Lenny didn't appear to be her type.

"I don't want the redhead, Hilary. I want you," Lenny admitted contritely. He tapped a tightly clenched fist against his leg and shot Garth another nasty look. His voice dropped repentantly. "I made a mistake, okay?"

"Well, Lenny, we all make mistakes, but I'm afraid this one can't be corrected that easily," Hilary told him.

Reconciling with Lenny? After he had treated her so shabbily? Hilary realized that was something she was going to have to think about.

"Come on, honey," Lenny coaxed. "Let's go somewhere and talk this thing over." He shot Garth another warning look.

Hilary looked at Garth, then back at Lenny.

"Go ahead. Don't worry about me," Garth offered, hoping they would leave him out of it.

Hilary realized she was about to do a devious thing, but she needed time to think. She just hoped Garth would play along.

"No, I don't think so. I'm here for vacation, and I'm staying." She slid in the booth next to Garth and slipped her arm through his. "With Garth."

Garth's eyes widened.

Lenny's upper lip curled ominously as his snapping black eyes openly accused Garth of trifling with his woman.

"I thought you were going to take the next plane," Garth reminded Hilary as he casually removed her arm from his.

Garth liked Hilary, and he would have helped her out if he could have. But he wasn't prepared to lose his life for her.

"I'm staying!" Hilary said. She firmly linked her arm back with his.

"Now, look"—Garth was beginning to lose his patience—"I don't want to get involved in this . . ."

Lenny's face resembled an approaching cloudburst. "Well, well, well! Ain't this cozy! You work fast, buddy boy!"

"No, this isn't what you think." Garth tried to explain, but Hilary was doing nothing to help. In fact, she seemed to be deliberately egging him on. "Tell him, Hilary . . ."

"Tell him what?" Hilary asked unconcernedly. She picked up the menu to study it.

"Tell him why we happen to be together." Garth decided to be firm with her. "Right now! I've grown fond of my neck!"

Lenny looked as if he were ready to blow a fuse.

"Leave Garth alone, Lenny. You're making him nervous," Hilary said obediently.

"Are you coming with me, or are you staying here with this jerk?" Lenny demanded. He was getting tired of begging. Lenny Ricetrum had never begged a woman in his life, and he sure wasn't about to start now.

Hilary carefully placed the menu back on the rack. "I'm staying with the jerk," she announced.

"Now just a minute . . ." Garth said resentfully.

Hilary patted Garth's arm reassuringly. "Go away, Lenny. Garth and I want to be alone."

Garth was dismayed. Every word Hilary said was clearly designed to give the erroneous impression that he and she were together. Really *together!* Garth had the growing suspicion that Lenny Ricetrum planned to squeeze him to death . . . slowly and painfully.

Hilary's reaction left Garth bewildered and just a little irritated. He had enough trouble without having an irate boyfriend on his tail. Not only was Hilary deliberately aggravating a man who weighed twice what Garth did, she seemed to be enjoying it!

The sound of a meaty fist crashing down on the table convinced Garth that Lenny was aware of the goading.

"Look, Ricetrum. I haven't moved in on your territory, but if the lady doesn't want to go with you, she doesn't want to go," Garth said. He stood up to face his adversary, trying to remember if he had ever made out a will.

Garth winced as the meaty fist hit the table a second time, rattling the dishes loudly again.

"Hey, you, back there! What are you trying to do, tear down the joint?" The proprietor of the diner shouted. "Either put a lid on it, or take it down the street!"

Thank God! Reinforcements! Garth's knees sagged with relief. He'd wondered just how long the owner would continue to keep his eyes glued to the football game on the portable black-and-white television set.

Lenny eyed Garth coldly. Hilary glared at Lenny with a look that could freeze hell over, and Garth wished to high heaven he'd never left Chicago.

"Well, you and ol' lover boy better watch your step," Lenny warned, deciding to let the matter lie for the moment. "But let me warn you, sweetheart, you'd better reconsider."

Garth put his arm around Hilary protectively. "Why don't you bug off, Ricetrum. Can't you see the lady's not interested?"

Garth's eyes suddenly bulged as Lenny pulled him up again and jerked the collar of his shirt into a tight knot, choking off his breath once more.

"Hilary, dammit! Tell him you'll at least think about it!" Garth gasped.

"Never," Hilary stated calmly.

"You better hope she gives it another thought, sucker. You'd just better hope she does!"

Lenny dropped Garth back down onto his feet, pivoted on the ball of his foot, and marched out of the restaurant angrily.

Garth grabbed his swollen neck and fell back in the booth limply.

He shot Hilary a murderous look as she sat calmly sucking up what was left of her Coke through a straw.

Stress? Joel Anderson had thought Garth was suffering from stress before? He should see him now.

Chapter Six

"OKAY, YOU WANT TO TELL ME what *that* was all about."

Garth was still shaken by the events of the past five minutes. From the moment he'd first laid eyes on Hilary, he'd wondered if she wasn't an apple short of being a bushel.

Now he strongly suspected she was—and it was beginning to look as if she were harboring a silent death wish for him.

Rubbing his aching throat, Garth waited while Hilary nervously twisted her straw into the shape of a distressed pretzel.

"That was Lenny—the man I told you about."

"I just about had that figured out."

Guiltily, Hilary dropped her eyes away from Garth's. "I should have warned you. Lenny has a nasty temper."

"I noticed that right away, too. What I didn't notice was that we were together—I mean, as in *personally* together!" Garth challenged.

Hilary hung her head sheepishly. "Oh, that . . . Well, I had to think fast. I'm sorry I involved you, but I knew Lenny would insist I return to Denver with him . . . and I don't want to."

"You don't want to!" Garth shook his head in disbelief. "I thought that's what all the water-works were about."

"Yes . . . but I need time to think." Hilary deposited the mangled straw in the ashtray. "Lenny needs to be taught a lesson. He can't just up and dump me, then waltz back into my life as if nothing happened." She had a little pride left.

"Fine! But from now on, pick another guinea pig," Garth warned. He reached for the check. "I came here looking for a little peace and quiet, and I don't plan to get involved in a lovers' spat."

"Lenny isn't my lover," Hilary stated flatly.

"Well, he sure isn't mine!"

Hilary's face suddenly softened. "I'm sorry, Garth . . . really."

"It's okay . . . And I don't want you to take this personally, but I think it's time we went our separate ways." Garth didn't mean to sound harsh, yet he felt it imperative to let her know where he stood. Fate had thrown them together constantly, but the time had come to part.

"Oh, I don't take it personally," Hilary assured him. "I think you're right . . . and I'm sorry about involving you the way I did. It won't happen again."

Garth straightened his collar petulantly, wincing when the material rubbed his bruised neck. "It's all right . . . but don't do it again."

"I wouldn't think of it." Hilary slid out of the booth and reached for the check. "Please, I insist on paying."

"That isn't necessary," Garth said dismissively. "I'll get it." He reached over and absent-mindedly tucked the blanket up closer around her neck. "You're...uh...you're showing too much..." Garth was finding it increasingly hard to keep his eyes off the tantalizing sight of the soft swell of creamy flesh the blanket was doing an inadequate job of concealing.

"Oh," Hilary glanced down, wondering exactly how much of her "uh's" had been exposed. "Thank you."

"You're welcome." *She sure has some figure*, Garth thought. He ran his eyes lazily over her petite form, which was draped enchantingly in the dark blanket. No wonder Ricetrum had blown his cool.

"About the check...I really wish you'd let me pay," Hilary persisted as she reached for her purse.

"It's not necessary," Garth repeated. He didn't want to stand there all night and argue over four dollars and twenty-eight cents.

"But I want to," Hilary insisted, and Garth found himself returning her smile.

He reached over and ruffled her hair good-naturedly. She had pretty hair, thick and lustrous. "I'll get the check," he stated firmly.

"You've been awfully nice about all of this." With a sparkle in her eyes that Garth found disturbingly appealing, Hilary reached for her makeup kit, and the blanket slipped a notch lower. She glanced up and smiled guiltily as Garth quickly averted his eyes. She tugged the blanket primly back in place.

"Oh, dear!"

"What now?" Garth noticed she was looking askance at the makeup kit.

"My purse . . . it's still in the hotel room."

"You mean you saved the makeup kit and left your purse?" He found that sort of feminine behavior hard to comprehend.

Hilary nodded miserably. "It had my plane ticket and all my money in it."

"Oh, bother!" Garth swore under his breath, realizing what her loss could mean.

She lifted her eyes hopefully. "What do you think I should do?"

"I don't know." Garth wasn't sure what *he* was going to do, but he knew one thing: He wasn't in any shape to be responsible for her too. "I'll take care of the check; then we'll try to figure out something."

"Thanks . . . I'll pay you back."

While he was paying the cashier, Hilary tried to decide what to do next. She couldn't expect Garth to take care of her. They barely knew each other, and he had made it clear that he was in West Creek for complete relaxation. He had been wonderful to her, but she couldn't continue to impose upon him.

She would have to call her parents and ask them to wire money, but she realized even that could take time. What was she to do in the meantime?

Garth returned from the cashier. They stood

for a moment. He smiled lamely, and she smiled back.

Garth barely knew her, yet he couldn't just leave her sitting in a diner wrapped in a blanket. But if he took her with him, he'd never get any rest. Her luck seemed to be as incredibly rotten as his.

"Do you know anyone else in West Creek you can call?"

"No." Hilary shook her head sadly. "I'll have to call my parents and have them wire me some money."

"That sounds good."

"It might take a few hours to get it."

Garth was relieved to hear she at least had a plan. "That shouldn't be a problem." Two hours ... two measly hours and then he could be on his way again.

"What will you do?" Hilary asked politely.

"I'll check with the hotel, but I think our clothes are gone for good. I was thinking maybe I should walk down to one of the department stores and pick out a few pieces of clothing to tide me over."

"Oh ... that sounds nice. Would you mind if I tagged along until my money gets here?"

"No, I suppose not," Garth agreed cautiously. He eyed her blanket worriedly. "Just be sure you keep that thing pulled up."

"Maybe I shouldn't go." Hilary quickly reassessed her state of undress. "I might embarrass you ..."

"I don't see that you have much choice. Besides, if anyone asks why you're wearing the blanket, we'll explain what's happened. Just keep the thing pulled up tight."

Obediently, Hilary hitched the blanket higher. "I will." She smiled up at him through lowered lashes, and Garth felt his pulse quicken.

Don't be getting any ideas about her, he warned himself. *She's nothing but bad news, Redmond. All you have to do is see that she's taken care of for another two hours; then it's so long, sweetheart.*

The reassuring thought made Garth feel better.

While Garth browsed through the men's department, Hilary phoned her parents in Denver. They quickly assured her they would send the money.

"Hotel fire! Are you sure you're all right? We thought you were going to be staying with Marsha!" Maxie Brookfield exclaimed.

"I'm fine, Mom. Honest. It was so late when I arrived that I thought I'd just stay at a hotel tonight," Hilary fabricated. She hated to mislead her mother, but she didn't want her to know her true predicament. Although Hilary had lived away from home for four years, her parents were still protective enough to worry about her if they thought she was alone in West Creek. Fortunately, Maxie didn't press the issue.

"Honey, don't you worry!" Simon Brookfield's voice came over the line to comfort his daughter. "We'll take care of the problem immediately. You're sure you're all right?"

"I'm fine, Dad. Just wire the money, and I'll pay you back when I get home."

As Hilary replaced the receiver a few minutes

later, she thought how nice it was to have parents. Especially understanding ones who asked very few questions.

Garth was examining a black-and-red flannel shirt when Hilary found him in the men's department.

He thoughtfully eyed his reflection in the full-length mirror, then turned and lifted his brows expectantly. "What do you think?"

"It's nice. You look good in red." *Actually, he would look good in anything,* Hilary found herself thinking. *Or in absolutely nothing . . .* She was shocked to have such thoughts about a complete stranger.

"Did you get through to your parents?"

"Yes. Daddy's making all the arrangements. He'll be calling me back as soon as the transaction is completed. I gave him the number of the store, and the manager said he would be happy to page me when the call comes through."

"Good." Garth said absently. He decided to take the shirt. "We'll just kill time until he calls back."

Glancing at Hilary, Garth felt a tug of compassion. She looked pitiful standing there in that blanket.

"Hey, why don't you pick yourself out a few things? I'll lend you the money, and you can pay me back when your money gets here," Garth offered casually.

"Oh, I couldn't. You've been too kind already."

"No, go ahead. You can't run around that way." He was beginning to resent some of the suggestive looks a few of the male shoppers had already given her. "Buy whatever you need."

"It would be so nice...if you're sure you wouldn't mind." Hilary jumped at the opportunity to rid herself of the embarrassing blanket.

"I'm sure." Garth disappeared into the dressing room to try on a pair of black trousers while Hilary went off to make her own selections.

She was trying to decide on an inexpensive coat when the saleswoman approached her. "Miss Brookfield?"

"Yes."

"You have a call at the counter."

"Thanks." She grabbed the midcalf-length burgundy coat and added it to the jeans, undies, gloves, and blouse she had already selected. Then she eagerly trailed behind the elderly woman to the service counter.

"Hi, Dad. Is everything taken care of?"

"Honey, now don't worry...They're having some sort of a computer malfunction at the Western Union office here, but the money's on its way."

"Good. How long will it take?"

"Well, that's the catch. You won't be able to pick it up until tomorrow morning," Simon explained apologetically.

"Tomorrow morning!" Hilary exclaimed, trying unsuccessfully to hide her disappointment. "Oh, Dad! Can't they get it here sooner than that?"

"I'm afraid not. Just have Marsha drive you to the Western Union office anytime after eight tomorrow morning. The money will be there waiting."

"But Marsha . . ." Hilary caught herself just in time. She realized she couldn't tell him Marsha was in Jamaica, while *she* was stranded in West Creek, penniless, with nowhere to spend the night.

"Hilary? Are you still there?"

"Yes. Tomorrow morning will be fine, Daddy. Thanks. I'll call you and let you know when I get the money," she promised. She quickly hung up before her courage failed.

The saleswoman had overheard the conversation, and Hilary suddenly found herself telling her about her miserable plight. She burst out into a fresh round of tears.

The clerk was just handing her a fresh tissue when Garth approached the counter with his arms loaded with garments.

"What's wrong now?" He dropped the bundle and automatically reached into his back pocket for a handkerchief. He knew Hilary well enough by now to know that she would go through her tissue in a matter of minutes.

Between sobs, Hilary recounted the details of her conversation with her father. At the conclusion of her tearful report, the saleswoman shot Garth an expectant look and leaned across the counter. "The poor little thing is in an awful predicament," she said sympathetically.

"I'm aware of that."

"Good! Then you won't just walk off and leave her?"

Garth eyed the salesclerk coolly. "I hadn't planned on it."

"There, there, dear! I'm sure everything will

work out all right." The motherly clerk tried to soothe Hilary. "This gentleman said he would stay with you."

"Oh, thank you, but I've been enough trouble to him as it is." Hilary accepted the handkerchief and blew her nose.

"Let's not panic," Garth said—for the sake of both women. He reached into his billfold for a credit card. "Put her purchases on here too."

The clerk nodded pleasantly. "If you'd like to slip into the dressing room and put these on, I'll make out the tickets," she told Hilary as she handed her a complete change of clothing.

While Hilary dressed, Garth paid for their purchases, then walked over to the elevator. Leaning down for a drink of water from the fountain, he started and jumped back as the flow spurted up to hit him full in the face. Reaching for his handkerchief, he remembered it was gone.

Sighing, Garth mopped the water off his face with the sleeve of his shirt. He found it hard to believe that just the day before he had been in Chicago—only mildly stressed out.

Hilary came out of the dressing room carrying the neatly folded blanket, her nightie, and her makeup kit. She located Garth and smiled, and he felt his stomach flutter. The jeans and blouse she was wearing fit her like a glove, and he was forced to admit to himself how attractive she was.

"You look better," he complimented her. He handed her the shopping bag with her other purchases inside.

"Thanks. What's that all over the front of your

shirt?" Hilary opened the bag and retrieved the coat and gloves. She slipped them on as he punched the button for the elevator.

"Water."

"Oh." Hilary didn't dare ask him how it got there.

They got on the elevator and rode to the ground floor. As they emerged from the revolving doors a blast of frigid air hit them in the face.

"It's getting colder," Hilary observed.

Pulling up the collar of his new jacket, Garth scanned the sky thoughtfully. "Yeah, it looks like rain."

They paused beside a streetlight, each sneaking an uneasy glance at the other. It would be the opportune time to part company.

"Well . . ."

"Well . . ." The thought of having to spend the night at a bus station or all-night café flashed horrifyingly before Hilary's eyes.

"I suppose we should check with the hotel and see what they suggest," Garth offered.

"Yes, that's a good idea."

They walked back to the Merrymont at a brisk pace, seeking shelter deep in the linings of their coats from the rising wind.

When they arrived it didn't surprise them to learn that the hotel had ceased operations for the time being. There was still a thick plume of black smoke drifting out of the windows of the fourth and fifth floors.

"Well, back to square one," Garth said as they walked back out to the street.

Feeling like an anchor around his neck, Hilary

knew the time had come to set him free. He had been nicer than the average person would have been, but she couldn't impose on him any longer. Already she was feeling a dependency on him that she shouldn't feel.

"Garth . . ." He paused and she turned to face him. She had to raise her voice above the rising wind. "You go on. I'll just hang around the lobby of the hotel until tomorrow morning."

"No, I couldn't do that—"

"Yes, you can. I insist. Just leave me your name and where I can return the money you loaned me, and I'll mail you a check when I get back home."

The thought was tempting, and she was making it easy for him. Still, Garth didn't feel he could just walk off and leave her. But Hilary insisted. She made him write down his name and address; then he stepped off the sidewalk to hail a passing cab.

"I promise I'll send the money as soon as I get home," she assured Garth as he hesitantly got into the waiting cab.

"You sure you'll be all right?" Garth felt torn. He didn't want to be responsible for her, yet he found himself reluctant to leave her.

"I'll be fine. Really!"

Garth reached into his back pocket and hastily withdrew his billfold. "Here's seventy-five dollars. See that you get a nice room at one of the other hotels and a good breakfast in the morning." He shoved the money into her hand before she could protest.

"Garth, I couldn't . . ."

Garth slammed the door and rolled down the window. "You can pay me back. Just be careful. There are a lot of weirdos around."

Hilary smiled and clutched the money to her heart. She was suddenly very sad to see her Good Samaritan go. "I will. You be careful too."

"I will."

She leaned over impetuously and kissed him. Her mouth felt warm and sweet on his. Garth closed his eyes, and he felt himself respond to the unexpected reward. The kiss sent a surge of desire through him. He was surprised at his reaction. A simple kiss shouldn't affect him that way.

The embrace was over before Garth knew it, and the cab was pulling away from the curb. He twisted around in the seat, watching as Hilary's now familiar figure grew smaller in the distance.

A feeling of loss came over him as the cab turned the corner and she disappeared from his view.

All the "what ifs?" imaginable flooded his mind as he sank wearily back in the seat. He had a headache; his nose was raw from his miserable cold; and now he felt like a complete ass for deserting her.

Suppose she couldn't find a hotel room? Suppose she ran into that airhead Ricetrum again. Suppose someone tried to pick her up . . . Garth's mind was spinning with all the ugly possibilities. He couldn't be her keeper! He was having a hard enough time coping with his own problems.

But the image of Hilary standing alone on a dark street corner rose up to haunt him. *Damn it, Redmond! You wouldn't leave a dog standing on a corner in this kind of weather, alone, unprotected...*

Unable to shake the guilt feelings, Garth suddenly leaned forward and tapped the driver on the shoulder. "Go back to the Merrymont."

"Did you forget something?"

"I guess you could say that." Garth sighed. He had no idea what he was going to do with her. He just knew he couldn't leave her standing on some corner.

As the taxi neared the hotel, Garth shook his head wearily when he saw she was sitting alone on a bus bench, her makeup kit and the shopping bag from the department store propped beside her. The wind was tossing her hair about, and just as he'd suspected, she was crying again.

Garth rolled down his window as the cab eased up to the curb. "Hi, good-looking. You fool around?"

Hilary glanced up, and her eyes brightened. "Only when I'm asked," she sniffed. She tried to make light of her misery, but she had *never* been so glad to see anyone.

"Well, I suppose you could get in, and we could discuss the possibilities," Garth suggested dryly.

He knew he was flirting with her, and for the life of him, he didn't know why.

Hilary grinned and hurriedly reached for the makeup kit and shopping bag before he changed his mind. "I suppose it's worth discussing," she conceded.

After all, she reasoned as she slid into the backseat of the cab next to his comforting warmth, she really didn't have much choice. And she had missed him like the devil the two and a half minutes he had been gone!

Chapter Seven

AS THE TAXI PULLED BACK INTO the line of traffic, Hilary jerked her gloves off with her teeth and unbuttoned her coat. "Where're we going?"

"Beats me. You got any suggestions?"

"Sorry, I ran dry several calamities ago," Hilary confessed. "Listen, I really appreciate your coming back for me."

"I thought you were going to get a hotel room," Garth reminded.

"I was...but I didn't know where to begin looking." Hilary's face suddenly broke out in a relieved grin. "Honestly, who would ever think two people could run into so many obstacles just trying to spend a quiet vacation?"

Garth was busy looking out of the window for a hotel or motel with a vacancy sign. He was barely listening to her prattle. "Yeah, who would ever think," he answered absentmindedly.

Hilary edged forward on the seat and peered

at him intently. "You're doing okay, aren't you? I mean, all this hasn't been too much for you, has it?" If the poor man had been under stress before, Hilary knew the last few hours couldn't have helped.

"No, I'm fine. How about you?"

She sighed. "I'm adjusting."

"Where to, buddy?" The cabbie peered in his rearview mirror, waiting for directions.

"To tell you the truth, I don't know," Garth confessed. "Would you have any idea where we can get a room for the night?"

"Around here?"

No, in Honolulu! Garth thought irritably. "Yeah, around here."

"For the entire night?" The driver sneaked another peek in the mirror and noted that neither one of them had luggage. They were both carrying shopping bags from Garfield's. It must be whoopee time again.

"There's a meat-packers' convention over at the Bellview and a pharmaceutical convention over at the Bell Tower." The cabbie took off his hat and scratched his head. "What with the Merrymont fire, I think just about everything in town's full up this evening." The cab turned the corner and shot down Gamin Boulevard. "'Course, I know a little place over on Fairfax that rents out rooms for a couple of hours or so..."

Garth felt his face turning a bright red at the cabbie's mistaken interpretation of his request. "Uh, no, we need something for the night," he mumbled.

The cabbie's mouth turned up at the corners in a tiny smirk. "Well, like I said, that's gonna be tough."

"Ask him if he knows someone who would just rent us a room for a little while," Hilary whispered.

Garth's gaze slid up guiltily to meet the cabbie's in the rearview mirror. "Are you serious?" he snapped out of the corner of his mouth. "He already thinks the worst."

"But if there's no hotel or motel vacancies, maybe there's a boarding house around that would be willing to rent us a room." Hilary realized it was a long shot, but at this point she was ready to concede they were desperate.

Seeing the immediate color flood Garth's face again, she added, "I wouldn't mind sleeping on the floor ... if you'll just spend the night with me."

"Uh ... Hilary ..." Garth knew the driver was listening to their conversation.

The cabbie grinned as he reached into his shirt pocket for a cigarette.

"No, really! I'll do anything you say if you'll just stay with me tonight, Garth."

While sitting on the lonely bus bench, Hilary discovered she'd lost whatever self-confidence she thought she'd possessed. She wasn't beyond begging Garth to stay with her. It hadn't taken but a few minutes to realize just how disconcerting it was to be completely alone in a strange town. Hilary would gladly sacrifice her pride if he would promise not to leave her alone again.

"I'll even pay you"—Hilary upped the ante hopefully—"as soon as I get my money."

Lucky devil! the cabbie thought enviously.

Garth's face turned several shades of red as he diverted his attention to staring out of the window again. "Why don't we stop at a restaurant and have a cup of coffee? We need to discuss this in private." Garth was determined to avoid the cabbie's widening smirk in the rearview mirror.

"Oh . . . Well, sure," Hilary agreed, wondering why both men suddenly had such strange looks on their faces. "You won't try to get away from me again, will you?"

"No . . . and I didn't try to get away from you earlier," Garth said quietly. He wished she would change the subject.

Hilary leaned back in the seat and let out a sigh of relief. "Good. I'd hate to have to call Daddy again."

Garth leaned forward and spoke curtly to the cabbie. "She means she had to call her father for money and . . ." He broke off lamely, realizing he could never explain the confusing situation. "Just pull over at the first restaurant."

"Whatever you say, Romeo!"

The taxi screeched to a halt a few minutes later in front of Red's Sirloin Parlor. Garth paid the amused driver as Hilary got out of the cab. He noticed she was limping again.

"How's the ankle?" he asked as he held the door open for her to enter the restaurant.

"I think it's getting worse."

"It looks as if it's swelling more."

That didn't surprise her. It was throbbing to beat the band.

"You get us a table, and I'll grab a newspaper."

Garth spotted the vending machines at the corner. As crazy as it sounded, Hilary's earlier suggestion of a boarding house might be their only chance to avoid sleeping on a park bench tonight.

While Garth went for the paper, Hilary asked for a table for two, and was promptly seated. As she sank into the comfortable red leather seat, exhaustion overcame her again. She realized she couldn't take much more of this merry-go-round. She was tired and grimy, and she longed for a hot tub where she could soak her ankle and a soft bed on which to rest. Was it only hours ago that she had experienced all those wonderful luxuries she had always taken for granted?

Hilary absently picked up one of the bread sticks the restaurant had provided and bit into it. Her eyes widened as she crunched down on something grainy.

Removing the foreign object from her mouth, she was dismayed to find it was a small piece of enamel from a tooth. She deposited what she had chewed in a napkin, and with her tongue she probed the jagged edge of a molar. She groaned out loud.

This had been the worst day of her life!

When Garth returned with the papers Hilary told him about the latest catastrophe, and he shook his head compassionately.

"I ordered coffee," she told him as he unfolded the paper and began scanning the classified ads.

"Good." He handed her a section of the ads. "Here, see what you can find."

"Okay."

"By the way, what time is it?"

Hilary glanced at her watch. "Eight-thirty."

"Brother!"

"What's wrong?"

"Nothing. I was just thinking that it's getting late to go looking for a room at a boarding house."

"Yes, I know."

The waitress brought their coffee and set it down before them. "Anything else I can get you?"

Hilary smiled. "No, thanks . . . unless you can recommend a good eye doctor, an ankle doctor, a dentist, and a place to stay the night."

The waitress walked away, smiling as if she thought Hilary was kidding. Hilary wished she had been.

"She didn't believe me."

"Who in their right mind would?"

They sipped their coffee and browsed through the ads, reading one out loud every few minutes.

"Here . . ." Hilary leaned forward and pointed to an ad in the third column. "This sounds like a nice one."

"I should hope to shout it does!" Garth protested. "Look at the price."

"Oh, yes. Sorry." She was leaning so close that he could detect a faint whiff of her perfume. For some crazy reason Garth suddenly felt himself becoming aroused.

Now that was *all* he needed to make his day, he thought irritably. he folded the paper shut.

"You keep looking. I'll call and check on a couple of these." He slid out of the booth and walked to the pay phone.

Hilary picked up her coffee cup and studied

him from under lowered lashes. She was enjoying his company. He was wearing a nice, clean-smelling aftershave...intriguing and sensuous. She took another sip of coffee. It seemed to her he got better-looking by the minute. Not pretty-boy handsome, but his face had enough interesting planes and angles to make a woman look twice.

Hilary wondered how many women there were in Garth Redmond's life, and she was surprised to feel an unreasonable twinge of jealousy at the thought. She barely knew him; yet she found herself feeling almost possessive.

Garth returned to the table in a few minutes, waving a piece of paper at her triumphantly. "These two are still available."

"Wonderful! Can we look at them right away?"

"I told them we'd be there within the hour."

The taxi pulled up in front of the first house, and Hilary looked at Garth and smiled. "It looks lovely."

"Right now, I'd settle for a pup tent," Garth confessed.

The landlady greeted them at the door with a warm and friendly hello. "My name is Mrs. Biggerton, but you can call me Mary," she said.

Hilary and Garth nodded and smiled politely.

"Mr. Biggerton always said our guests should call us John and Mary—God rest his soul." Mary dabbed at the corners of her eyes. "John was such a good man."

Lamely, Hilary and Garth nodded again.

"The room . . . ?" Garth prompted.

"Oh, yes, the room. Just follow me, dearies."

My, my, Mary thought. *What a lovely couple they make*. She was reminded of herself and her late husband. She and John had been just about this young couple's age when they had bought this old house. *How grand first love is!* she thought as she led them up the carpeted stairway.

"It's a lovely, lovely room. Nice big windows facing the south. Very quiet. Old Mr. Whitlock has the adjoining room, but he doesn't give anyone a minute's trouble," Mary promised as she unlocked the door and motioned them into the room.

Garth saw all he needed to make a quick decision. The room had a bed, and it appeared to be clean. He turned to Hilary who quickly gave her approval with a hasty nod.

"It looks good to me," she agreed.

"Good. We'll take it."

"Oh, my!" The landlady smiled at them benevolently. "I was hoping you would say that. Now if you and the missus will follow me, we'll take care of the registration."

Garth was about to clarify the *missus*, when he saw Hilary's warning look.

They walked back down the stairway, listening to Mary chat about her pet canary, Wiladeen, who was feeling under the weather. "I'm afraid she's caught a draft, poor thing. And with the weather predicted to turn so bad...well...I only hope Dr. Saddler can drop by before too much longer."

Garth glanced at Hilary. He wondered if a draft could be fatal to a canary.

Hilary lifted her shoulder bitterly. If it were *her* canary, it would be.

As they entered the front hallway, Mary glanced out of the picture window and noticed that the taxi was still waiting at the curb. "Oh, dear! If you'd like to get your luggage, I'll wait here for you," she offered. The cab's meter was running, and the poor little things were probably having to watch every penny, Mary reasoned. She felt sorry for young people today. Everything was so expensive.

Hilary appreciated Mary's concern but quickly pointed out, "We don't have any luggage..."

She realized immediately that she'd said the wrong thing.

A giant iceberg suddenly floated into Mary's eyes. "You don't have any luggage?" she asked.

"No... You see, we actually need the room for just one night...because all the hotels are full..." Hilary's voice trailed off lamely as the iceberg suddenly grew in size.

"One night?"

"Yes, you see—"

"Why, the two of you should be ashamed of yourselves!" Mary marched over to the door and yanked it open self-righteously. "Go! Out of here with you! I run a decent, God-fearing establishment, and I don't hold with any of this kinky one-night stuff."

"Excuse me, Mary, but we're not—" Garth started to protest, but Mary cut him off abruptly.

"*Mrs.* Biggerton to you! Why, John would roll over in his grave if he thought I was party to such goings-on. The very nerve!" Mary stuck her nose in the air. "Out!"

"But, Mary..." Hilary tried to explain again, embarrassed by the woman's mistaken impression. "You see...no, we aren't married, but we were staying at the Merrymont and—"

"Oh, *please*, young lady! Spare me the details!" Mary pressed a hand over her thundering heart. "Mind you now, I'm not one to moralize, but you two should be ashamed of yourselves. Your parents certainly would be!"

"You don't understand..."

But Hilary's attempted explanation was ignored as Mary pivoted on one foot and stalked away. "I'll have no part of this! No, sir, not in this house! And I'll thank you to show yourselves out!" Mary was still ranting about "today's decadent society" as she disappeared through the kitchen doorway.

Hilary turned to confront a red-faced Garth. "You devil, you! Are you trying to corrupt me?" she deadpanned.

Garth sighed as he ran one hand through his hair. "I have the distinct feeling the room isn't available anymore."

"Strange, I have that same feeling."

They quietly let themselves out the front door.

"I don't know what you're laughing about," Garth admonished as they got back into the cab. "It's close to ten o'clock, and we still don't have a place to spend the night."

"I know." Hilary settled herself in the backseat and picked up the classified ads again. "But we will," she predicted optimistically.

At the next stop they were admitted inside the house by a big burly man who constantly winked at Hilary whenever Garth's head was turned. Recalling the bad impression they'd made on Mary Biggerton, Hilary cringed to think how this insinuating clod would misconstrue the situation.

Hilary heard Garth's quick intake of breath as the man unlocked the door to the apartment and let it swing open.

The small room was appalling. Beer cans were strewn across the coffee table, and there were several bags of trash standing in the middle of the kitchen floor. Just how long they'd been there, only heaven knew. If the sight hadn't nauseated Hilary, the smell certainly did.

She tried not to breathe as she trailed closely behind Garth. She hoped he was as horrified as she was, yet she was resolved to yield to his decision. Whatever he decided, she would have to accept.

Glancing at the soiled spread that was draped haphazardly across the sagging bed, Hilary reminded herself that she really wasn't *that* tired. She could sit up in a chair all night and let *him* have the bed.

Garth continued to pretend polite interest in the room. True, they were desperate, but nobody could be *this* desperate, he thought glumly. He was surprised that the man had the nerve to show the apartment without first having bulldozed the place out.

"It's a little messy," the landlord granted. "The ol' lady don't get off work till eleven, but if you want the room, I'll send her up as soon as she gets home. She can spruce it up a little." He ripped the tab off a beer can and took a long swallow as his eyes ran over Hilary suggestively. "Won't take long, once she gets her butt in gear."

Hilary clamped her hand over Garth's arm and began to squeeze tightly.

Garth glanced at her questioningly.

"My foot . . ." Hilary shuddered as a large brown roach scurried across her shoe and disappeared under the bed.

"Damn bugs! The exterminator was here last week, and the little varmints have been runnin' wild ever since." The landlord set his beer can down, jerked the metal bed away from the corner, and proceeded to stomp the offending creature into a greasy pulp.

So much for available room number two.

"Well, now what?"

In the taxi once more, Hilary sucked in the welcome fresh air and tried to forget the unspeakable carnage they had just witnessed.

Garth struggled to make a decision he'd avoided all evening. It looked as if he'd be forced to make it now.

"My grandparents have a beach house," he finally admitted.

Hilary glanced at him in disbelief. "Here . . . in West Creek?"

"Yes . . . but I didn't want to go there until tomorrow night."

"Why not?"

"My cousin Dorothy, her husband Frank, and the most obnoxious kids I've ever encountered—

that's why not," Garth confessed. "But even *they* are beginning to sound good."

"Are they staying at the cottage?"

"Yes, but they're supposed to leave tomorrow night. As much as I hate to admit it, I don't think we have any choice but to join them."

"I can stand it if you can," Hilary assured him.

Garth wasn't sure he could, but he figured his options had just run out.

The taxi eased to a stop in front of the cottage on Oceanside Drive. The weathered bungalow was surrounded by neatly manicured hedges. Garth paid the driver, grabbed the two Garfield shopping bags, and escorted Hilary up the sidewalk.

"What are we going to tell your cousin?" Hilary fretted. She could imagine how Dorothy would view her staying with Garth.

"I don't know about you, but I'm telling them good night. Then I'm going straight to bed."

"Not me. I'm heading straight for a hot bath."

"I don't see Frank's station wagon around anywhere. They must be out sightseeing." Garth reached under the mat to retrieve the extra key.

"I feel terrible just barging in like this."

"Wait until you meet Frank and Dorothy. You'll get over it."

"Garth!" Hilary frowned, and he grinned.

They stepped through the doorway, and Garth flipped on the lights. Setting the shopping bags on the small love seat, he walked into the living room, switching on lamps as he went. Hilary followed closely behind as her eyes appreciatively scanned the homey cottage.

"This is really nice," she said gratefully.

"Yeah, I always thought so. It has all of Gram's personal touches." Garth's smile was affectionate as he pointed toward the multicolored afghan that was draped across the back of the sofa.

"Did she do these?" Hilary was closely examining the finely detailed cross-stitched pictures that adorned the south wall.

"Yeah, those too. Wait until you see the kitchen—if the kids have left it standing. Grandpa is a carpenter by trade, or at least he was until he retired. He did all the cabinetwork."

Hilary followed him into the kitchen, and Garth switched on the lights.

If the living room echoed Garth's grandmother's creativity, the kitchen proved that his grandfather was equally talented. "My goodness, this is lovely!"

"You really like it?"

Hilary walked over to the cabinets and ran her hand over the polished oak admiringly. "This is exactly the sort of cabinet I'd like in my own home someday."

Garth smiled and thought of how Lisa would hate the cabinets. They wouldn't be modern enough for her. "Grandpa always says when I get married he'll build me a house."

Hilary's gaze met his shyly. "And are you planning on getting married soon?"

"No...not soon. How about you?" Garth regretted mentioning the subject as he saw the sadness come into her eyes. "Sorry, I didn't mean to remind you of Lenny."

"That's all right. Lenny and I never discussed marriage," she admitted.

"I date a woman who'd like to discuss it, but I'm not ready yet," Garth said.

"Oh."

Glancing at the kitchen table, Garth noticed a note propped against the ceramic salt shaker. He picked it up and read it, then released an audible sigh of relief. "Looks like we may have gotten our first piece of good luck."

Hilary glanced at her watch. "Let's note the hour, for posterity's sake," she joked.

"Looks like Frank decided to leave a day early so he could rest up before going back to the office."

"Oh. Well, at least that will make it easier for you." Hilary pulled a chair away from the kitchen table and sank onto it gratefully. She began absentmindedly rubbing her swollen ankle.

"That ankle still bothering you?"

"A little."

Garth knelt down and took her foot in his hand. The ankle was red and swollen to twice its normal size.

"Sit right there, and I'll have you fixed up in no time," he promised.

He rummaged beneath the kitchen sink and produced a small porcelain pan. He put the tea kettle on the burner to heat water, then poured a small amount into the pan a few minutes later. After adding cold water, he tested the temperature, then carefully slipped her shoe and ankle hose off and lowered her foot into the basin.

"How's that?"

"Fine." Actually, **Hilary** thought it was pretty close to heaven.

While she soaked her ankle, Garth rummaged through the pantry and retrieved a small first-aid kit. "Gram's always prepared," he explained as he opened the lid and reached for the Ace bandáge. "When you're through, I'll wrap it for you."

While Hilary indulged herself, Garth made them each a cup of tea, and they lapsed into an easy, relaxed conversation.

"So you're a flight controller," Hilary mused aloud. "That must be very interesting."

"Yes, I've always liked my job, but it can get hectic at times."

"Tell me something—how in the world do you keep all those planes from running intó one another?" Hilary asked.

Garth laughed. "Well, I don't. At least, I'm not responsible for *all* of them. Let's see, how can I explain it simply? The east-bound flights fly at odd altitudes—twenty-seven hundred, twenty-nine hundred, or thirty-one hundred feet, etcetera. West-bound flights fly at even altitudes."

"But doesn't that bring them dangerously close to one another?"

"No, not at all. They're separated by distances of a thousand feet vertically, and ten miles laterally."

"Then you agree that flying is the safest way to go?"

"The safest way *to go?*" Garth grinned. "We try to avoid that phrase; but yes, I believe the skies are safer than they've ever been, despite what you hear to the contrary. Between 1981 and 1985, the airlines flew one billion passengers through twenty-six million takeoffs and landings, with an average fatality rate of ninety per year. Compare that to the hundred and twenty-three people killed daily in car accidents—that's an average of forty-five thousand deaths a year. And flying is even safer than walking, which takes seven thousand lives a year."

"I don't mind the flying. It's the circling—when my plane hasn't been cleared to land—that makes me nervous," Hilary confessed.

"It shouldn't worry you. It's just a normal holding pattern when traffic's stacked up. The planes are still separated by a thousand feet, and they're being closely monitored on radar. When a plane at the bottom of the stack is cleared to approach and land, then the others are individually and systematically instructed to descend a thousand feet."

"Simple," Hilary jested.

"At times," he agreed.

It was nice to talk to each other. Hilary and Garth's moods were less pessimistic by the time Hilary had removed her foot from the basin a half hour later. She surveyed the foot and grinned. "It's beginning to shrivel." She gingerly lifted the waterlogged foot, and Garth reached for the towel. "I'll get that for you," he said.

"You don't have to. I can . . ." Hilary began to protest. She suddenly felt extremely shy. She reached for the towel, knocking it from his hand.

Bending to retrieve the linen, they found their

faces inches apart. The unexpected closeness caught them both by surprise.

"I can do that," she said softly.

"I'd like to do it for you."

Hilary had a fluttery feeling in the pit of her stomach. Garth's look was warm and suggestively intense.

As if a magnet were drawing them together, their mouths slowly moved toward each other. They touched.

His lips were sweet and inviting as they lingered on hers, caressing and light. Hilary closed her eyes and felt the room begin to tilt crazily. She held her breath, hoping he would take her in his arms and deepen the kiss. But as suddenly as it had begun, the embrace ended.

Garth cleared his throat and handed the towel to her. "Maybe you're right. You dry the foot, and I'll wrap it."

Hilary touched her tongue to her lips. She could still taste his presence. "All right."

When the ankle was properly wrapped, Garth suggested they go straight to bed. "There's only one bedroom, so I'll take the sofa," he offered.

"Please, take the bed. I don't mind sleeping on the sofa."

"The sofa will be fine. I'm so tense I'll have to take a sleeping pill to relax. Believe me . . . I'll be out in five minutes," Garth assured her.

Rummaging through the shopping bags, Garth found the package of T-shirts he'd purchased earlier. "You can sleep in one of these."

"Thanks. Would you care if I took a bath first?"

Visions of Hilary naked, soaking in a hot tub, rose up to tantalize Garth.

"No. Make yourself at home. There's a bathroom second door to the right. I'll use the one off the utility room."

"Thanks. Well, I guess I'll see you first thing in the morning."

"Yeah . . ." Garth's eyes moved over her lazily. "If you're up first, Gram keeps the coffee in the refrigerator."

"How do you like your eggs?"

Garth's eyes unwillingly dropped to the gentle swell of her breasts, and he was mortified to hear *his* voice saying, "Fried . . . with double yolks."

Chapter Eight

HILARY AND GARTH SAID GOOD night, and Hilary walked down the hall to Garth's grandparents' bedroom. She was still smiling.

The way Garth had looked at her a few minutes ago and the crazy· way her pulse had jumped when his gaze slid admiringly over her breasts ... Well, maybe Lenny wasn't going to be as hard to forget as she'd first thought.

Hilary opened the door and switched on the lamp beside the bed. The small bedroom emerged in a warm light. The furnishings were homey and comfortable, and the full-sized brass bed beckoned invitingly.

In minutes Hilary had slipped out of her blouse and jeans and had drawn a tub of hot water in the adjoining bath. Instead of a leisurely soak, however, she found she wanted to wash as quickly as possible and get into bed.

At Garth's suggestion, she availed herself of

Grace Redmond's liberal assortment of creams and lotions sitting on the vanity. Then she slipped into the T-shirt he'd handed her earlier.

The garment totally engulfed her petite frame, and Hilary found herself running her fingers sensually over the soft material, thinking about its owner.

Hilary knew Garth had never worn the shirt, yet she found herself visualizing how the material would lie against the broad expanse of his chest...the way it would mold and cling to all those muscles...With that tantalizing thought, she felt the beginnings of desire. It was strange. She would ordinarily be thinking about Lenny; yet now it was Garth—a man she had known for such a short time—who suddenly dominated her fantasies.

She pulled back the fluffy comforter on the bed and climbed between the crisp sheets. The mattress welcomed her tired body with a cushioning embrace. Outside, a shutter banged against the side of the cottage, and Hilary could hear the breakers rolling in from the Atlantic.

It seemed as if the wind had been picking up steadily all evening. Hilary hoped it wouldn't interfere with plane departures the following morning. She planned to go to Western Union and collect her money, then call the airport and book a flight to Denver. Soon this whole crazy escapade would be a memory...with the exception of Garth. Hilary had a feeling he was going to linger in her mind a good deal longer.

She lay in the dark, going over the past few hectic hours with a surprising fondness. How unexpectedly they'd come into each other's life.

Had his pulse raced as erratically as hers did when they touched? Snuggling more deeply within the folds of the comforter, Hilary warned herself that she was becoming much too attached to Garth Redmond.

For all she knew, he could be in love with the "Lisa" he had mentioned earlier...And there was Lenny to contend with...And Hilary didn't know a thing about Garth, other than the fact he was attractive...kind...understanding...incredibly gentle.

The memory of his unexpected kiss set off a series of flutters in the bottom of her stomach as she eventually drifted off to sleep.

Garth had to manhandle the stubborn sofa cushions. He unfolded the thin foam mattress from the metal cage of the sofa, then rummaged for ten minutes before he found an extra blanket and pillow in the hall closet.

As he passed Hilary's room, he wondered if she was asleep. He had heard her moving about earlier, but all was quiet now.

Running his tongue over his lips, he could still taste the faint traces of her lipstick. Why was it that one kiss had aroused him so swiftly, so unexpectedly, so fully that he had had to fight the urge to make a pass at her? Crazy, that's what it was. The woman was not only dangerous to his libido but together they made a dangerous couple. It was as if a curse were on both of them, yet Garth found Hilary increasingly appealing.

Slipping off his shoes, he climbed into bed,

then tried to remove his pants beneath the sheet. Snagging his sore toe in the metal frame of the sleeper, he bit his lower lip to stifle an agonizing moan.

Damn! Might as well try sleeping on a bed of nails!

The thin slice of foam rubber, which someone had mistakenly labeled a mattress, had a tendency to curl up slightly at either end; and the metal support bar across the middle seemed determined to become embedded in the base of his spine.

Rolling back out onto the floor, Garth reached for his trousers and withdrew the small packet a doctor had given him a few months ago when he'd complained of a succession of sleepless nights. The strong medication was to be taken only when necessary, but Garth knew, at the rate he was going, he had to have it now.

He walked into the kitchen, drew a glass of water, and popped one of the pills into his mouth. A few moments later he was back in bed, trying to find a safe harbor away from the tormenting support bar.

As the sleeping pill began to take effect, Garth's eyelids drooped heavily. Hilary's image floated temptingly before him. Hilary...sleeping in the next room, in his shirt...unrestricted...unencompassed...eggs...

Garth groaned and rolled onto his stomach. He slammed the pillow over his head to block out the sound of the wind and his confused thoughts.

* * *

Lori Copeland

Sometime around three in the morning, Garth flipped over on his back. He could hear the wind howling outside the beach house.

Ordinarily he was a light sleeper; but under the influence of the medication, he found it nearly impossible to open his eyes. Trying to fight off the effects of the sleeping pill, Garth finally managed to sit upright in bed.

He shook his head in an effort to clear his vision. His eyes narrowed as he focused on the large protuberance at the bottom of his bed. Groping at the bulge in the blankets, he jumped when he heard a feminine voice respond in a sleepy tone.

Sometime during the night, Hilary had crawled into bed with him. She recoiled when a hand touched her bare bottom.

"What in the...Hilary, is that you?" Garth leaned over and heatedly addressed the bulge.

"Yes" came the muffled reply.

"What are you doing?"

"Trying to sleep."

"In *my* bed?"

"Yes."

Garth sighed and ran his hand through his tousled hair. "You want to come out of there?"

It was hard enough for Garth to ignore his growing attraction to her. Now she was in his bed...

There was a slight pause; then Hilary slowly emerged from beneath the blanket. She was embarrassed he'd caught her, but she quickly decided that the sense of security she'd felt while snuggled safely under the covers was worth the sacrifice. It had been either join Garth in his bed, or continue to lie petrified in her own while her mind amplified the sound of the wind as it slapped angrily at the beach house.

Hilary crept out of the sheets, up the long, muscular length of his body, and settled easily on his chest. It was much wider than she had first estimated. He was bare-chested and undeniably gorgeous. Hilary wasn't usually so audacious; yet she felt completely at ease lying on top of him.

Garth's eyes met hers distraughtly. "*Now* what are you doing?" The feel of her lying pressed tightly against his bare chest sent his hormones on a rampage.

"The wind is blowing," Hilary explained lamely, realizing that he was probably going to demand that she go back to her own room.

"So?" His voice was still thick with sleep.

"So ... I was frightened ..." Her fingers slipped through the thick mat of hair on his chest and lingered there.

"Frightened? Why were you ... Stop that!" Garth removed her hands, but she quickly wrapped her arms around him and buried her face in his neck.

"Please, I've always been terrified of the wind," Hilary pleaded. "Just let me stay here with you for a while."

Garth tried to shift her, aware that she was going to be shocked if she moved in the wrong direction.

"Look"—he eased her to his side, settling her in his arms as he would a small child—"there's nothing to be afraid of. It's just a little wind."

"I was in a tornado once," she confessed, trying

to offer him some sort of explanation for her radical change in behavior. "I was terrified."

Garth felt a shudder ripple through her, and he pulled her closer. "Okay, if it makes you feel any better, you can stay with me for a while." He was too tired to think straight, and she was doing crazy things to his libido. But it was a mistake to let her stay, and he knew it.

Hilary sighed, and her arms tightened around his neck appreciatively. "Thank you."

Garth lay back on the pillow and closed his eyes for a moment. He felt fuzzy and lightheaded from the medication. He drifted off for a moment, thinking about Hilary in his arms. He desired her. Wouldn't any man in his right mind? But he wasn't thinking clearly. They'd known each other only a few hours, and Garth wasn't about to jump into what could easily become a sticky situation.

But she felt incredibly good in his arms. Soft and tiny like a kitten . . . and she smelled so feminine. The tantalizing scent drifted over Garth . . . Her bare legs were next to his, and they felt as smooth as silk next to his hair-roughened ones.

Garth stirred restlessly. "Hilary . . . about you and Lenny Ricetrum—"

"Please, I don't want to talk about Lenny."

"Are you sure? You've been pretty upset about him." Garth absentmindedly began to caress the outline of her bare thigh. Maybe if he reminded her of Lenny she'd realize that they were putting themselves in a dangerous position, lying this close . . .

"Lenny seems like a million years ago," Hilary confessed as she snuggled more deeply into his arms. It wasn't Lenny who was upsetting her. It was Garth. Hilary was afraid he would realize what his hand was doing—and stop.

But his hand continued to meander slowly up the silken length of her. Supple fingers paused once or twice to massage the small of her back.

Hilary, secure in the realization that he *did* realize what he was doing, began to relax.

"You shouldn't do that," she protested half-heartedly when he touched pleasure points, causing a quickening of her pulse. She hated herself because she couldn't manage to sound more convincing.

"Just relax," he murmured smoothly, and his hand continued its alluring path up her spine, sensuously kneading and exploring her satiny skin. Even in his sluggish state, Garth knew he should stop. But he couldn't—even if he'd wanted to. Wasn't she openly inviting him to take advantage of the situation? Together in the same bed, she was clinging to him as if they were already lovers.

His mouth lowered slowly to search for hers, and a thrill shot through him when he found hers eagerly waiting.

They kissed, their soft murmurs of pleasure blending as his hand moved under the T-shirt to her bare breasts.

The kiss deepened, and Hilary felt herself go limp in his arms as the gusts shook the house with growing ferocity.

She realized that what she was doing was rash and totally out of character, yet she was returning his kiss with a reckless abandon, pressing ever closer...encouraging his advances...almost begging for them.

Had the past few hours indeed pushed her over the brink to insanity?

Garth shifted his weight, and his kisses became more ardent as he pressed her back against the pillows.

"Garth..." Hilary murmured as their mouths parted a few moments later. He nibbled warm kisses down the column of her neck. "Is there another woman...?"

"Another woman?"

"Is there someone special in your life?" Hilary hesitated to ask, but the answer could make a difference.

"No." Garth started to kiss her again, and then he paused. Lisa seemed so distant since he'd left Chicago. Almost as if she no longer existed in his life. "No, that's not quite true." He amended what he'd said. "I've been seeing a woman for the past few months, but we're not engaged."

"Do you plan to marry her?"

"No." The finality of his answer surprised him. A heavy weight felt as if it had suddenly been lifted off his shoulders. "No, I don't," Garth repeated again more firmly. "I just realized that."

"What we're doing is reckless," Hilary warned, teasing his mouth with the tip of her tongue. "We barely know each other."

"I know."

"I don't make a habit of this."

"That's nice to know." He rolled over with her in his arms and began to slide the T-shirt up over her head.

"Garth." Hilary's eyes met his, and he saw confusion clouding the pools of glistening blue sapphires. "I don't want you to think I'm easy." She had gone mad. There was no longer any doubt in Hilary's mind.

"I don't think that." He kissed the tip of her nose, then took her mouth again as his fingers began to arouse her with an expertise that left her breathless. Garth was careful to keep his own desire in check as their passions began to soar. Hilary heard his suppressed moan, and her own spiraling needs urged him on.

Garth murmured her name urgently as the storm continued to build.

Hilary was suddenly seized with panic. What was she doing in his arms, about to let him make love to her? She didn't know a thing about him. It seemed imperative that they know *something* about each other!

"How many children are there in your family?"

"What?"

"Children . . . do you have any brothers and sisters?"

"Two younger brothers."

"I have an older sister. What's your favorite dessert?"

"Cheesecake."

"I favor lemon pie."

"That's nice." Garth's mouth took hers fiercely.

"School?"

"What?"

"Where did you go to school?"

"In Chicago . . . Why?"

"Are you a college graduate?"

"Yes...Are you?"

"Yes." They rolled over, and Garth lay on top of her now.

"What about your grades?"

"They were okay...I made the Dean's honor roll."

Hilary felt her heart sink. She'd been lucky to eke out passing grades.

"What kind of a car do you drive?"

"Damn it, Hilary! Do we have to discuss this right now?"

"No, I just thought we should know something about each other."

"I know I'm going crazy," Garth whispered. "Let's talk later."

Hilary decided she'd found out all she needed to know.

In his arms she found a joy, an awareness she had never known before. He was gentle yet firm, demanding yet giving, eager to have her experience the ultimate fulfillment along with him. She knew she was falling in love and was powerless to stop it.

Garth suddenly groaned as he lost control. He joined her in completion, and they soared and spiraled in the climax of their loving. Tears rolled unabashedly down Hilary's cheeks at the beauty of the moment.

"What's the matter?" Garth whispered once the tides of passion had crested explosively, then slowly began to ebb.

"It was so...perfect."

He smiled and wiped the wetness off her cheeks

with his thumbs. "It isn't anything to cry about."

"I cry when I'm happy."

"And when you're sad . . . and when you're hungry . . . and when you're—"

Hilary tenderly covered his mouth with her hand. "True. I'm a mess."

"No, you're beautiful," Garth corrected her. Hilary was sure she saw something very close to love in his eyes. "And you've made me very happy." Their mouths met again affectionately.

"The wind is getting worse," Hilary murmured a few moments later as Garth settled her in the crook of his arm.

"If it'll make you feel better, I'll take a look outside," Garth offered sleepily. "Those old shutters have always been loose, and when they rattle it makes the wind sound worse than it really is."

"I would feel better . . . but be careful."

"I planned on it." Garth slid out of bed and immediately stubbed his sore toe on the metal leg of the bed. He hopped painfully on one foot as Hilary wadded the corner of the sheet in her mouth to keep from laughing.

He looked at her incredulously. "You think this is funny?"

Hilary quickly sobered up. She shook her head, no.

Garth stepped into his pants and yanked the zipper closed. "I'm going to lose that toe if I hit it one more time!" he grumbled.

Hilary agreed and stuffed the sheet into her mouth again, her eyes crinkling with suppressed laughter.

Garth reached over to tickle her ribs, and she

collapsed on the pillow. They wrestled on the unsteady frame for a few minutes before it threatened to collapse. He finally kissed her again and got up. His head spun like a top, and he groped for support.

"Damn! I should never have taken that sleeping pill."

"How strong was it?"

"Enough to knock a bull moose out cold for twenty-four hours."

Hilary grinned. "Go check the shutters; then we'll both try and get some sleep."

"Believe me, Ms. Brookfield, there are very few women I would go out at this hour to check a shutter for," Garth complained.

He slipped his jacket on and opened the front door. The sudden impact of the violent wind threatened to knock him off his feet. "Holy..." he exclaimed. It was pitch-black, but from where Garth stood he could see that the trees lining the cobblestone walk were practically bent over double in their surrender to the strong gales. In the distance he could hear the roar of the breakers rolling in from the ocean.

"What's the matter?" Hilary was waiting just inside the door.

"The wind... It's going crazy."

"I told you so."

"Those breakers have to be at least four feet high," he exclaimed.

"Is it a hurricane?"

"I don't know. Stay where you are." Garth shut the door, and Hilary crept back into the warmth of the bed.

She plumped the pillow, keeping one ear tuned to the wind as she thought about the way Garth had made love to her. Was it possible that only a few hours ago she was crying over a lost love, and now she could barely remember what Lenny looked like?

Was it possible to fall in love with a man so totally, so completely, in such a short span of time? Or was it merely the strange set of circumstances she and Garth found themselves in that caused the strong attraction? Hilary wasn't sure.

Intimacy was an act she'd never taken lightly. She viewed sex as a serious commitment moment, but she didn't know how Garth felt about the subject. Hilary rolled over and stared at the front door. Where was he? He'd been gone only for a few minutes, she reminded herself. He couldn't possibly have had time to fix the shutters...But then it was so dark and windy out there. What if something had happened to him? Panic seized her as she hurriedly slipped out of bed. Wrapping herself in the blanket, she hobbled to the door and pulled it open.

Oh, my gosh! She held her breath in awe. She had never seen such violent winds. "What is it?" Hilary had to shout to make herself heard.

Garth was busy trying to secure one of the flapping shutters. "What?" He cupped a hand to his ear questioningly.

"I said is it a hurricane?" Hilary shouted.

"Hurricane?"

She nodded.

"I don't think so. I think the season's over." Garth leapt back up on the porch as an icy rain started to plummet down from the overcast sky.

Hilary went in search of a towel as he shrugged out of his wet jacket. Moments later she returned and handed him the towel.

"If it isn't a hurricane, what is it?"

"I have no idea. I suppose it could be a hurricane, but they're usually over by mid-November." Garth vigorously rubbed his hair dry with the towel. "But by the looks of things, I'd say we're in for something more than a typical winter storm."

"With the way our luck's been running, I'd have to agree."

Garth glanced up and grinned. "Let's see... What could be worse than a hurricane?" he prompted.

"Typhoon?"

"I doubt it. We're on the Atlantic side."

"Not for long," Hilary predicted. "Not the way that wind is blowing."

Garth pitched the towel on a chair and walked into the kitchen to switch on the radio. He scanned the range of the dial but couldn't find a weather report. He set the dial on an easy-listening station, realizing that most stations have periodic weather announcements.

Hilary kept glancing out of the window and pacing back and forth across the floor nervously. Garth was still trying to fight off the effect of the sleeping pill, so he wandered back into the living room and draped himself across the sofa.

"Are you going to sleep—in this storm?" Hilary asked.

"No." Garth yawned. "I'm just resting my

eyes." His voice trailed off sleepily as he began to get warm.

Hilary shook her head in disbelief, then went into the kitchen to get closer to the radio.

Garth nodded off briefly, only to be awakened a few minutes later by Hilary tapping on his shoulder.

"Huh?" He tried to force his heavy lids to open.

"What's a 'ziggy'?"

"A what?"

"A *ziggy*."

"Some sort of a model . . . I think." Both eyes drooped shut again.

Hilary shook his shoulder. "No, that was Twiggy! What's a *ziggy*?"

"Damned if I know." Garth tried to cover his ears with a pillow, but Hilary blocked the effort.

"Listen, Garth. There's something really strange going on. Wake up!" She reached over and turned up the volume of the small radio she had brought in from the kitchen.

". . . We interrupt this broadcast again for an updated report on the winter-storm watch. The National Weather Service has issued a severe winter-storm warning for the entire coastal region. Winds gusting up to fifty miles per hour, unusually high tides, and surging waves are expected. The National Weather Service has urged residents to complete all safety precautions and evacuate to higher ground inland as soon as possible."

Hilary listened wide-eyed as the weather forecaster continued his gloomy report.

"The severe coastal storm is being attributed

to the nearly straight-line configuration of the earth, sun, and moon. It is estimated that this alignment takes place once in every eighteen and a half years. *Syzygy* is the technical term for this celestial lineup, which occurs when the moon is aligned directly opposite the earth and sun, or between the two bodies. Both sun and moon are far south of the equator; and the moon is at perigee—its closest approach to the earth in a month. Either alignment causes a bulging of the tides in some areas of the earth. Keep tuned for updated reports—"

Having heard all he needed to for the time being, Garth reached over and switched off the radio.

"What are you doing?"

"Eighteen and a half years! And the syzygy picks this time to show up again!" Garth smacked his pillow angrily.

Hilary watched as he slowly rolled to his feet, trying to focus his vision.

"Where are you going?"

"Apparently this thing is going to get a whole lot worse before it gets any better. We've got work to do."

"Don't you think we should leave?" Hilary trailed helplessly along behind him as he went in search of a rain slicker.

"And how do you suggest we do that—call a taxi?" he asked dryly.

"We could try."

"Check the phones. I'm betting most of the lines are down in this area."

When Hilary picked up the receiver, she was

met with an ominous silence. Her face grew pale. "What will we do?"

Garth paused and pulled her up to his chest. He tipped her face up to give her a brief, reassuring kiss. "I'm sorry. I know you're scared, and I have to admit I'm a little concerned myself. But we'll be fine."

"I'm frightened."

"After what we've been through? Living through a little 'ziggy' should be a breeze!" He made light of their predicament.

"Are you going out again?"

"Yes. We can't just sit here. My grandparents keep a good supply of plywood out in the garage. They've lived through a few coastal storms in their time." Garth smiled encouragingly. "Quit worrying."

"Oh, Garth! This is all my fault."

"Why?"

"I saw that 'ziggy' word mentioned in the newspaper, but I didn't bother to read what it meant."

"It's *syzygy*." Garth pronounced the word *SIZ-uh-jee*. "And don't feel guilty. I'm the one who's at fault. I knew about the storm watch for this area, but as of yesterday the forecasters hadn't been able to predict how serious it would be. Besides, I was so preoccupied with my own problems that I didn't pay much attention."

Hilary appreciated Garth's attempts to minimize her fear. "Do you really think we'll be safe here?"

Garth nodded. "I'd better get at it, though. I've got a lot of nails to drive."

"I'll help."

"What about your ankle?"

"It's fine." Hilary forced herself not to limp as she turned toward the bedroom to get dressed.

Garth caught her arm to detain her. "Hey, lady"—he pulled her back into his embrace and kissed her again with incredible tenderness—"you're okay, you know that?" he asked when their lips finally parted.

"Thank you. I've been hoping you'd notice." They kissed once more; then he swatted her bottom playfully and sent her on to get dressed.

Nailing the bulky sheets of plywood over the windows was a slow, tedious process. Especially when one of the carpenters was trying to fight off the sluggish aftermath of a sleeping pill, and the other one was trying to keep her weight off the sprained ankle she kept forgetting about.

Despite deep yawns and countless ouches, the work was eventually completed.

Around midnight the tired twosome stood back to assess their work. Garth watched Hilary's eyes as they reflected pride in their accomplishment.

She'd sure proved to be made of stronger stuff than he would have expected from the weeping, helpless girl he'd encountered twenty-four hours ago. If she hadn't held the awkward sheets of plywood, Garth would still be struggling to nail them to the window frames. She'd taken time out to brew a pot of strong coffee, and they had drunk several cups as they continued to work.

"I wish we'd had enough plywood to cover the garage windows," Hilary brooded.

"They'll be easy enough to replace."

With the work completed, Garth changed his mind about staying through the brunt of the storm. "Maybe we should try to get to higher ground, now that the house is secured."

"All right. But first"—Hilary pointed to a faint light in the distance—"we need to see if those people need our help."

Garth glanced at the cottage occupied year-round by the Johnsons. They were near his grandparents' age; and the last time Garth had seen Ben, arthritis had taken its toll on the aging man's hands.

The self-designated rescue team hurriedly headed into the wind and crossed the yard.

Ben and Esther Johnson welcomed the offer of assistance. Hilary and Garth pitched in and worked throughout the night, praying that their efforts would save the cottage from complete destruction.

"Don't you think we should try to get to higher ground, Ben?" Garth asked as the last of the windows was sealed off.

"Nope. Me and Esther's been through some pretty rough times. We'll be staying."

Garth glanced at Hilary, who smiled. The strain of the past few hours was evident on her pretty features. "We'll be staying with you—if you don't mind," Garth said.

"Nope. Welcome the company."

The brunt of the storm was predicted to hit around three that morning. Ben, Esther, Hilary, and Garth sat huddled in the Johnsons' living room to wait out the raging winter storm.

Around two o'clock, Esther and Ben nodded off to sleep.

"Are you doing okay?" Garth whispered as he cradled Hilary in his arms. They were sitting on the sofa, listening to the rain pounding on the weathered roof.

"I'm fine. Just a little tired." Hilary yawned as she rested her head on Garth's shoulder. She was exhausted, but she had never been happier. "How's your cold?"

"I hadn't thought much about it. I guess it's better."

"Good. You tired?"

"Yeah, bushed." Garth sighed as he stretched long legs out in front of him and rested his head against hers.

"Garth...about what happened earlier."

Garth didn't answer for a moment. Somehow he sensed he wanted to talk about the intimacy they'd shared, but he wasn't sure he did. He needed time to sort through his mixed feelings. Though he couldn't explain it, he knew Hilary had touched a portion of his heart that no other woman had ever touched before. Finally, he responded to her prompting. "What about it?" he asked softly.

Hilary moved her head until it rested comfortably on his chest. Her finger toyed lightly with the button on his shirt. "I'll never forget tonight...or you."

Garth stroked her hair affectionately. "I won't forget either." She felt so small and helpless in his arms...so *right!*

"Will you call me occasionally?"

Garth chuckled. "What do you want me to call you?"

Hilary sighed. "Darling ... sweetheart ... honey ..."

He sighed and buried his face in her hair. He wasn't sure if she was teasing or not.

Hilary laughed, and she could tell he was considerably relieved. "Just call to say hello once in a while. Let me know how you are ... where you are ..."

Hilary couldn't imagine not ever seeing him again, but she knew it was entirely possible, once they went their separate ways.

"Sure. Why not? And you can give me a ring every now and then."

She decided to pay him back for his earlier jibe. "What sort of ring do you want?"

"Is this where I'm supposed to say 'a wedding ring'?" Garth asked calmly.

Hilary raised her face to meet his, her heart suddenly in her eyes. "Of course not ... Unless you want to."

Garth chuckled at her candor and kissed her deeply, drawing a response from deep within.

When their lips parted many long moments later, he promised softly, "I'll think of you often."

"Make sure that you do!" Hilary wanted more—much more. But it was a start.

"I'm hungry."

"Me too." Their mouths touched, lingered, reluctant to part.

"We'll eat a steak ten inches thick when this is all over," he promised, trailing a finger through a damp strand of her hair.

"You'll have to buy it for me," she reminded him.

"I'll buy you the moon if you want it." His mouth closed hungrily over hers again, sealing the promise with another long kiss.

Exhausted from the hard work and the all-night exposure to cold winds, they settled down in each other's arms and dozed, secure in the knowledge that, at least for the moment, they still had each other.

Chapter Nine

THE WINTER STORM RAGED FOR hours. Fierce winds pounded at the thin sheets of plywood nailed to the windows, and cold rain poured from repeated cloudbursts, promising the aftermath of severe flooding.

It seemed Mother Nature was intent upon showing the true force of the power she held over the elements. Even the salty sea responded to her show of uncompromising strength as it hurled its brutal waves against the deserted shoreline.

Hilary lay listening to the wind. Her stomach rolled turbulently as she thought of being devoured by the angry ocean. The only thing that kept her from succumbing to her terror was the comfort of Garth's arms. With him by her side, she felt she could endure anything.

The storm continued for what seemed like endless hours before it finally began to abate. With dawn came the calming of the ruthless winds, although the rising sun was still obscured behind a thick mass of clouds.

"It looks like it's about over." Ben stood at the front door of the cottage and viewed the aftermath of destruction, thankful that the cottage had survived another onslaught.

Garth stirred on the sofa and gently nudged Hilary. "Come on sleepyhead. We need to check on Gram's cottage."

"Is it finally over?" Hilary sat up self-consciously, trying to arrange her tousled hair into some semblance of order.

"It's still raining, but the winds are beginning to let up." Garth was anxious to view the storm's damage.

Hilary and Garth stepped out onto the porch a few minutes later. The ravaged remains that greeted them were distressing.

Trees were down, their sharp, splintery ends a mere mockery of the splendid strength they had once possessed. The front lawn of the cottage had been turned into a small lake.

Garth and Hilary descended the steps to wade ankle-deep in icy water. It was no longer pouring, just an icy drizzle fell from the clouds.

"Your cold, Garth . . . It will get worse," Hilary fretted as they sloshed their way across the yard.

Garth sneezed and pulled the slicker up closer to his face. "Watch where you're going. There's a lot of debris."

Shattered pieces of wood drifted past, fragments of small abandoned boats that had fallen prey to the pulverizing winds. In the distance they could see a deserted beach house bobbing, roofless, in the turgid waters. The structure had been too weak to withstand the main onslaught of the storm.

Garth threaded his way along the beach while Hilary followed, clinging to his jacket for stability.

"And what, fair lady, should we do on this third day of our lovely vacation?" Garth joked as he stopped long enough to sneeze a couple of times into his handkerchief. "I'm sick of all this relaxation! Let's do something exciting!"

Going along with his sudden spurt of joviality, Hilary pretended to give the matter serious thought. "Oh, dear, I don't know. There's so much we haven't done, yet. Earthquakes, locust plagues, aviational disasters—"

"Oh, sorry. I almost covered that one on my flight to Raleigh, but everything turned out all right at the last minute."

"Honestly?"

"Honestly. The landing gear malfunctioned on my plane," Garth admitted.

"Well, I suppose that makes up for the blowout my cab had on the way to Stapleton ... and for my sprained ankle."

"Yeah, I suppose that makes us even-up on good times."

They looked at each other and grinned. "At least *you* aren't half blind," Hilary said accusingly. "I lost my contact at the airport."

"I know. I stepped on it."

Her mouth dropped open. "You *what!*"

"I can see ..."—Garth ignored her astonishment and went on listing his miseries—"I just can't breathe because of the pneumonia I got when my cab was stuck in traffic, and I was forced to run the rest of the way to O'Hare."

By now, each of them was striving hard to keep a straight face.

"You had plenty of time to buy cold pills during the layover in Raleigh," she said reproachfully.

"No, I spent those particular eight hours handing out clean handkerchiefs to some strange— and I do mean strange—woman who was crying every time I looked up."

"How sad!" Hilary's grin widened. "You didn't have cold pills in your luggage?"

"I didn't *have* luggage by that time."

"But you could have purchased some when you arrived at your hotel."

"Oh, by then I had my luggage back," he conceded.

"You did?"

"Yes, only the hotel burned down, and I lost it again."

They lost their composure at the same time and began laughing over their ridiculous string of bad luck. Hilary sagged weakly against him, and he almost went down in the water.

"You should have seen your face when Lenny grabbed you around the throat!"

Garth steadied himself and looked at her incredulously, shocked that she would have the gall to mention the humiliating incident. Hilary dissolved in a new round of merriment.

"You thought that was funny? You're sick! That baboon could have broken my neck!"

Hilary nodded sympathetically. "I know!"

She dissolved in laughter again, but Garth shook his head in disgust. He hadn't found Lenny Ricetrum all that amusing.

When Hilary's giddiness had finally passed, Garth reached over and pulled her to him for an overdue good-morning kiss.

"Hell of a vacation, Ms. Brookfield, but you've definitely made it worthwhile," he said a few moments later.

"Thank you, Mr. Redmond. We must do it again sometime."

As they neared the Redmond cottage, they were relieved to see that it was still standing. Garth didn't even mind that its shingles were all curled or that the windows of the garage had been blown out during the night. As they drew nearer, the waters were beginning to recede.

"My feet are like blocks of ice," Hilary complained. She huddled more deeply into the lining of her jacket.

"Mine too." Garth sneezed again.

Until last night his cold had seemed to be getting better. This morning there was a tightness in his chest, and the cold water he was standing in set him shivering with a renewed chill.

Garth reached over and took Hilary's hand as they walked around the corner of the garage. "I want a hot cup of coffee and some dry clothing."

The sight of Lenny Ricetrum sitting on the front porch was the last thing Garth had expected. Hilary stopped abruptly when she saw him. She tugged warningly on Garth's jacket as he trudged on toward the porch, ignoring the unwelcomed visitor.

"Uh-oh . . . Look who's here."

"I noticed, but *he* can move on this time."

"But, Garth . . ."

Garth ignored her protests, and they continued walking toward the cottage. Personally he planned to ignore the two hundred and twenty pounds of foreboding flesh sitting on the doorstep.

Lenny stood up and crossed his arms. His look openly dared them to try and walk past him.

Garth had just about had it. What was supposed to have been a relaxing vacation had turned into a nightmare of unbelievable proportions. From the very start of this bizarre journey two days ago—*just two days ago*, Garth thought despairingly—he'd run into one disaster after another. Now, to add to his problems, he'd become intimate with Hilary Brookfield, who just happened to have an ex-boyfriend who was big enough to hunt bear with a switch.

What had he done to deserve this?

The sight of the baboon who had earlier tried to twist his neck off, who was now trying to block the entrance to *his* home, kindled a spark of anger in Garth.

"How did you find us, Lenny?" Hilary demanded as they approached the porch.

"Let's just say I'm not as dumb as you think I am."

"I didn't say I thought you were dumb. I just thought I had made it clear that I was going to need a little time to think about our situation—"

"Can it, Hilary!" Lenny interrupted curtly. "This is between me and ol' lover boy right now."

"My name is not *lover boy*, Ricetrum, and I don't appreciate your talking to Hilary in that tone of voice," Garth warned. His brown eyes sparkled with a stubbornness Hilary had never seen there before.

"Lenny, I want you to leave." Hilary hurriedly stepped between the two men. She was afraid Lenny would actually hurt Garth this time.

Garth calmly set her aside.

"But, Garth!"

"I can take care of this, Hilary."

"Hilary, I told you to can it!" Lenny snapped.

"And I told you, I don't want you talking to Hilary like that." Garth stepped forward, meeting Lenny's cold stare with one equally glacial.

"Oh, yeah? How would you like me to talk to you—with these!" Lenny doubled up his two beefy fists and shook them threateningly at Garth.

Garth stiffened with resentment. "Be my guest!"

Hilary clamped her hand over her mouth as Lenny suddenly sprang from the porch like a panther.

The force of a man twice his weight slamming into him so abruptly promptly knocked Garth back flat on his back. Lenny gripped Garth's head, landing a brutal punch to the right eye. It split the skin wide open on impact. Blinded by mud and blood, Garth struggled to deliver his own blows.

Hilary stood paralyzed with fear, watching the

unfairly matched pair as they rolled around in the mud. The tumbling finally halted with Lenny sitting straddled across Garth's chest.

"Come on, Ricetrum! Can't we discuss this like two adults—" Garth's plea was cut off as another meaty fist slammed into his mouth. He swore and rolled his head to one side to spit blood.

The two began frantically wallowing around again at Hilary's feet. She realized she'd have to do something—and fast.

The sight of blood oozing from the cuts on Garth's face gave her the strength she needed. She crouched aggressively as her temper surfaced in full force.

"Lenny, you get off him this instant!" Like a mean bantam rooster, Hilary flew between the two struggling men.

In her eagerness to assist Garth, she slipped and fell facedown in the mud. She paused only long enough to rake away the gook from her eyes. Crawling the rest of the way on her hands and knees, she pounced on Lenny's back.

"What are you doing?" Lenny tried to shake the unexpected wildcat off his back. But Hilary's fingers grabbed a hunk of his black hair and jerked painfully. Lenny let out a yell, and the momentary distraction afforded Garth a well-targeted right to Lenny's face.

As Lenny's hands shot up to protect his nose, Garth was busy trying to free himself. Lenny's fruitless efforts to sling Hilary off his back left her head spinning long after his attempts had slowed down.

"I said let him go, Lenny!" Hilary enunciated

in an ominous voice just before she yanked hard on his hair again.

"*Ouch!* All right, all right! Damn it, Hilary! Let go of my hair!"

Finally giving up on his hoped-for reconciliation, Lenny lifted himself from Garth, whose face was completely covered with mud.

Lenny made a feeble attempt to straighten his dishevelled clothing. He could take a hint. It was obvious that Hilary was no longer interested in him.

Reaching up to rub his smarting head, Lenny gave it one more try. "I'm warning you, Hilary. I'm flying back to Denver in an hour, and if you don't come with me right now I'm washing my hands of you—permanently."

Hilary rose to her feet unsteadily, her clothing covered with thick mud. "Well, happy trails to you!"

Lenny shot her a dirty look and stalked off angrily to his rented car. Moments later he wheeled out of sight.

Garth sat up and stared at the muddy woman who had come to his rescue. Even with her hair dripping filth, Hilary was nothing short of beautiful as she hovered over him and offered her hand in assistance.

Garth lifted one brow wryly. "Happy trails to you?"

Hilary shrugged. "I couldn't think of anything better."

Though he realized he would have a shiner later on, Garth couldn't remember when his spirits had been higher. Hilary had flatly refused to go back with the jerk.

Hilary put a protective arm around Garth and helped him carefully to his feet. "We'd better get you into some dry clothes."

"*We?*" Garth grinned.

"You're sure a frisky little devil—right after the tar's been beaten out of you!" Hilary chided. She decided to ignore his suggestive tone. "Lean on me."

"I didn't get the tar beaten out of me," Garth protested. "Ricetrum's going to have a black eye too." He draped his arm around her neck and nuzzled her ear playfully. "Um . . . you taste like mud!"

Hilary avoided his amorous advances and pointed him in the direction of the cottage. "Let's get you into the shower and rinse off some of this mud before it sets like cement."

"Will you get in with me?"

She blushed. "You're getting awfully bold."

"It's our vacation! We should have a little fun," Garth complained. He felt good. She'd actually refused to go back with Ricetrum!

While Hilary adjusted the water temperature in the shower, Garth examined his injuries in the mirror. He decided he hadn't come out all that badly. He could've been dead!

He licked the salty blood off his split lower lip and frowned. "Why couldn't you have been dating a hundred-pound weakling?"

Hilary grinned. "You did okay."

"I did, didn't I? Did you see that right punch I threw at him?"

"I saw. It was impressive. Come over here."

Garth obeyed and she helped him—clothes and all—into the shower. When he was safely in the stall she started to close the door, but he reached out and grabbed her hand.

"Now, stop—"

"Get in with me."

"No!"

"Yes! You know something?" His eyes met hers, and Hilary felt she could see right into his soul. And it looked as if he had feelings that he couldn't comprehend himself.

"No, what?" She knew she shouldn't take the bait, but she did anyway.

"For a minute I was afraid you would go back with Ricetrum," he confessed.

"Would that have bothered you?"

He smiled back at her. "Yes . . . I think it would have."

Hilary felt the return of butterflies in her stomach. "I'm glad. Lenny Ricetrum is history, as far as I'm concerned. I'm not sure what I ever saw in him."

"I'm not either. I didn't think he was your type," Garth admitted as he pulled her into the shower with him. He wrapped his arms around her waist possessively. "Kiss me."

Hilary didn't wait to be invited twice. She moved into his waiting arms, and they exchanged a long, satisfying kiss.

"Are you hungry?" he murmured sexily against her lips.

"Ravenous!"

"Me too!"

They both knew they weren't talking about food.

With a control that had his insides trembling, Garth's hand captured her chin and his thumb gently caressed her lips. "Thank you."

"For what?"

"For standing up for me against Lenny."

Hilary could feel the sweet pulse of desire coursing through her as he began to peel away her muddy clothing. "I can't explain how I felt when I saw you were in danger..."

"Try!" Garth urged as he quickly stripped out of his clothing, then pulled her close so that her bare body was pressed against his.

"I was frightened...I was so afraid Lenny would hurt you...and I didn't know what I would do if he did." Hilary's words dissolved as she felt the touch of his lips on her breast.

"You're beautiful," he whispered as the tip of his tongue moved with unbearable lightness across her skin. Waves of pleasure surged through her as he continued the sensuous assault. "And desirable...exciting..."

Hilary curled her fingers into the thick mass of his hair, pressing her body against his solid, comforting length. Nibbling lightly at the lobe of his ear, she added one other description, which only served to send a hot shaft of desire ricocheting through him.

"And very wicked!" Garth scolded.

"That wasn't wicked."

"Who told you it wasn't?" His mouth caught hers demandingly.

After a long, arousing kiss Garth whispered his

own observation, and she laughed softly.

"You're terrible!"

Garth chuckled and gave her a big bear hug. "You know what?"

"No, what?"

"This has been a terrible vacation, but I can't remember ever feeling as good as I do right now."

Hilary laughed, sharing his jubilant mood. She was happy, but she had to remind herself to keep the whirlwind relationship in perspective. The feelings were still too new for her to hope they could ever last.

As the hot-water heater's supply began to run out, Garth lifted her into his arms and stepped out of the shower.

"Garth ... we shouldn't," Hilary warned. Barely controlled passion was clearly evident in his eyes now.

"Why not?"

"Well, last night ... was last night. When you go back to Chicago, and I return to Denver ..." Her voice trailed off lamely. Her body throbbed with longing; she wanted him as badly as he wanted her.

He looked into her face, full of defenseless love, and assured her gently, "I can't imagine ever forgetting you."

He moved to the brass bed and laid her down tenderly. Then his hands were in her hair, drawing her closer and stilling her murmured protests with the perfect union of their mouths. Soft rays of sunlight filtered through the sheer material of the drapes as he sought to weaken her resistance as surely as she was weakening his.

He brought her body flush against him, proving his need for her. A tender light shone in his eyes as he whispered in a voice made more urgent with desire. "If it's the short period of time we've known each other that bothers you, then I won't make love to you again," he promised. "But I'm afraid you'll have to be the one to make that decision."

"Until I met you, I would have never dreamed I could be so reckless," Hilary confessed.

"Reckless? I don't think what we have is reckless."

"It is for me, Garth. I want permanence in life ...and I think it's too soon for us to commit ourselves to such a relationship. We barely know each other."

"No, not yet. But in time..." Garth lowered his mouth to take hers. The rational words lingered, but the desires of the flesh were more persuasive.

Lavishing her throat with feather kisses, he warned again. "Say the word and I'll stop."

Hilary thought he wasn't being fair. Her hazy mind didn't have the slightest idea of what "the word" would be.

"I don't want you to stop," she confessed and drew a shuddering breath. He was kissing her with a seductive torment that was more eloquent than words.

"Maybe there isn't any word that could stop me," he conceded. His mouth moved down the perfumed length of her, touching her here ...and there ...and there ...

Maybe nothing could stop him from claiming her again, Garth realized.

Maybe this crazy roller coaster he had been on would turn out to be the real thing.

Maybe . . . He would think about it later.

Chapter Ten

HILARY WAS THE FIRST TO awaken. Her hand moved to caress the warm form lying next to her. When it came in contact with a masculine, hair-roughened thigh, she smiled. She hadn't been dreaming. Garth had made love to her again— no, it had been more than making love. Something wonderful and exciting had taken place last night, and she was sure he'd felt it too.

She sighed and rolled toward him as his arms drew her tightly against his bare length. He was still asleep, and he looked so peaceful that she was sure there was still a special warmth that lingered from their spent passion.

The little clock sitting on the nightstand drew her attention. She gasped softly when she realized they'd slept for a straight fourteen hours!

Turning back to Garth, she teasingly traced the dark circle under his left eye—Lenny's legacy.

Black eye or not, he was the most handsome

man in the world, she thought wistfully. More important, he was a good man...perfect husband material. Hilary sensed he would be wonderful with children, and she'd bet her last her dollar he would even love his mother-in-law. He just seemed to be the type.

Propping herself up on her elbows, she tenderly brushed her lips across his bare shoulder. "Mrs. Garth Redmond. Hilary Redmond. Garth and Hilary Redmond," she whispered, liking the sound of all three.

Garth moved and his eyes opened slowly. Hilary smiled and kissed the tip of his nose affectionately.

"What are you doing?"

Sorry that she'd disturbed him, mostly because she'd been caught, Hilary said guiltily, "Tasting."

"Tasting?"

"Yeah." She poked the tip of her tongue in the crease of one of his dimples and licked him playfully.

"What do I taste like?" he mumbled.

"Um...like...gentleness, passion, kindness—things like that." Her mouth found his, and they kissed a long, leisurely good morning kiss.

When their lips parted, Garth gazed into her eyes lovingly. "I didn't know you could taste things like gentleness and kindness."

"Not all men taste like that." She absent-mindedly traced his lower lip with the tip of her finger. "But you do, Garth."

"You give me too much credit."

"No, I don't. You're wonderful."

Garth was embarrassed by her praise, but he loved it. "You think so? Come here." He pulled her on top of his chest and kissed her again. "Let's see what you taste like."

Hilary closed her eyes and savored the butterfly kisses that he sprinkled across her forehead, her nose, finally coming to rest against the fullness of her lips, his tongue gently probing the warm moistness of her mouth.

"So . . . what do I taste like?"

Garth gazed into her passion-laden eyes and said softly, "Let's see." He paused, gliding his tongue back across her lips, tasting, sampling her sweetness. "I think you taste like . . . gentleness, kindness, and passion."

"But I don't have all those qualities. I anger too easily; I have no patience at times; and while I'm not a mean person, I'm not necessarily overly kind." She hated to admit it, but it was all true.

"What about passion?"

"Well now, passion is possible," she confessed humbly.

"Possible!" Garth lifted a dark brow dubiously, and she grinned.

"Well, maybe probable," she amended, vividly recalling the night before.

"I should think so!"

"Want me to prove it?"

"I thought you'd never ask!"

Entwined in the warm embrace of each other's arms, they gently rolled over, and Garth hungrily captured her mouth again. As their insatiable need for each other flared up again, Garth buried his face in the full softness of her hair and confessed she actually tasted sweet—very sweet. For the next thirty minutes they made love with such ardor that it left them both spent.

With passion temporarily appeased again, Hilary lay quietly in his arms. Garth wondered why she'd suddenly grown so still. He glanced down and nudged her gently. "Hey, sleepyhead, don't drift off on me. It's getting late."

"Um . . . just a few minutes . . . two winks at the most," she pleaded.

Garth glanced at the clock and was astounded to see the time. "Not a chance! I'm starving. Let's forget breakfast and find ourselves a nice thick steak."

The thought of food enticed Hilary to move ever so slightly beneath the sheet. Prying one eye open, she bargained, "And a hot, fat, baked potato—drenched in butter and sour cream?"

Garth nodded sleepily.

"Salad, rolls, and lemon pie?"

"Cheesecake."

"Both!"

"Good Lord!" He smacked her on her bare fanny and rolled out of bed. "How do you keep your figure, eating like that?"

"I just don't worry about it. I usually eat anything I want and suffer terrible guilt later."

Garth chuckled, recalling how Lisa forever counted calories and became outraged when he refused to do the same. "I'll buy you anything you want. Let's just get a move on."

"All right, but I get the shower first." She playfully tossed her pillow at him as she sprang to her feet and headed toward the bathroom.

Intercepting the flying pillow with one hand, Garth sat up in the bed and watched as she disappeared through the doorway. "Want some help?"

"No. Not if you want to get to the restaurant anytime in the near future," she called back.

Garth rolled out of bed and went over to the door. He rapped loudly. He could hear the sound of water running, so he knew she would be standing beneath the warm spray now.

He remembered all too well how beautiful she looked with her silky skin glistening, the gleaming beads of water sliding down the length of her supple frame...

"Just a shower—I promise I won't start anything," he pleaded as he pressed his face against the closed door.

Hilary laughed and shouted above the stream of hot water, "Not a chance. You could be lying."

"No, I promise."

"I thought you were hungry!"

There was a meaningful pause. Then, "I am."

At the suggestive innuendo in his voice, Hilary felt herself weakening. The hot-water heater did tend to empty its supply rapidly—and he did have that miserable cold...She tried desperately to rationalize what she was about to do.

"Please!"

With a resigned sigh, she stepped out of the shower and unlocked the door.

"I knew you'd break down." Garth grinned and reached for her slippery body as she tumbled willingly into his arms.

"I told you I was weak."

"I remembered." Garth ran his hands exquisitely over her bottom while he kissed her, then let them drop back to his sides repentantly. "Okay, I promised. But may I at least soap your back?"

"Only if you'll shampoo my hair too," she bartered as she stepped back into the shower and turned to face the spray of warm water.

"I don't know how to shampoo your hair," he protested.

"You shampoo yours, don't you?"

"I don't think it will be the same."

By the time Garth had lathered her hair, Hilary looked like a creature from outer space.

"Garth! You've used too much shampoo," she complained, spitting the soap bubbles out of her mouth.

He was unconcerned. He was too busy sculpting various animal shapes out of the white froth.

"And here is an attack zebra!" he announced, scooping up a handful of the soap suds and backing her into the corner of the shower.

"Garth, no!" She dodged as he—and the attack zebra—masterminded an offensive on her body that eventually ended with another round of lovemaking.

Later, while she dried her hair, Garth dressed and headed for the Johnsons' cottage to call a taxi.

The level of the small lake in the front yard had descended more rapidly than he'd expected. He was glad its icy waters no longer sloshed over the tops of Silas's old rubber boots.

It was more than two hours before the cab arrived.

As they settled themselves in the backseat, it occurred to Hilary that she hadn't phoned her parents as she'd promised. She'd even forgotten to pick up the money they'd wired her.

"Garth, before we find a place to eat, could we stop by the Western Union office and pick up my money? I was supposed to have picked it up hours ago. My parents are probably sick with worry."

"Of course. I had forgotten all about the money. I suppose we'd better stop by the Merrymont and file an insurance claim while we're at it."

"I suppose so." Hilary snuggled closer to him.

"After we've had dinner." Garth leaned over and nibbled on her ear.

"By all means. Let's eat first."

By the looks of things, the small town of West Creek was still in a state of emergency. Utility workmen were busy repairing fallen power lines, and merchants were removing the bulky sheets of plywood that had saved their plate-glass windows. In the lower-lying areas, families could be seen sweeping the icy waters out of their flooded homes.

Hilary's money was waiting when they arrived at the Western Union office. She signed the required forms, collected her funds, then phoned her parents in Denver.

"Daddy?" Hilary began hesitantly. She wasn't sure if her parents knew of the storm.

"Hilary! What on earth happened to you? We

heard on the news about a storm back there, and we were worried sick when we didn't hear from you!" The sharp tone of her father's normally mild voice assured her they knew the full extent of the damage caused by the syzygy.

"Daddy, I'm fine," Hilary said soothingly. She glanced at Garth and made a patient face. "The storm wasn't as bad as the news media made it sound."

Garth grinned, realizing she was trying to downplay the extent of the nightmare they had just weathered.

"When you didn't call us back, naturally we assumed the worst. Your mother's been having fits!"

"I'm sorry, Daddy. Lines are down, and I wasn't near a phone that worked. Tell Mama I'm fine. Really!"

"I will, baby. Is Marsha all right?"

Hilary looked at Garth and smiled. "She's fine, Daddy. Couldn't be better."

"Are you going to cut your vacation short because of the storm?"

"I think so. I'll let you know what I decide."

When Hilary said good-bye and hung up the phone, Garth looked at her tenderly. "That was nice of you."

Lisa would have played the crisis to the hilt; yet Hilary had gone out of her way to spare her parent's feelings. Garth admired her more every hour.

"What was nice?"

"The way you deliberately spared them extra worry."

"Why should I worry them? The storm's over, and I'm still in one piece."

"It was still nice of you." Garth leaned over and kissed her.

"Well . . ." Hilary wrinkled her nose at him lovingly. "I've had a good example to live by lately."

The taxi left the Western Union office and drove to the restaurant. Fortunately for their growling stomachs, the Steak House had escaped severe damage.

Garth eyed the broken neon sign outside the restaurant. "How do you want your *teak*?" he teased, making playful reference to the S that had been sucked away by the strong winds.

Hilary smiled, thinking how nice it was to be able to enjoy life again.

Garth escorted her from the taxi and offered her his arm. Hilary graciously accepted it, and with a look of pride etched on his face, he guided her into the restaurant.

"How's the ankle feeling?" He had almost forgotten about her injury.

"What ankle?" she grinned. "How's the cold?"

"What cold?" Garth bantered. The words were barely past his lips when another sneeze hit him.

In no time the hostess had them seated and served. Hilary couldn't remember when a baked potato had ever tasted so good. Garth remarked that his steak was prepared exactly the way he liked it, and he savored every bite with exaggerated pleasure.

Over coffee and cheesecake, the lightness of

their mood slowly shifted, becoming more serious.

Garth reached over and picked up her hand, then kissed the back of it gently. "I'm glad we've had this time together."

Hilary sensed that the hour she'd been dreading had finally arrived. For a second she considered confessing that she had fallen in love with him. But at the last moment she changed her mind. She wasn't sure he was ready to hear that yet. He had never talked of the future.

"I'm glad we have too, Garth."

"The past few days have made me think about a lot of things..." His words faded as he groped for a way to express his feelings. He wasn't exactly sure what they were himself. She'd just come out of a bad relationship, and it was too soon for her to start a new one. As for him, he certainly didn't want to jump into anything he couldn't get out of later if he wanted to.

Hilary absentmindedly toyed with her coffee cup, keeping her gaze from his. She wanted desperately to tell him how she felt, but she was afraid. If she expressed her love, and he didn't share the feeling...

"Hilary, I guess what I'm trying to say is..." Garth paused, poking his fork at the half-eaten cheesecake.

"Garth, you don't have to say anything," Hilary told him. She didn't want to hear the dreaded "It's been nice, but see you later, kid" routine. She'd rather part with the fragile hope that what they'd had was real. Maybe with a little time, Garth would realize it too.

"Hilary . . . I need a little time—"

"Garth"—she reached over and covered his hand with hers—"you don't have to explain. I know." He was struggling with his doubts, and she wasn't going to push.

"I'll call you . . . And you stay in touch with me." Garth's troubled eyes searched hers for an answer she didn't have. "Okay?"

Hilary sighed. At least he wasn't shutting the door entirely. It was more than she'd expected but achingly less than she wanted.

"Okay."

Garth felt a sinking sensation in the pit of his stomach. Had he hoped she might argue with him? "Okay, we agree to keep in touch?"

"Yes, of course." Hilary squeezed his hand reassuringly.

His gaze grew incredibly tender, and he held on to her hand tightly. "You're one hell of a woman."

"Thank you." Her own eyes glistened brightly with unshed tears. "You're quite a man."

Forcing a front of bravery, Hilary quietly excused herself and left for the sanctuary of the ladies' room before the telltale tears could slip down her cheeks. Once she was safely behind closed doors, she gave into the heartfelt sobs. She would never see him again, she agonized. He would go back to Chicago and forget that Hilary Brookfield had ever existed.

Torn between an aching heart, which told her to stay and try to change his mind, and a rational mind, which cautioned her to leave before she got in any more deeply, Hilary reluctantly admitted to herself what she had to do.

She'd go back to Denver first thing in the morning. Maybe getting back to a normal routine would help her get her life in order.

When Hilary returned to the table, she was dry-eyed and wearing a bright smile. Over second cups of coffee, she told Garth of her plans to leave for Denver on the early-morning flight, reasoning that she really should be getting back to the office. "I left on such short notice, and with Marsha gone ..." Hilary shrugged. "I think I've had all the 'vacation' I can stand."

They both laughed nervously.

"I guess maybe I'll do the same thing," Garth admitted.

They looked at each other, and Hilary wasn't sure if she had the strength to leave.

"I'll get the check," she said softly. "I have the money this time."

Later they rode to the Merrymont and quietly filled out the small mountain of insurance forms, then called the airport and made their reservations for the next morning's flight.

As they left the counter Garth put his arm around her and drew her close to his side. "Stay with me tonight."

"I was thinking about getting a room in town," she confessed. She knew that if she spent the night with him, she'd be helpless to leave when morning came.

"Please ... one more night," Garth urged.

Hilary shook her head ruefully. "What am I going to do with you?"

Garth's adoring eyes sent her the silent answer.

"Oh, I almost forgot." She rummaged through her purse after they were seated in the taxi. "Your money."

"Keep it. Consider it a get-acquainted present." Garth smiled.

"Thank you, but I couldn't." Hilary tucked the wad of bills into his jacket pocket.

Garth removed the money and pressed it firmly into her hand. "If you insist on paying me back, wait until you get home. Please."

"Okay, but I will pay you back," she insisted, realizing she didn't want to spend their last few precious hours together arguing. "I'll put a check in the mail tomorrow."

She suddenly sneezed.

"You getting sick?"

"I think I'm getting your cold."

"Hm!" He grinned and winked. "I wonder why!"

They shared their last few hours together in the beach house beneath a darkened sky now ablaze with glittering stars.

"It feels like I'm saying good-bye to my best friend," Garth confessed as he cupped her face and tried to memorize every feature in the soft rays cast by the lamp at the bedside.

"I'd like to be your best friend," Hilary whispered.

Garth sipped at her lips as if they were warm wine. "Granted, my fair lady . . ."

It was a long time before their passion could be appeased. It was late when they finally dropped into an uneasy sleep, still entwined in each other's arms.

During the night they slept fitfully, waking every hour to look at the hands on the clock.

When daybreak arrived, few words were exchanged as they rose and dressed for their early-morning flight. They carefully avoided looking at each other as they packed in strained silence.

At the municipal airport on the outskirts of West Creek, they sat quietly as they awaited the plane.

The short flight was uneventful, and all too quickly they had landed at Raleigh-Durham.

This time a lengthy delay, such as the one they had experienced three days earlier, would have been welcome, but both departures were running right on time.

Hilary's plane was the first scheduled to leave.

"Well, I guess this is it." She forced her voice to remain cheerful, although her insides were tied in knots.

"Yes, I guess it is." Garth ran a hand uneasily through his hair. "You will keep in touch?"

"Sure." Hilary smiled and patted the side of her purse. "I've got your number written in three different places." She knew she didn't need the reminders. She'd memorized the number before the ink had dried.

"Well, they're playing my song," she said as the second call for Flight 527 come over the intercom.

Garth suddenly reached out and caught her to him. "Take care of yourself..."

"You too..." She was suddenly crushed against his broad chest.

Even through the thick fabric of his jacket she

could detect the beat of his heart. It was all she could do to refrain from crying out her pent-up love as he lifted her off her feet and kissed her more passionately than ever before. She was breathless and teary-eyed when the final boarding call sounded.

He gently lowered her back to her feet, and his eyes met hers solemnly. "I'm holding you to your word, Hilary. Don't forget me."

"I won't," she promised, and they kissed one last time before she broke away and ran blindly down the jetway.

Chapter Eleven

THE FOLLOWING DAYS PASSED with painful slowness. Hilary spent long hours at O'Connor Construction Company, where she was preoccupied with agonizing memories of Garth.

They both had remained true to their promise to keep in touch. They corresponded via telephone or cards almost daily.

Even Lenny Ricetrum had kept his promise to wash his hands of Hilary. He'd quit his job at O'Connor's, and someone had mentioned that Lenny was seeing a recently divorced brunette.

The news didn't bother Hilary. She discovered she didn't care if Lenny's newest flame had purple hair—as long as he stayed away from her.

The sound of the five-o'clock whistle signaled Hilary that Day Number Ten had passed. Feeling disheartened, she put on her coat and headed to her empty apartment. Gary Franks had called earlier and asked her out for dinner, but Hilary confessed she would be terrible company.

It was becoming harder and harder to face the four walls that had become her self-imposed prison. She fantasized that Garth would magically be there waiting for her one night, but she knew that wasn't likely to happen.

Hilary arrived home and held her breath with anticipation as she checked the mailbox. When her trembling fingers retrieved the large manila envelope with Garth's return address scrawled across the corner, she felt her heart soar. A big fat letter was stuffed inside. Hilary unfolded its neatly written pages, and a pink check slipped to the floor. She frowned, scooping up the check she'd sent to him for the clothing he'd bought her.

Trying to read the letter and unlock the door at the same time proved to be impossible, so she paused in savoring every word just long enough to jiggle the door to her apartment open. Once inside, she didn't bother to remove her coat as she sank down on the sofa to finish the letter.

"Oh, Garth, I miss you," she whispered, wiping the back of her hand over eyes that were now filling with tears as she read his casual chitchat.

The telephone rang, forcing her to restrain her tears. She grabbed for a tissue and prayed the caller would be Garth.

"Hi, honey!" Simon Brookfield's voice came cheerfully over the wire.

Feeling her heart take a nosedive, Hilary sighed. "Oh, hi, Daddy."

"What's this 'oh, hi, Daddy' stuff? Are you all right?" Simon had noticed that something had been bothering his daughter ever since she'd returned from vacation.

"I'm sorry. It's been a long day." Hilary apologized for her obvious distraction. "How's Mama?"

"Fine. She wants to know if you'd like to come for dinner tonight. We haven't seen much of you since you got home."

"Dinner? Tonight?" What if Garth should call while she was away? No, she couldn't take the chance. It was foolish to sit and wait for his call, but then Hilary would be the first to admit Garth had that effect on her.

"Thanks, Daddy, but I'm really tired tonight. I thought I'd take a nice hot bath and go to bed early."

"Are you sure, honey? You've been spending a great deal of time tucked away in that apartment of yours lately. We miss you."

"I'll make it up to you, I promise. Maybe one night next week."

"Okay, hon. Anytime will be fine with your mother and me. Just give us a call."

"I will."

"How's the cold?"

"I think I'm finally getting over it."

"You're sure nothing's wrong?"

"Dad, I'm not a child," Hilary reminded him patiently.

"I know, I know. But just because you're grown doesn't mean we don't still worry about you. You just wait—"

"Until you have children of your own!" Hilary finished for him, then laughed softly. "Okay, I'll make sure they keep me up nights worrying, just the way I do the two of you."

"You won't have to go out of your way to do that," Simon chuckled. "It comes with the job."

"Good night, Dad."

"Good night, dear. Don't forget about dinner next week."

"I won't."

Hilary hadn't much more than placed the receiver back onto its cradle when the phone rang again.

"Hello." She was careful not to allow her expectations to soar again.

"Hi, babe!" The familiar baritone voice immediately turned her knees to pulp.

"Well, hi there!" Hilary deliberately kept her voice casual, although she had to sink onto the nearest chair. "I just got your letter . . . and my check. What's the big idea?"

"Don't panic. I can explain."

"Then start explaining. And it'd better be good. If not, this check goes back in the mail—first thing tomorrow morning," she warned.

"You'd actually be so crass as to send a present back?"

"Present? What's the occasion for such a generous present?"

"Your birthday?" he offered.

"Uh-uh. My birthday isn't until July. How quickly one forgets," Hilary teased.

"I didn't forget . . . You never told me," Garth said softly.

"You never asked."

"Okay, I'm asking you now. When's your birthday?"

"July twenty-eighth."

"So I'm a little early. Take the check and buy yourself something nice."

"Oh, Garth! I love you!" The words were out before Hilary realized what she'd said.

There was a significant pause. Then, "You what?"

Hilary realized that her impulsive declaration of love had completely stunned him, so she tried to patch up the confession by appearing to make it more of a blanket observation. "Of course I love you. How could I not love a man who helped me through three of the most miserable days of my life?"

"Oh . . . that kind of love."

Had she heard a distinct let-down in his voice, or had she only imagined it?

"Exactly when do you think it happened? Was it when you soiled my handkerchiefs, or when we hand-wrestled for the Samsonite?" Garth tried to mask his disappointment with teasing.

"I think it was shortly after you called me Harry," Hilary decided.

For a moment there was another silence; then Garth said, "Well, I guess I'd better get myself in gear and get ready for work. I just thought I'd call and see what you were up to."

"Garth . . ." Hilary stalled, wanting to tell him she did love him—and not just because he had shared those three days with her. She loved him because he was special. She loved him because he was Garth.

"Yes?"

"I'm glad you called."

Hilary was positive she detected a slight unevenness in his voice this time. "I think about you a lot, Hilary."

"I think about you, too."

"Lenny giving you any trouble?"

"No, I haven't seen Lenny lately."

"Well, I need to go. We've been in school recently. They've started a new landing program that's designed to clear up the lengthy delays in flight schedules." Hilary heard his weary sigh. "It's been a nightmare."

"Is the weather bad?" She wanted to prolong the conversation, yet she knew she shouldn't delay him.

"It snowed a little today."

"Well, thanks for my birthday present."

"Yeah, keep in touch."

"Yes . . . you too."

"Good night."

"Good night."

The following week more presents arrived. First, Hilary received three dozen white roses. Garth called that evening to explain that their arrival was an early Valentine's Day gift.

Hilary accepted that. Valentine's Day was only three weeks away, she rationalized, wondering if he really thought the flowers would last until then.

When a large flacon of Joy was delivered two days later, it was Hilary who called Garth. Her jubilant thank you was casually dismissed with the assurance that the perfume was an early Christmas present.

"Garth, it's only the last day of January!" Hilary protested.

"Yeah, I know. But I like to get my shopping done early. I beat the rush of last-minute shoppers that way."

As the days turned into a full month, Hilary knew their phone bills would be astronomical. She dreaded the day when AT&T tallied up their conversations.

The weather in Denver took a turn for the worse, dumping a record-breaking snowfall the first week in February. More diligently than she watched *Dallas* or *Falcon Crest*, Hilary found herself watching the weather report every night to see what the weather was doing in Chicago.

Until she'd met Garth, she'd never cared about the forecast. But with the increased pressures bad weather brought to the air-traffic controllers, Hilary's nightly prayers now ended with a Please, let there be clear skies in Chicago tomorrow!

Garth came to dread the long nights. After having spent two nights in Hilary's arms, he had yet to experience the restful sleep he'd shared with her in West Creek.

Scanning the forecast printout sheets for the Denver area, he wondered if his "snow bunny" would ever again melt in his arms the way she had at the beach house.

Sometimes Garth would call Denver on his break when he could feel the pressures mounting. Hilary could always tell when he was calling from the control tower. His voice would be tense. But after five minutes of chatting he seemed to relax and become his old self again.

"You're good for me," Garth confessed one night, and Hilary assured him that the feeling was mutual. She always felt warm and needed after they hung up, even in the loneliness of her apartment.

March arrived, and with it came Hilary's first phone bill. She let it sit on the coffee table for two days before she had enough courage to open it.

"Good grief!"

She knew she couldn't afford to keep up with the tremendous cost of calling Illinois every other night. It would be cheaper to fly there and talk to Garth in person.

She paused as she seriously toyed with the idea. Well, why not? For much less than one month's telephone bill, she could fly to Chicago and spend an entire weekend with him. She threw the bill in the air exuberantly. Why not?

It wasn't the huge phone bill that convinced Garth it was time to put a stop to the cat-and-mouse game.

He'd always come home tired, even before Hilary came into his life. But now he'd always wake up feeling exhausted, having spent night after night tossing and turning.

Garth didn't mind obsessing about Hilary during his every waking moment . . . he just preferred that she be in his arms while he was doing it.

He tried dating Lisa a few times but finally admitted that she was out of the picture. Lisa had taken the breakup as he'd expected—very badly. She was furious and nasty.

But Garth didn't care. All he could think of was Hilary.

Hilary, in the meantime, frequently drove out to Stapleton International Airport, where she would gaze longingly at the control tower. She tried to visualize Garth's world.

She was still debating whether or not to fly to Chicago. Suppose Garth would resent her for just dropping by. It was possible. He'd never once suggested they try to see each other again. In the end, Hilary decided that was a chance she'd simply have to take. She couldn't endure another week without seeing him. As she gazed at the distant tower, she thought of the man she loved who was hundreds and hundreds of miles away. The constant roar of jets taking off and landing reminded her of the awesome responsibility of Garth's job, and she felt the sting of tears filling her eyes.

Garth needed her. He needed someone to come home to...someone who could share his life, someone who would love him...care for him... nurture him...

Garth Redmond needed her.

On her lunch hour the following Friday, Hilary purchased a ticket on a late-night flight to Chicago.

It was the day before Valentine's Day. She would plead that she couldn't find a stamp and wanted to deliver his card personally. Garth could hardly object, since he had used much flimsier excuses himself when her presents had been delivered.

The afternoon seemed to drag by without end. Hilary spent most of the time correcting one typo after another on the countless stacks of invoices she'd attempted to type.

Ten minutes before the five-o'clock whistle blew, Hilary was out warming the engine of her car. She figured there was no sense in wasting precious time. This way, the motor would be purring like a kitten when she punched the time clock.

At exactly one minute after five she was out the office door. She was home by five-thirty, a new record for a drive that usually took close to an hour.

She packed a sufficient amount of clothing and personal items to get her through the weekend, then took a taxi to the airport.

The night before Valentine's Day! Hilary's heart raced wildly with the knowledge that, with any luck, she would be spending it in Garth's arms. She prayed he wouldn't have other plans for the weekend. The thought was too disturbing to dwell upon.

Hilary exited the cab and raced toward the busy terminal, paying no heed to the small patches of ice still lingering on the walkways. All of a sudden she found herself slip-sliding across the frozen glaze, groping wildly to retain her balance.

Dropping the suitcase, Hilary grabbed for a handrail just moments before she would have spilled to the ground. But not quickly enough to prevent her left ankle from twisting painfully.

She grabbed the injured ankle and groaned out loud. There was something about Stapleton and her ankles that just didn't mix! She thought of the last "fly the friendly skies" effort she'd attempted and prayed this wouldn't be another disaster.

She took small comfort in the fact that the right ankle had since healed. It was her left one that was killing her now. Retrieving her suitcase, she hobbled on, praying that she wasn't on another roll of bad luck.

In a rush to board her flight, she limped right past the handsome man who was just dashing out another door.

Garth stopped abruptly and whirled around as he saw Hilary limping in the opposite direction.

He saw that she was carrying a suitcase, and his heart nearly stopped. She was on her way out of town just as he was coming in. The realization shot a surge of panic through Garth, and he called out to her hastily retreating form the first thing that came into his mind.

"Hey, what's wrong with your ankle?" he shouted, puzzled that, after all this time, she was still hobbling.

The sound of Garth's voice brought Hilary to a skidding halt. He *had* come for her! She knew it even before she turned around.

"Garth!" Hilary's eyes lit up like two Christmas trees as she dropped the suitcase and came flying toward him, forgetting all about her throbbing ankle.

Garth caught her up in his arms, and they

kissed long and hungrily, ignoring the way they were blocking the flow of traffic.

"Garth, darling! What in the world are you doing here?" Hilary exclaimed as their mouths finally parted long enough to exchange a few brief words between snatches of eager kisses.

"I could ask you the same thing." Garth grinned. She looked even better than he had remembered.

"I . . . I was on my . . . I asked you first!"

"I'm here to see my girl," Garth said simply, then took her mouth in another possessive kiss.

It was forever before they could will their mouths apart long enough to step aside finally and let the other passengers pass.

"No kidding—why are you here?" Hilary insisted as he carried their bags over to the side and set them down.

"I was just passing through Denver, and I thought I'd stop in and ask you to . . ."

"I would love to have dinner with you." Hilary accepted before he could finish the invitation.

Garth grinned and kissed her once more. "Who said anything about dinner?"

"Oh, uh . . . I thought you were going to ask me . . . to have dinner with you." Hilary could feel an embarrassed flush spreading across her face.

"No. Dinner isn't exactly what I had in mind."

"I'm sorry . . . What were you going to suggest?"

"Well, since I couldn't find a stamp to mail your Valentine card I thought I would personally deliver it, and then—"

"Oh, Garth! That was my line!"

"Your line?"

"Yes! I was on my way to see *you*, and I was going to say I couldn't find a stamp for your card, so—"

Garth laughed and they were suddenly kissing again. When their lips parted much, much later, he gently cupped her chin and lifted her face to meet his. "I was on my way to ask you if you weren't busy this weekend, would you consider marrying me?" he finished.

"Marry you?"

"That's right."

"Well . . . yes. Of course."

"I was hoping you'd say that." Slowly his mouth covered hers.

All of a sudden his words sank in, and Hilary's eyes widened in disbelief. She broke off the kiss and let out a shriek of delight as she threw her arms around his neck and hugged him so tightly he found it hard to breathe. "Marry you! I can't believe it! When? Now? Of course I will!"

Garth chuckled and tried to loosen her grasp but finally gave up and hugged her back. "Why do you find that so hard to believe?"

"You've never said you loved me," she said accusingly, still finding his proposal hard to believe. Garth had just asked her to marry him!

"Maybe I've never said it in so many words, but I thought you might get the hint," Garth chided. He thought of the horrendous stack of florist, phone, and department-store bills lying on his desk at home.

"Oh, I love you!" Hilary kissed him over and over, not caring in the least that they were making a scene. "To heck with all these flimsy excuses! Let's go to my apartment," she suggested in a breathy whisper against his ear. "I want to give you your Valentine's gift ... in person."

Garth growled suggestively. "I hope it's what I've been wanting for weeks."

Hilary winked. "I would have sent it earlier if I could have found a big enough stamp."

Garth quickly picked up both pieces of luggage, and they started out of the airport, with Hilary clinging possessively to his arm.

"Is your ankle still bothering you?" he asked.

"Would you believe I slipped on the ice and sprained it again?" she complained.

"Same one?"

"No, the other one this time."

Garth threw his head back and laughed, feeling like a million dollars as they walked out of the terminal into the frigid night air.

Snow was beginning to fall in thick, puffy flakes that stuck to the frozen ground the moment they landed.

"The weatherman's calling for eight inches by morning," Hilary warned.

"Well, naturally!" Garth looked at her wryly. "What else would Brookfield and Redmond expect when they're together?"

Hilary grinned and wrinkled her nose at him. "Say what you want, but I think we'll make a perfect team."

Garth leaned over and tenderly kissed away the remains of the large snowflake that had just landed on her cheek. "You bet we will, Brookfield. The *very* best."

DANCE *of the* FLAME

ELAINE BARBIERI

**Elaine Barbieri's romances are
"powerful...fascinating...storytelling at its best!"
—*Romantic Times***

Exiled to a barren wasteland, Sera will do anything to regain the kingdom that is her birthright. But the hard-eyed warrior she saves from death is the last companion she wants for the long journey to her homeland.

To the world he is known as Death's Shadow—as much a beast of battle as the mighty warhorse he rides. But to the flame-haired healer, his forceful arms offer a warm haven, and he swears his throbbing strength will bring her nothing but pleasure.

Sera and Tolin hold in their hands the fate of two feuding houses with an ancient history of bloodshed and betrayal. But no matter what the age-old prophecy foretells, the sparks between them will not be denied, even if their fiery union consumes them both.

_3793-9 $5.99 US/$6.99 CAN